# Last Kiss
# Goodnight

Also by Teresa Driscoll

*Recipes for Melissa*

# Last Kiss Goodnight

## TERESA DRISCOLL

bookouture

Published by Bookouture

An imprint of StoryFire Ltd.
23 Sussex Road, Ickenham, UB10 8PN
United Kingdom

www.bookouture.com

ISBN: 978-1-910751-84-8
eBook ISBN: 978-1-910751-83-1

This book is a work of fiction. Names, characters, businesses, or-
ganizations, places and events other than those clearly in the public
domain, are either the product of the author's imagination or are
used fictitiously. Any resemblance to actual persons, living or dead,
events or locales is entirely coincidental.

*for Peter, James and Edward*

# PART ONE

Moscow
Nov 1960

My Martha,

I write, guessing and fearing this may not reach you. But what else to do? Three years now with no word...

Friends tell me I should give this up. But I find that I just cannot.

And so I will continue to write, preferring to dream, to hope, to pray that just one of these letters will somehow get through to you. I do not want to believe the alternative; that you choose not to reply...

Please don't let that be the reason...

And so if these are the lines to finally reach you then let me reassure you that I have been writing constantly via your father's address. And above all – please, please do not believe that it is too late.

If I cannot find you, then come and find me, Martha. I beg you.

I love you still and I will love you always. Everything I said to you was the truth, I swear. And everything I do in this crazy life I now lead, I still in my heart do for you.

I would never have left if I felt it would turn out like this. Never.

Please Martha. Do not give up on us.

Your Josef x

# CHAPTER 1

## Aylesborough-on-sea – 1976

Her behaviour is ridiculous. This Kate knows but cannot help.

Even as she darts forward to claim the front seat on the bus, she can imagine sitting further back, watching herself with professional concern. This strange unrecognisable self. This woman now anxiously spreading out her three hessian bags to discourage anyone else from joining her. A woman displaying all the classic symptoms of compulsive behaviour – taking the same bus on the same days and arriving ridiculously early (despite the absence of queues) to ensure she can enjoy the same seat.

Of course she should give this up. Break the pattern while she still can. But what Kate knows also is that alone on this front seat, high over the world, with the smell of the sea spray and the gulls calling overhead, she will, for a time at least, feel safe.

She checks her watch – eight minutes and *twenty eight, twenty nine, thirty seconds* to go – and opens the local paper. A sigh.

It will feel better once they pull away. Once the speaker system crackles into use. Yes. Very soon she will be able to relax. Eager now for the familiar commentary. The scripted jokes.

It is her tenth trip with the Open Top Tour company and Kate has today managed to negotiate a discount on her tickets, lying that she is researching tourism for a book.

In the first week, she took the bus twice – Monday and Wednesday – but is now opting for all three tours on the winter schedule, building her week around them. The pleasure for Kate is two hours out of the house yet with no requirement to either talk. Or walk. Two hours away from the packing boxes. Two hours away from Toby.

She has lied to him too about this new addiction, inventing research at the local library for an imagined Open University course. It made him smile, hoping some new project might help. *It's good that you are getting out again, Kate. Really good.* But no. Kate closes her eyes. Ashamed.

It is not good. All a lie.

'Can't keep away then?'

Kate is relieved to recognise Mike's voice – the least intrusive and most surprising of the tour guides – a tall, undernourished man with a striking, Roman nose. Dark hair. Dark horse. All the guides have the gift of the gab, the patter perfected, each following the same script, but Mike always adds a little something new each time. Some nugget of information dug out here, some observation picked up there.

She folds her paper, turns and manages a smile, confident he will check her ticket quickly – knowing better now than to take the conversation any further. She turns back then to look ahead as the diesel engine chugs into gear and the bus pulls away, her breathing slowing, her heart steadying. Waiting for the smells. Peanut butter sandwiches remembered from bus trips in her childhood. Fish and chips from the tourists on the benches below. Diesel and fumes from passing traffic. And then the clear, glorious salt of the sea spray.

Kate closes her eyes to begin her swim; arm over arm, slow and confident – heading towards the lighthouse in the distance. It so calms her. To swim in her mind's eye. Searching in the safety of the daylight. Imagining each stroke through the clear, cool water – ahead of her the beacon of white and red…

*No longer manned, of course. Most lighthouses are becoming automated these days…* Mike's voice fades as she swims further and further, faster and faster – the light beckoning; the water re-freshing. Her arms rhythmic and strong. Left. Right. Left. Right. Pounding through the waves to the purr of the engine and the beat of Mike's scripted monologue...

*Now, if you take a look to the left, you will see the double doors of the Old Ropery...*

On and on she swims. And daydreams. And drifts. Floating periodically on her back for a breather once to catch the eye momentarily of a young man sleeping rough in the bandstand of the park just visible over the hedge, then turning over to continue her swim. Left. Right. Left. Right. Until suddenly, as the bus turns onto Willow Street, there is a jolt.

Kate surfaces and opens her eyes as Mike pauses briefly then apologises for the congestion, caused by – a *bloody BMW driver – 'scuse my language* – who is trying to squeeze into the last remaining parking meter by the quayside. Kate leans forward to take in the scene. The BMW is stuck at a forty-five-degree angle, ready to reverse into the parking space but now unable to move, blocked by a white Transit van which has turned from a side street and cannot reverse because of the traffic behind it.

Kate watches, amused, as the BMW and Transit drivers both emerge from their vehicles to start remonstrating. As a little crowd gathers, Mike thinks *passengers might be interested to know that the little shop to their right – the Minstrel's Place – is the only building in Willow Street to have survived the Blitz...*

But Kate is no longer listening. She is not interested in the Minstrel's Place, nor indeed in the drivers' escalating dispute. For something unexpected has caught her eye.

A man eating a pasty is now blocking her view and she has to lean back to correct the angle and see more clearly. Infuriatingly, the man steps back himself, his considerable stomach blocking her line of sight yet again so that now she has to lean forward.

And then suddenly, a clear view. And there she is. A strange woman sitting alone on the middle bench, overlooking the quay.

Knitting.

Kate moves her head, as she processes the picture – zooming in slowly as she tries to work out why the image so jars. For it is not just the knitting which seems out of place on this blustery November day but the *whole* picture. As if it is in the wrong frame.

The woman is striking – very high cheekbones and a neat, perfect nose – and yet oddly dishevelled, with unkempt long hair drawn back in a rough ponytail. She is wearing an oversize coat, secured at the waist with a large black belt which clearly belonged once to a man and not to the coat or the woman in question. She is wearing short, green wellingtons and has three plastic bags alongside her on the bench.

But what is most odd, what has caught Kate's eye, is not only is this faux bag-lady clearly too young for the job, but that she is knitting what appears, from Kate's position, to be a baby's matinee jacket. A beautiful lemon colour, with the wool tucked safely on top of the first bag so that it will not fall onto the damp pavement. And it is this paradox – the contrast of the pale, baby lemon alongside the general grubbiness of the woman – which has caught Kate's eye.

Kate pauses for a moment, staring all the time as the needles click, click away, and tries very hard to censure her response. In her head, her professional voice whispering the first warning. *No, Kate. No.* Toby's voice follows louder and more strained – *You need to rest, Kate; take better care of yourself* – and then finally her doctor's familiar tut-tutting. But Kate ignores them all, bites into her lip and makes the decision very quickly, so that in no time at all she is tucking her paper back into her bag, gathering up the rest of her things and hurrying down the spiral stairs.

From his commentary position alongside the driver – *passengers might like to know that the waiting time for a berth in the ma-*

*rina is now two and a half years* – Mike raises an eyebrow as Kate heads for the door. 'Sorry, Mike. I've got to go…' and then she is stepping, almost tripping, off the bus, all eyes of the six ground-floor passengers following her.

Back at street level, Mike's voice in the distance, Kate feels for a moment the familiar sense of anxiety which permeates so much of her life now, but takes in a deep breath against it and moves all her bags into her left hand so she can tuck the hair blowing across her eyes behind her right ear.

Years in her job have given her a confidence in approaching strangers – even (some might say especially) *odd* strangers – but today Kate does not feel confident as she moves towards the figure still click, clicking away at her task on the bench. What she feels is an unsettling mixture of both apprehension and inexplicable compulsion.

The woman knitting does not look up and Kate decides to fetch tea to excuse and assist her intrusion. A prop.

There is a mobile van parked alongside the quay, popular with the fishermen, so Kate queues there, all the time watching the woman, whose eyes only stir from her work when a gull hops down alongside for a few minutes, searching beside the bench for scraps of food.

Clutching two mugs of tea (the man apologises for the chipped mugs but *fishermen so hate that horrible polystyrene* and *can you please return them?*), Kate walks tentatively over to the bench, trying but failing not to spill the drinks, which are over-generously poured to the point of surface tension.

The woman pauses as Kate sits, eyeing the mugs curiously and looking around for a moment as if for the person to whom the second drink is to belong.

Kate runs her tongue around the inside of her top lip. 'I hope you don't mind but I thought you might like a cup of tea. Warm yourself up?'

A knowing expression flashes fleetingly across the woman's face before the eyes settle, her gaze hardening. 'I prefer coffee actually.' The tone is pointedly neutral and she pauses then to assess Kate's reaction, which is to blush, first with embarrassment and then irritation, not at this woman's apparent ingratitude but at her own clumsy stupidity; for bumbling in so awkwardly. Setting herself up for this.

But then as suddenly as Kate feels the flush deepen – hotter and hotter – the woman's expression softens.

'The thing is I can only drink tea with vast quantities of sugar.' A different tone now. A tilt of the head. 'Albert at the van would have put sugar in, if you'd told him it was for me. Two huge spoonfuls. Appallingly bad for me.'

An olive branch? Yes. A definite change of tone. And now the woman is reaching out for her tea, but Kate keeps a firm hold on both mugs, then nods and marches straight back to the van, hot tea scorching her hand as she manoeuvres the mugs for the required two spoonfuls of sugar – glancing back anxiously at her bags left alongside the woman, half expecting her to run off with them. Some con. Some scam over sugar which she tries regularly perhaps?

And then Kate is back – sitting alongside the woman who is now smiling and sipping her tea. The bags untouched.

'So – God squad, is it?'

'I beg your pardon?'

'Well – free tea usually involves the big man upstairs. You into all that, then?'

The woman's voice is a surprise – deep and rich. Almost certainly privately educated and Kate finds herself laughing out loud. God squad? She – Kate Mayhew, who believes in absolutely nothing right now?

'No. Sorry. Not my thing at all – faith. You?'

The woman shakes her head and only now, as Kate moves her foot, accidentally knocking over one of her own bags, does she notice there are actually six between them lined up neatly alongside the bench – three plastic and three hessian – a sight so odd it prompts her to laugh again, then unexpectedly add the truth. 'I'm a social worker actually. Off duty. In fact, off my rocker just now, if the doctors are to be believed. *Extended sick leave.*'

'Oh.' And then Martha – as she is to introduce herself – looks at Kate very earnestly as if she has confessed to some crime, and Kate wonders if it is the job or the alleged breakdown she pities...

When, in fact, it is something else entirely.

For Martha is reading the unexpected on Kate's face – this strangest of frissons between them – wondering now which question will come next.

What she is knitting?

Or *why* she is knitting?

# CHAPTER 2

It is the birds not the bus which wake Matthew in his bandstand.

He hears the open-top tourer hovering along the hedge, its lower floor invisible. Catches the eye too of a rather strange woman on the upper deck, fussing with her bags. But Matthew closes his eyes then as the diesel engine draws away, to listen again to the birds, so glad that they should wake him here – relieved for his first thought to be music and not the cold.

As if just for him, they repeat their call now – three notes, three times over. And then Matthew smiles as he identifies them, not the birds but the *notes*, picturing them on the music page; subconsciously moving his fingers inside the sleeping bag as if at the keys of the piano.

A G E flat.

And again. A G E flat – the last note held long and soft.

Even as a very young child, Matthew could do this. Name musical notes – recognising them instantly in the same way most people recognise colours. For a long time he took the gift for granted, presuming everyone could do it, for him just the norm; some genetic quirk like the curl to his hair or the paleness of his eyes which made his father inexplicably wince and look away sometimes when he did not know Matthew was watching through some distant reflection.

Not until he was nearly eight did Matthew learn that his gift had a name. Perfect pitch.

And was rare.

*One in ten thousand people*, his music teacher told him the day it was discovered in a singing class. *Do you have any idea how lucky you are, child? What I would give…*

Matthew remembered the envy in his teacher's voice as he tested him over and over. Note after note, as if he might catch him out in some trick. Some mischief.

But there was no trick. Matthew could not explain how he knew a note's name with no reference point. No tuning fork, hints or help. He just did.

Yawning now as the anaesthetic of sleep wears off, he stares for a time at the lattice blanket which the light casts over him – filtered and smudged through the wooden trellis of the bandstand. Odd to see something so striking here. It reminds him of a photographic exhibition his mother took him to once – trees, pylons and telegraph poles, all in black and white with their shadows casting strange shapes. Some elongated. Some stumpy and distorted. Matthew moves his own shadow now to obliterate the mesh of dark and light, then stretches his body against the discomfort of this new life – young bones practising for old age, his nose still struggling against the smell.

He pulls a face at the memory of the drunk who relieved himself so close to his sleeping bag two nights ago, laughing at Matthew's outrage as the smell woke him – still new enough to the streets to be shocked. To mind the smell. To mind the loathing in the drunk's eyes.

No more car parks, Matthew decided that night. No more hanging around the regular haunts with the others – the bus shelter, the arcade by the fish and chip shop. To hell with safety in numbers.

He is cold from his first night in the park but the bandstand, though small, has kept out the worst of the wind, and he likes this solitude.

And the birds.

Matthew glances around to check he is not being watched then reaches down inside the sleeping bag to find his wallet, tucked into his back pocket. He has just thirty five pounds left; enough still to set him apart from the others. Enough still to go home. To give this up. But not a lot now to separate him from his choice.

Above him the trees shiver in the cold wind and then, through the leaves, Matthew watches his father's eyes glaring at him. His mother a step behind – her eyes softer but red-rimmed from crying, the pupils large and pleading.

'You choose, Matthew.' His father's voice – so angry. 'You and your bloody music. You go and you *bloody well choose, son.*'

And then their faces dissolve into the pattern of clouds against a cold, blue sky. Matthew sits up and hugs his knees to his chest, still zipped inside the warmth of his sleeping bag as the birds continue their melody.

Twenty years he has lived with his perfect pitch, never questioning its origin. But now things are different. And Matthew's father is wrong.

There is no choice.

# CHAPTER 3

'You haven't forgotten tonight?' Toby's voice is distorted, followed by the sound of gargling and spitting.

Damn. The *party*. Kate clicks the front door shut behind her and throws her keys onto the hall table – too hard so that she watches, helpless, as they slide across the polished surface and fall onto the carpet. She meant to pick up her dress from the dry-cleaner's. The clock, just visible through the door ajar into the kitchen, confirms it is too late now. 5.30pm. The shop shut. Her mind is whizzing through her wardrobe as Toby, teeth finished, emerges from the bathroom at the top of the stairs, rubbing his hair with a towel as he looks down at her.

'So how was the library?'

'What?' Kate feels her brow tense as she leans to pick up the keys, still mentally trawling through her rack of clothes.

'The *library*? How's it going? The research?'

The calm of the sea air slipping away – the familiar anxiety seeping slowly back into its place. She breathes slowly. 'Oh fine. Fine. Quite busy today.' She can wear the red dress. Yes. It is clean. It will do.

Toby begins rubbing his hair again.

'I thought you were picking up your dress?'

Kate reaches for the post stacked alongside her keys on the table, to avoid her husband's eyes.

'Decided black was too formal. I'm going to wear the red.'

She is already heading through to the kitchen, clutching the letters and weaving her way around the three packing boxes stacked beside the understairs cupboard.

'I said we'd be early, if that's all right?' Toby's voice crescendoes down the stairs with his footsteps as he follows her. 'About seven. Shall I run you a bath?'

'I'll shower.'

Black.

White.

Yes.

No.

Toby stares at his wife.

'Fine.'

She does not look back at him, thinking instead of the time, forever ago, in a different life and in a different bed that smelled of their flesh and their sweat and their longing. That different world in which he told her, time and time over, their limbs interwoven, of that very first time he stared.

The story of how he watched her across the room of the party at her shared flat, the night they met; utterly transfixed as she danced. She had noticed him too, but remembered it quite differently. She had thought, you see, that she was the one who had been sneaking glances. But no.

Apparently, from across the room, he had been watching her too; mesmerised as she danced – a drink still in her hand, eyes closed, which was why she did not realise. He had remembered very precisely what she was wearing. Dark jeans and a cream linen top with a long line of tiny buttons down the front. In bed in those early days he would trace his finger down her flesh, explaining how he had dreamt of doing this as he stared at the buttons that first evening, wondering if the top pulled over her head or if the buttons would have to be undone.

One by one.

He told her that he had never imagined he would get the chance to find out.

A friend who had watched him staring and staring as she danced had been blunt. '*Out of your league, Toby.*' Kate had been described then as choosy. *Difficult.* The truth, over which they later laughed, was Kate had knocked this friend back.

For herself Kate remembered only that she was surprised how few people she knew at the party – most invited by her flatmates. And then, as she decided on fresh air, she noticed this tall and slightly aloof man standing on his own. Lovely eyes.

Later he would tell her that she reminded him of a painting. He was looking at her hair…

She called it frizzy. He called it pre-Raphaelite.

Kate, having no idea yet of his interest, had hatched a plan to escape the heat. She fetched a kite from her room and asked if he would like to fly it with her – worrying then, even as she shaped the words, that this sounded too contrived. When, in fact, the truth was she genuinely liked kites – had a collection of four or five. Old-fashioned kites with wooden frames in bright, childhood colours. Red, green, yellow and blue. She told him there was a beautiful common just a few minutes away. And the wind was perfect.

'I'm Kate.'

'Toby.'

Both staring then. Eyes locking for the first time – each of them separately and secretly – hoping and daring to imagine.

Toby looking at those buttons…


Across the room at this new and very different party, she can feel him watching her again in the red dress. But this time not with longing – instead with a new and now familiar look of helpless concern which these days she so hates.

She is drinking too much, this she knows – can hear her own laughter just that little bit too loud. Two glasses of champagne. Three.

At one point she catches Toby's new business partner Mark exchanging a worried look with his wife and so she switches to water and escapes to the hall, leaning back against the wall. Fresh paint. A tad chalky against her bare shoulder. She strokes the wall, feeling the soft dust. Limewash? Yes. She recognises it from samples she had painted on a wall upstairs in their old home. Never finished…

She thinks she is alone; thinks she has stolen another moment. Like on the bus with the gulls and the guide and her ridiculous hessian bags.

And then she sees Toby watching her through a mirror at the other end of the hallway and she can hear the echo of his voice from last night, lying in their sad crisp, cotton pyjamas; same bed but a million miles apart now.

'It's no good just pretending it didn't happen, Kate.' That awful look in his eyes; the realisation that he knows exactly what she is doing. In this new place with these new people.

In their shiny new house with the three, terrible boxes still unpacked in the hall. On her bus with all the imaginary swimming. And the endless *searching…*

'We can't just pretend it didn't happen, Kate. It won't work. Shutting it down. Pretending it didn't happen. That's not going to work.'

# CHAPTER 4

Matthew examines the distinctive coffee shop logo on his bright red mug then turns back to his paper – fidgeting with the highlighter pen in his left hand. He scans the catering section first. Can he bluff his way as a chef? Probably not. Silver-service waiter? At a push. Dishwasher? Certainly. Matthew draws a box around two adverts which look promising and sips his drink.

He will need to smarten himself up. Take another swim at the local leisure centre for the excuse to use the showers ahead of any interviews, but is hopeful. Yes. He needs a job fast, one which will not check background too closely, and he will have to find somewhere to stay too. Catering offers the best chance of a room thrown in, but if that isn't an option he will try meantime for a hostel bed. Sleeping rough is no longer a runner. He is less streetwise than he supposed – discovering only when he returned to the bus station that the park he used last night was a regular pick-up point. A couple of lads, mistaken for prostitutes, were beaten up there only the previous month.

After finishing with his paper, Matthew turns to his map and finds the site easily. The now derelict Millrose Mount Hospital – to be renamed Millrose Mount Village – is about two miles out of town.

His mother gave him the name. After the row. *You won't tell your father. He'll kill me, Matthew. He made me promise…*

He stares at the folds on the map and tries to picture how patients might have arrived there in the past. Van? Sedated? Straitjacket? He can conjure only extreme pictures. The truth of his connection here still so impossible to give shape.

Matthew folds the map and decides to walk. Save the bus fare. No surprise there is only one route in and out, and on the long, steep approach road he is thinking about all his research at the library. The papers written by the architect who designed this place. He is wondering, most of all now, if the huge portal entrance looked to those patients in the past as it looks to him now. Like an enormous mouth.

Screaming.

And then he sees the phone box opposite Millrose Mount. Checks his watch. Decides – yes. Is soon inside tapping his foot, waiting for someone to pick up, praying it will not be his father.

'Hello. *Mum*?'

'*Matthew*. Matthew, is that really you, love?'

There is a clatter of something falling to the floor. He imagines a tin of polish. Duster in her hand. Always with the dusting…

Then bleeping. The machine is impatient. Wants more money *now*. Matthew drops his coins in his panic and almost loses the connection as he crouches, scrabbling for the money and managing finally to slot a ten pence into the opening.

'Hello? Hello? Matthew… are you still there?'

'Yes – Mum. It's all right. Listen – I just wanted you to know I'm all right.'

There is sniffing now at the end of the line and Matthew can picture her exactly – her left fist clenched and tap tapping away at her jaw.

'You're coming home, love? Yes? You're coming home?' He imagines a duster scrunched into a tight, tight ball in her hand, her voice rising higher and higher.

Again the blessed beeping. This time Matthew shovels in one, two, three coins.

'Is he there? Is Dad there?'

More sniffing.

'No. He's out.'

'And has he calmed down?'

Silence.

'He'll come round, Matthew. If you'll just come *home*, love.'

Matthew's lower lip is trembling and he has to use his teeth to steady the flesh, biting just hard enough for it to hurt.

He wants still to be angry with her. Not to miss her so much. Not to be so bloody afraid.

'Just tell me where you are, love. I've been frantic. We'll come and get you. Yes?'

Matthew can hardly bear the pain in her voice. And for a moment she is standing right there in front of him, smiling as she straightens his tie for school. *There.* She kisses his forehead and runs her fingers through his curls. His skin feels wet from her kiss but he does not wipe it.

He would like to tell her how this really feels. To not know who you are. To stare in the mirror and feel invisible, like a ghost. He would like to ask her straight out how she could do it.

Lie to him *all those years.*

But then the beeping again. And Matthew sees the note. Middle C. Bleep. Bleep. Bleep.

C C C

'I'll ring you again…'

And she is gone. The woman who is not his mother. Not really. And Matthew has absolutely no idea how to feel – the note of the dialling tone held long and harsh now.

G sharp.


'Can I help you?'

As Matthew leaves the phone box to approach the site office there is a man in the doorway, hands on hips. He is wearing a white hard hat with the logo Millrose Mount Village – a hat which has clearly not been correctly adjusted for his head and perches too high on his brow, making him look ridiculous. He is wearing quite a well-cut suit. Evidently not a builder, then.

'I just wanted to have a look around, if that's allowed?'

'Sorry?' the man looks worried. Matthew imagines he may be quickly doing the maths – the mental check that he is too young. To be a former patient.

'My parents are hoping to move to the area. I'm starting college here. We were wondering—'

'So they might be interested in *buying* one of our conversions?' The man's expression changes completely. New best friends.

'Yes. They asked me to call in for a brochure.'

'Oh right. Come this way. Please. Please. Follow me.'

And now the besuited man is leading Matthew inside the Portakabin where he presses a glossy leaflet into his hand and asks for his parents' address so that he can post on the full sales pack once it is ready. *Expected any day from the printers.*

Matthew says he will arrange for his parents to call in themselves and wonders how long the project is expected to take? He is staring out of the window at the fencing and the skips and, in the distance, two JCBs parked alongside a large mound of gravel.

'A couple of years for all the infrastructure, but we're thinking that some people will want to do their own design work. Buy off-plan. Work with a blank canvas. The potential is just staggering.'

'And you've had much interest? I mean, people don't mind the history? We just wondered if everyone was comfortable. You know. The idea of it… being a psychiatric place, I mean. In the past.'

The man grins. 'Believe me, one day this will be the norm. One day, people won't blink at the idea. This is the chance to be first. To get in before the prices rocket. Ten, twenty years from now, they'll be converting old places like this all over the country.

And trust me, you won't find a more impressive building than this one. The design – extraordinary for its day. Really.'

Matthew smiles. He does not want to give away just how much he already knows about the architectural heritage of this building. But it is not the architecture that interests him. He leafs through the brochure, which assures him that nowhere else can so much floor space be purchased for the money. He is skimming for background on the use of the hospital – its true history – declining tea as he makes it to the final page, his curiosity unsurprisingly disappointed.

Matthew checks his watch, closes the brochure and makes his excuses. *His parents will definitely be in touch. Very soon.* And then, in the doorway, as if an afterthought, so as not to arouse too much suspicion. 'I was wondering about the history of the place? I don't suppose there are any records? Anyone who used to work up here?'

The man's smile fades just a little and he bites his bottom lip, reassessing Matthew.

'You're not a journalist, are you?'

'Goodness – no. I just thought it might be interesting. If we're going to be living here one day, I mean.'

'I think there's stuff in the town library. Quite a lot about the architect. Samuel Cribbs. His papers. They may be able to help.' The salesman's tone is cautious now; the hope of commission fading from his face.

Matthew nods his thanks and reassures that he will pass on the brochure and his card to his parents.

'I'll get them to give you a call.'

The man's weak smile confirms he no longer believes him.

# CHAPTER 5

At the café overlooking the quay Martha is smiling as Kate rushes in – flustered. They have met twice more for tea and coffee at the mobile van – each separately but equally surprised at their strange, and as yet unexplained, rapport. But today Kate has suggested breakfast. The guilty pleasure of a proper fry-up. Indoors. Sit down. Her treat.

'I'm so, so sorry I'm late. Have you ordered, Martha?'

And then Kate is cross with herself for misjudging the traffic, noticing the fresh stains of egg and ketchup with tiny crumbs of fried bread on the large white platter. Damn. She planned to pay. Her idea.

'Look – I really am sorry. I'll settle up. And get more tea… yes?'

Martha shakes her head. 'It's OK, Kate. Taken care of. You get your own.'

Kate is now puzzled, her brow tensing as a large woman emerges from behind the counter, bumping past her to manoeuvre into the seat next to Martha and with a thud places a large photo album on the table. The woman, sporting enormous sweat stains under each arm matched only in scale by the most extraordinary smile, squeezes Martha's shoulder and then turns the pages of the album.

'Just look, Martha. So *beautiful*. How can I thank you?' A strong Italian accent. Warm, friendly tone.

Kate leans forward to see, upside down, a series of pictures of a family group standing alongside a font, with a baby draped in a long, white shawl. The woman then narrows her eyes, querying the intrusion.

'I'm sorry. Introductions,' Martha is smiling. 'This is Kate – a new friend of mine. Kate – Maria – an *old* and very dear friend of mine.'

The two women nod politely.

'Martha knitted the shawl for my granddaughter.' Maria turns the album so Kate can see properly. A beautiful, highly intricate piece of work like crochet – Kate suddenly understanding the free breakfast.

'You are very welcome, Maria. I'm glad it went so well. And how is the baby?' Martha is beaming.

'Gorgeous.' Maria puts one hand to her chest, a long exhalation then. 'She does not sleep, of course. But these young mothers – they expect too much.' And then spying the growing queue at the counter, Maria squeezes Martha's shoulder again before disappearing off to deal with her customers.

Martha sips some more tea as Kate finally sits.

'So you're a regular around these parts then, Martha? When you suggested here, I didn't realise…'

Kate is now taking in Martha's transformed appearance – new clothes – still tatty but clean. Her hair washed and loose today, which makes her look much younger – Kate realising that she is probably quite close to her own age. Late thirties. Forty, tops.

'Yes. Maria and I go back a bit. I spend most winters here. People are very kind. Look out for me.'

'And you've found somewhere to stay OK?'

'The hostel, yes. The usual.' She pulls a face, suddenly looking at her watch. 'Damn.'

'Is anything the matter?'

'No. No – but I need to be somewhere.' She finishes her tea in one swig. 'You can come if you like, unless you want to stay on? For your breakfast?'

'No, no. I'm fine. I'll eat later.'

'Come on then.' And now Martha winks. Patently teasing.


Just minutes later and Kate understands why Martha laughed off the offer of a lift. Wendy's Wool Shop, their destination, is precisely two doors down. The same enviable view of the quay from a glorious bay window and the interior – Kate's idea of heaven.

As if frozen in time, the shop smells of the past; an aroma of care and attention. Beeswax. Something akin to lemons. And all the shelves in immaculate order. Rows and rows of wool – categorised by grade and colour with the prices neatly recorded in smart black pen on square white cards.

'Oh – Martha, it's so good to see you. I'm so sorry I was away when you got back.' The woman behind the counter exchanges a warm hug with Martha. 'I so wish I had a spare bedroom you could use. You do know that?'

'I'm fine. The hostel's OK. You're not to worry.'

And then the wool shop owner is stepping back to hold Martha at arm's length for a moment, appraising her outfit, Kate all the while smiling awkwardly in the background.

'Salvation Army? The Lord forgive me, but we can do better than that. I've put a few bits aside. Out the back.'

Martha turns to Kate and beckons her forward to the counter, repeating the sequence in the café. Wendy-Kate. Kate-Wendy.

'You're new in Aylesborough then, Kate?'

She trots out her script – her husband, an architect, moving his business, their desire for a healthier, quieter life by the sea, but it is soon apparent that Wendy is struggling to concentrate and, as Kate pauses, the shopkeeper's gaze moves back to Martha – the smile broadening as she scurries out to the back of the shop, reappearing with two large bags: one stuffed with wool and notes, the second with clothes. For a time the women babble amiably about mutual acquaintances. Which wool is popular just now. The trends. The frustrations.

'Quite a few orders.' Wendy is rummaging through various notes in the bag with the wool. 'A lot of tank tops and waistcoats, I'm afraid.' She pulls a face. 'I blame that Leo Sayer character myself. I know they're fiddly, but see what you can do. There's no hurry.'

And then, as two customers appear at the counter holding patterns for tank tops, which makes Wendy colour, there are more hugs and Martha is juggling the bags as they move aside to let Wendy get on with her work. Only at the door does the convivial mood change ever so slightly as Martha turns and Wendy speaks more quietly.

'I'm sorry, Martha. No letters. I've asked around for you. Nothing.'

And then they are back on the bench where they first met, sipping tea once again from chipped mugs – Kate still completely disorientated.

'So you knit then to *order*, Martha?'

'Sometimes. Wendy's very persuasive and I enjoy it. Helps with the pennies when there's not much work about.'

'But you can't make much, *knitting*, surely?' Kate immediately regrets her tone. 'I'm sorry. I didn't mean for that to sound patronising. Forgive me.'

Martha just sips her drink and for a time the women look pointedly out to the water where a fisherman is tidying the nets on his boat, watched closely by the gulls circling above – the boat rocking ever so gently so that the man has to stand with his legs wide apart as he works.

'I know it's not really any of my business, but do you mind me asking why here? Why Aylesborough every winter?'

She would like to ask about the letters really. *What letters, Martha?*

'And would you mind if I lied as you did to Wendy back there?' There is no disapproval in the tone. Just a directness which feels as surprising as it is refreshing to Kate, who sits in silence, wondering what on earth to say. Should she admit that she is secretly pleased to have been caught out? Pleased for someone to see through her?

The fisherman is now tossing overboard some scraps from a large plastic bucket, which sets the gulls into a frenzy of squawking, the two women turning to look at each other for just a moment – yet another brief holding of eye contact; this strange acknowledgement of something Kate does not yet understand – before their gaze is drawn away to a man muttering to himself as he marches to the library next to the wool shop, a huge black folder under his arm, bearing the large logo of the development up on the hill – *Millrose Mount Village*. A logo which Kate has spotted subject to sometimes comic but mostly coarse graffiti on various billboards around the town.

Kate watches the man go into the library and opens her mouth to ask Martha how she knew that she was lying back there. But Martha looks so relaxed, still no judgement or disapproval on her face, and so Kate changes her mind.

Says nothing at all.

*Moscow State Orchestra*
*1960*


*My Martha,*

*I keep telling myself this will be my last attempt to reach you. And then I change my mind. And write again...*

*Friends are still saying that it is time – way, way overdue – to let this go.*

*Are they right?*

*As you see, I am in Moscow still – rehearsing for a new tour. We are to play the Debussy Sonata and I always find it so difficult... Do you remember the first time that I played it for you? At your father's home?*

*I will certainly never forget.*

*Sometimes I wonder if these letters are even leaving Russia. Other times I imagine it is your father who refuses to forward them. Destroys them, even?*

*At night sometimes I lie in bed and imagine still the worst thing of all. That my friends have been right all along and I am now some kind of embarrassment to you.*

*But the hell for me is in the not knowing.*

*That is the worst thing, Martha. The thing I find so impossible to live with. Thinking of you. And not knowing if you ever think still of me.*

*Your Josef x*

# CHAPTER 6

Day three in Alyesborough. Matthew glances at his watch and scratches his head. Bad decision to use the leisure centre soap on his hair. Even a long rinse has left it dull. Unbearably itchy. He brushes his shoulder, instinctively turning to the nearest shop window to double-check his reflection. He pushes his chin up and tilts his head, the shift in the angle then dissolving the mirror so that he is looking *through* the window.

Matthew closes his eyes immediately. No. He is no kind of believer in fate. And he does not have time for this.

*No, Matthew.*

He is already pushing his luck for his interview. Keeping his eyes firmly shut, he lifts the rucksack gently from his shoulder and lowers it to the ground, all the time trying to ignore the music in his head – the movement of his fingers. Twitching. He has played one like it only once before. Grade three. He remembers the cool of the ivory – picturing the small crack on the upper C which he could feel clearly against his fingers during the forte passages. But most of all he remembers the tone – the exquisite tone which has never quite been equalled. Before or since. And he remembers too the sick feeling in his stomach as he left the cold, draughty exam room in the city museum with a sense of utter bereavement.

Matthew opens his eyes now and stares, leaning forward to take it in properly. A rosewood case with ornate flowers looped in bowers around the side – too fussy for most tastes but a gem nonetheless. He can picture the craftsmen assembling it, smiling all the time with pride, and watches the scene play out, wondering if their banter is in German – the piece from the New York factory or Hamburg?

He cups his hand into a peak over his eyes to deflect the sun, surprised and embarrassed suddenly as a man walks into view alongside the piano with a large yellow duster in his hand.

Matthew leans back and stands very straight, keen to avoid eye contact. Too late. The man is beaming from ear to ear and then, horror of horrors, *beckoning*.

Matthew looks over his shoulder and turns back, frowning, to find the man now laughing at him and beckoning again. No – *you*. Yes – *you*. Matthew blushes, furious with himself for not marching on by. He signals at his watch that *sorry, he is in a hurry. Has no time.* But the man is having none of it and laughs, swinging the door open, the duster still in his hand, and as a small bell tinkles middle A above his head stands there expectantly. So that in the end Matthew has absolutely no choice but to go inside.

'Arrived yesterday.' The man is breathless with excitement, prowling around the piano like a great cat stalking its prey – taking small, measured steps as if any sudden movement might make the instrument panic, hitch up its wooden skirt, rise onto the tips of its metal claw feet and run for the hills. 'I can't believe it either.'

'I beg your pardon?' Matthew pushes his rucksack with his foot to rest alongside a stand of sheet music.

'Sorry. But I saw you gawping.'

Matthew closes his mouth, aware only now that it is wide open, and checks his watch again. This is ridiculous. The hotel job sounded perfect – even a room thrown in. It would be crazy to miss the appointment. And what is this, anyway? A conversation with no beginning. The man is clearly barking.

'I know it's madness. For a little shop like this, I mean... to tie up so much money in one piece. But it's not a risk. Not *really*. I mean, they sell themselves, don't they? I have a friend who's made a fortune with them.'

Still the man walks around the piano, as if needing to take in every angle.

'He's an authorised dealer – in Bath. Can help with parts. Advice. Liaising with the factory. They guard their reputation, of course. Quite understandable. But if I do a good job. With the restoration, I mean.'

Matthew moves towards the piano and runs his finger over the case – smooth, bar a few tiny ridges where the decorative inlay needs attention.

'Is it in tune?' Matthew tries middle G. Slightly out. Just below concert pitch.

'Twelve thousand parts apparently. In every one. Astonishing, isn't it?' The man finally stops stalking to sit suddenly on a piano stool positioned alongside a much humbler upright model.

'I'm going to spend the first month just assessing her, of course. Take it slowly. I've done rebuilds before. But not a Steinway. Never a Steinway grand.'

They are both staring at the keys, the man grinning again.

'Go on then.'

And now he is hurriedly positioning another stool in front of the grand – gesturing for Matthew to sit down.

'I beg your pardon?'

And then the man tuts as if Matthew has said something completely ridiculous.

'You're wondering how I know you play?' The tone is high-pitched and teasing but affably so. Not sarcastic. 'Young man, I have been in this business *all* of my life. No one looks at a piano like that unless they play.'

Matthew raises his right eyebrow and can hear his father's voice. *Don't do that with your eyebrow. It's rude, Matthew. Looks so bloody superior.*

'I have watched people gaze through that window for a generation,' the man is smiling. 'And trust me – there are only three looks. First – those who don't play. All they see is a piece of furniture. You can watch them weighing up the measurements. The colour. Trying to picture how it will fit the proportions of their room. The same way you might look at a sofa or a chair. Then there are the people who *wished* they played. Or wished they played better. Regret in their eyes.' At this he sighs in sympathy. Sad for them. 'And then there is the third group. The ones, as you know very well, who do not look with their eyes at all.'

Matthew for a moment is unnerved to be read this well. And this quickly.

'*Please.*' He is waving now for Matthew to sit down. 'Anything you like. I'm a pretty average pianist these days. Spot of arthritis, sadly. Would love to hear how she can really sound.'

Matthew, obedient, finally sits and feels his stomach somersault – nervous not of his eccentric audience but the fear of disappointment, like a child with a large box at Christmas, afraid that the gift inside may not live up to the dream.

Chopin or Debussy?

Matthew holds his breath. Flexes his fingers. Undecided. A few notes then changes his mind. Debussy. Yes. He closes his eyes and begins again, slowly and tentatively. And then as the tone confirms his best hopes, a smile – his shoulders relaxing as he plays a few more bars and then, beaming, on through the whole piece – eyes wide open, with his new companion grinning a *told-you-so*.

And not until the piece is done do either breathe properly. Or speak. Both astonished that, even ahead of all the work required, it can sound like this. Like a cloud of magic has passed through the shop – freezing time and holding them there in some strange and mesmeric bubble. The spell cast.

'Tea.' The man has to cough to clear his throat. To compose himself. 'I'll make us tea. I'm Geoffrey, by the way.'

Matthew looks at his watch – resigned now. The hotel job lost.

'Matthew. And yes, please. Tea would be just lovely.'

Through Mozart and a few lighter pieces, Matthew assesses there is a lot of work to be done. Several of the notes are failing completely. Others sticking. And the pedals need major attention too. But for all that, the piano is a dream. The tone beyond wonderful.

He teases his new companion, finishing with Chopsticks as Geoffrey emerges from the back office with a tray and, inexplicably, three mugs. After offering Matthew milk, Geoffrey explains the spare drink.

'I'll just pop next door with this. To Wendy. In the wool shop. I always do the morning cuppa. She does the afternoon. Won't be a tick.'

Matthew stops then – stunned that this complete stranger is about to entrust his shop to him. Even in the brief moment that it would take to deliver the tea, a dishonourable person could at worst be into the till and away – at best leg it with a stack of the music books on display.

'You shouldn't go trusting your shop to a stranger, you know.'

'Shouldn't I?'

And then the bell tinkles above the door again as Matthew watches Geoffrey emerge onto the pavement outside to collide almost immediately with a man he recognises – the salesman from the old hospital who is carrying a large folder bearing the development's logo. *Millrose Mount Village*.

'Stupid bloody idiot!' The developer jumps back as a slurp of hot tea cascades down his trousers. 'What the bloody hell are you doing?'

Geoffrey steadies himself to appraise the man very carefully, just as he sized up Matthew – the conclusion clearly less pleasing this time. 'I'm very sorry. You must be in a hurry.'

The salesman snorts, glancing momentarily into the shop so that Matthew has to turn away – keen that he should not be recognised – and then marches off, muttering that people *ought to be more careful. Look where they're bloody well going...*

Geoffrey does not reply but smiles weakly at Matthew and disappears for just a few minutes before returning a little breathless. 'Half a cup better than none, I suppose. Wendy can be quite busy on a Wednesday. Now. Where were we?'

And then a whole barrage of questions. So what is Matthew doing in Aylesborough-on-sea? And where is he staying? And when Matthew confesses he is roughing it until he finds a job, Geoffrey ushers him, almost exploding with excitement, to the desk at the other side of the room where, to Matthew's astonishment, is a small, faded sign. *Part-time help needed. Musical experience essential.*

So that, within half an hour, it is all agreed. A trial period. Twenty five hours a week at first. Yes. Matthew can play and serve customers while Geoffrey keeps the other side of the business going – piano tuning – which these days means closing the shop. Losing sheet music sales and the like.

And Matthew, quietly wondering what *these days* refers to, is saying – *surely you'll want references* until Geoffrey gives him the same look which answered his question about how he knew that he could play. And Matthew stops. Realising he is in danger of insulting him.

# CHAPTER 7

Kate and Martha meet next on the beach.

'It's why I wear wellies.' Martha, hands on hips, is teasing as Kate minces her way along a river of seawater, trying to decide where to cross. The stream divides the beach in two, widening much further back into a rock pool through which three children are wading, carrying fishing nets.

Kate finally decides to leap for it but lands short, Martha then roaring as she stands momentarily bemused – ankle-deep in water.

'I don't know what I was thinking with these canvas shoes.' Kate steps out of the stream to shake her right foot, spraying water, her shoe and sock sopping. 'You're right. Wellies next time.'

They walk then for a time in silence, something Kate likes very much with Martha. Not to have to do small talk. Finally, as they reach rocks on the far side of the beach, Martha sits and takes out a flask provided by Maria from the café, lifting a spare cup by way of invitation.

'Oh yes, please. Perfect. You know, Martha, it's really funny, isn't it, how with some people you can feel OK very quickly. Truly relaxed, I mean. And with others you never get to that point.' She accepts a biscuit, wrapped in a napkin. Again made by Maria.

'God. These are delicious, Martha. Maria is seriously good.'

'She is.'

Martha takes a deep breath and for a moment Kate worries that she has embarrassed them both; crossed a line by mentioning the rapport. Said too much? And then...

'I don't think you can ever call it. Who you'll click with.' Martha is examining her own biscuit very closely. 'I think, to be honest, it's probably best not to try to analyse it. Just be glad when it happens.'

'Yes. You're probably right.' Kate then turns to watch the children fishing with their nets in the pool. 'I used to do that with my father. Rock-pooling. Between us, I think he was secretly sorry never to have a son. Never quite sure how to play it with me at home. The dolls. The doll's house and all the girly jazz. But when we went on holiday – he sort of came into his own. Relaxed more with me. He used to take me rock-pooling a lot. Collecting crabs in buckets. I loved it.'

'So do you not have any siblings, Kate?'

'No.'

Martha pauses for a moment, brushing biscuit crumbs from her coat. 'Me neither.'

'Though I never minded, actually. Probably makes me sound very selfish. but I rather liked it.' Kate narrows her eyes. 'People always assume it must have been lonely, growing up, but I had lots of friends. Never minded at all.'

Martha takes in a long breath and then glances up to the hill in the distance on which perches the large and imposing outline of what Kate assumes is Millrose Mount Hospital. The site now has ugly fencing all around it, which rather spoils the view.

'I'm assuming that fencing will come down when they redevelop?'

'Sorry?'

'Up there. The old hospital. That's the one they closed because of the TV documentary, isn't it?'

Martha shrugs.

'I read about it. In all the papers. Awful story.'

'Before my time. Maria probably knows.' Martha is suddenly glancing at her watch. 'In fact, talking of Maria, I really ought to get back. I said I'd help her out.'

'Oh right. Yes, of course.' Quietly Kate is disappointed they are short of time today but she finds a smile. Does not want to seem needy. Martha loves working in the café and it is amusing to watch her and Maria together. Maybe she will pop in later to join them both for a quick drink and a chat. Yes. Kate feels lucky to at last have this new option. Somewhere to go. People to talk to.

And so they sit for just a little longer before retracing their steps, Kate this time taking a longer run-up to successfully clear the river.

'So the bus trips, Kate. You still doing the open-top tours?'

'Sometimes.' Kate doesn't remember sharing that she was a regular.

'It's just I noticed you a few times. Before you noticed me, I mean. Up on that top deck. It's the hair. Hard to miss…'

'Oh right. I was doing research. For a project. On local tourism.' And then Kate feels this instant pang of guilt; an unease which spreads very quickly through her so that she stops suddenly, which makes Martha stop in her tracks also, turning to face her.

'Actually, no. That's a complete lie, Martha. I was taking the bus tours to kill time.'

Martha frowns.

'I mean, I've never not had a job to go to before. And this situation – this blessed extended sick leave thing. It's completely thrown me.' Kate is surprised to have said this out loud for the first time but there is something about being with Martha which makes everything feel different. Confusing and strange but also a relief somehow. Permission to be herself. Like that moment on the quay when Martha knew immediately that she was lying.

Martha remains very still, just looking. The salt in the air. The salt on Kate's lips. Both of them just standing. Waiting, apparently, for Kate to go on.

'The thing is, Martha, we moved here to try to make it all a bit easier. A change of scene. But the truth is, I still don't really know what I'm supposed to *do*. With my days, I mean. It's not like a holiday, this. With a holiday, you make the most of time, because you know soon you are going back to being busy. This? This is completely different.' Kate can feel her heart rate increasing. For so long she has stuck to her script. Worn the brave face. Told everyone *how marvellous it is to have so much free time. Wonderful. I'm so lucky.*

Martha tilts her head and reaches out her hand to touch Kate's arm. Kate expects a momentary touch. But instead Martha keeps her hand there, resting on Kate's elbow. And somehow it feels the most comforting thing that anyone has done for her for a very long time.

'It's actually the thing that is driving me completely mad. All this time on my hands, Martha. I honestly have no idea what I am supposed to *do*.'

*Moscow State Orchestra*
*1961*

*My Martha,*

*I have just a few minutes to scratch a few lines, so forgive how short this is. A dancer friend is being sent over to France to help sort the new line-up after Nureyev's defection.*

*This friend has posted letters for me before and can be trusted. Also, I am addressing this via Margaret your housekeeper – hoping it has a better chance of reaching you.*

*All is chaos over Nureyev. Many people in our circle are very, very angry – fearing repercussions. But me? Oh Martha, I am absolutely overjoyed.*

*Now at last I believe that this can be done.*

*I have so much more to say but my friend is hovering at my door so know this only...*

*I am due to tour both Europe and America myself very soon. Everything is sold out, so we are all praying it will not be cancelled, even with all this Nureyev fallout.*

*So – providing this tour does go ahead, I am going to do it, Martha. Defect.*

*I really am going to get away... and find you.*

*Always and forever,*

*Your Josef x*

# CHAPTER 8

'You are joking.'

Kate pushes two more towels into the washing machine, aware that she is overloading it.

'Tell me you're joking, Kate.'

'Jesus.' Unable to close the door, even with her full weight pressed against it, Kate realises she is in danger of forcing the hinge, so pulls out one of the towels and tries again, triumphant as the door finally clicks into place. 'She's nowhere decent to stay.'

'That's not true, Kate, and you know it. And for God's sake, stop that, will you? *Please.* We need to talk about this properly.'

'It won't be for long.'

'How do you know that? Give this Martha the green light to move in here and what possible incentive could there be to leave? We'd be stuck with her.'

'She's a nice woman. Really interesting. You'll be surprised.'

'She's a *bag lady*, Kate.'

'More traveller, actually.'

'Bag lady. Traveller. Hippy. Dippy… Whatever. You've met her, what – four, five times at most? You know absolutely nothing about her background and suddenly you want her to live with us? I mean, you must see this is complete madness. She could be a nutter. Murder us in our beds. This isn't My Fair bloody Lady, you know.' Toby is now pacing, something he always does when completely exasperated. He has this slightly funny gait when he gets wound up like this and, even though she is genuinely sorry to upset him, Kate cannot help being just a tiny bit amused, especially by the Eliza Doolittle reference.

She bites her lip against a smile, which she knows could tip things entirely the wrong way, and turns to the clothes just emptied from the tumble drier on top of the washing machine – folding them quite needlessly into colour-coded piles. Whites. Brights. Mids.

'We get on, Toby. Me and Martha. Really clicked. And I think it will do me good.' It is perhaps wrong of her to play this card. Below the belt? But, like so much of her behaviour these days, she simply cannot help herself and so plunges on. 'And in any case, I've asked around and checked her out officially. Not a drinker. No drugs. Not really a bag lady, as I said – just eccentric. A misfit. Travels with gypsies sometimes. Picks fruit in France… that sort of thing. Spends the winter here each year. A lot of people vouch for her. She normally uses a hostel, but it's not great…'

'But it's not *normal*, for God's sake – to live like that, is it? And it's not normal to take people in just because…'

As Toby stops very suddenly – apparently at a complete loss – his face begins to change. The mood changes. He looks all at once sad and lost rather than cross – the very expression Kate so hates. She pauses also. A terrible frisson of guilt – right through her.

Toby still thinks that time can save them and there is a part of Kate which wishes very much she could find some way to believe him. Loves him all the more for trying so very hard. But a bigger part of her knows a different and starker truth. That for her, at least, time will make no difference whatsoever.

Just as she confided in Martha, without her job, she doesn't even have anything to *do*. And so – yes. Why not help Martha? Something nice. Something good. Something to distract and to fill this terrible phase in which Toby – her sweet, kind but wholly deluded Toby – still believes that waiting, that the simple passage of time, is going to magically change things.

Kate folds the dishcloth into two. Then four. Silently she taps the flesh beside her thumb. The counsellor taught her that. *Three. Four. Five.* To count or tap – anything rhythmic and soothing – when it all feels too much.

'Will you at least think about it, Toby?' *Nine. Ten…*

'You need to rest still, Kate. And we both need space. I mean – I know you mean well. I do understand that. And I love that you're the kind of person who wants to do this kind of thing. But it's just not the right time. To have some complete stranger – some misfit – to stay.'

Kate slots the washing basket back into its place – the middle shelf of a tiered stainless steel rack in the utility room – and stands, her knees creaking their protest. She is eager for an excuse to escape this and so checks her watch, feigning surprise.

'Look. I've got to go. I'll be late for the library. We'll talk some more properly tonight – yes? I know it's a lot to ask. I do see that, Toby. But I honestly think the company will be really good for me. Just for a little while. Will you at least think about it? *Please?*'

And then she pauses, staring for one brief, rare moment right into his eyes, which surprises them both – she jolting physically as he refuses to look away.

'OK then, Kate, so how about this? How about I promise to think about this Martha staying for a while if you think about the boxes in the hall?'

Kate feels her shoulders tense. Still he will not look away.

'I know it's hard, Kate. But we can't just leave them there. We have to decide what to do.'

For a while Kate says nothing, Toby reaching out then to hold his palm gently against her face – the gesture so very tender that she can hardly bear it.

Kate wants to hold his face in her hands too. To be a different person. She wants to tell him that she is so sorry for how she is, that she still loves him and that they are going to be all right. But she can't do it. Can't lie. Not about this. She can lie about the library and about the non-existent research. But not this...

'OK? So I think about Martha and you think about the boxes. What we're going to do about them.'

In her head Kate says that she honestly wants to try. But for now the words just won't come out of her mouth.

# CHAPTER 9

Matthew is freezing. The heating in Aylesborough's library a complete joke.

'We've reported it,' the librarian confirms as Matthew tests the metal radiator – barely tepid.

He decides to keep his coat on as he sits at his regular table by the window, the copy of Samuel Cribbs' diary in front of him again. The original in the large display case is impressive. This copy less so. Some of it faded and difficult to read – with sketchy notes from the local history society.

Matthew read through these notes previously, along with Cribbs' opening on his inspiration for the building, but he ran out of time and is hoping today to find more clues about Mill-rose Mount's day-to-day life as a hospital. To his disappointment there is nothing on the shelves about the building's recent and controversial history. Just this diary.

Matthew stares at Cribbs' now-familiar sketch on the front and feels his fist clench involuntarily. He really does not want to believe that this is where life began for him. Born? In a place like this? In truth, Samuel Cribbs' book is unlikely to be of much use. Certainly what he has read so far hasn't helped, but with no up-to-date records, it is better than nothing.

Matthew flicks through the pages. Ah, yes. This is where he got to last time... September 14th 1869... and, according to the diary, an *exceptionally fine, bright day for the season*. It was, Samuel

Cribbs noted, a special day. Returning to Millrose Mount to celebrate its first anniversary up and running...


He had needed a moment to himself, away from the rest of the visiting party, Cribbs explained. Yes. A moment to reflect as he stared at the wall alongside the large door, which bore the copper plaque unveiled just a year ago, when he had been so heartily applauded at the opening ceremony of Millrose Mount Hospital. He remembered how the cord had become entangled and the little velvet curtain would not at first sweep aside to reveal the plaque's dedication. He blushed at the memory of his embarrassment then, tugging at the cord over and over until Mr Smitherleigh, who had been in charge of all the arrangements, swept forward to rescue him.

The sun today shone bright, reflecting like a beam off the copper plaque, which he suspected might well have been polished especially for his return visit. *Millrose Mount Hospital, opened September 1868 by its architect Samuel M. Cribbs.* (He had been very insistent about the M, being oversensitive with regard to his cousin Dr Samuel J. Cribbs, with whom he was so regularly and infuriatingly confused.)

Though he had been nervous a year ago, it was a nervousness born of vanity, he realised now. The feedback on the building project was so good, all the site visits so promising that he had been almost certain the day would be a success and was nervous, in truth, not for fear of failure or reproach from his peers but because he feared his expectation of plaudits was perhaps too high. His ego too swollen.

Today's nerves were entirely different. For today Samuel Cribbs was, for the first time, to see the building fully occupied. In action. And it was the thought – how could he put this – of the *patients* which now frightened him.

Matthew looks up to find the young library assistant watching him. He smiles but, embarrassed to have caught his eye, she begins pulling out drawers, pretending to check the cards inside. She is attractive, the assistant – nice eyes – and Matthew smiles again before returning to his reading.

When he had been designing the building, Mr Cribbs reflected, he had persuaded himself of a caring, fatherly approach to the people who were to occupy it. He had listed their needs. He had been practical. Thoughtful even. Hadn't he come up with the novel idea of the central exercise area? But the reality was something else entirely. For Samuel Cribbs (whose family genes were blessedly free of mental impairments) had no real experience of so-called 'imbeciles'. Of lives rendered unfortunate – some might say useless – by some cruel accident of birth.

In truth, today he had no idea what to expect. And he was *afraid* as he paused, aside from the party gathered, all ready, to tour on this first anniversary of the building's completion.

So he was perhaps the most surprised (the rest of the party coming from the medical profession and thus being more enlightened in these matters), as they were eventually ushered inside by the doctor who was to be their guide, by the scenes which greeted them.

They began in the kitchens, which Mr Cribbs was pleased to note were functioning as splendidly as he had hoped. The proportions perfect. The noise was considerable, of course – the clattering of pans and dishes and oven doors, punctuated by instructions issued by some of the many staff scurrying about. But the overall impression was one of remarkable order. Yes. Almost military order. And what was to come as the greatest surprise of all was his discovery, in conversation with the superintendent, that a good fifty per cent of the people he had assumed were staff were actually patients.

Mr Cribbs, on discovering this, glanced around in amazement, trying immediately to distinguish between the two. Patients? Or paid help? It was nothing short of miraculous, and he began to smile. Relaxing now. Congratulating himself on the part that he had played in this achievement – in providing the right environment for such a healthy routine for these people who, at home, no doubt would not have been allowed to put the kettle on.

The food was passed in large, covered dishes to lines of people who were waiting in the corridors with trolleys ready, presumably, to be wheeled away to the wards. Again, from the varied clothing it was difficult to be sure whether these people were inmates too.

From the kitchen, the visitors were moved to the bakehouse, where patients (their status confirmed by a supervisor) were operating the machinery to knead the dough before expertly shaping it into loaves for the ovens. And no, Mr Cribbs was assured, there had been no record of any serious accidents. *The hospital was very proud of its safety record.*

A sample ward was next on the tour, where the party were shown first the dayroom – four tables each set for twenty patients to take their lunch – and then the sleeping quarters. Thirty inmates per room, overseen by two nursing staff. And along the route, as the group negotiated the ample corridors and stairways, Mr Cribbs was informed that, yes, the vast majority of the running of the whole establishment was undertaken by the inmates. Millrose Mount Hospital, in effect, was run by Millrose Mount Hospital. He had helped to create not just a building but a self-sufficient community.

Mr Cribbs paused as his party was led ahead up the main stairway of the block towards the visitors' reception room where he suspected sherry and lunch would now await them. He knew that to the west was the wing he had been asked to design with 'special facilities', for the most unfortunate; those intent on harming not just themselves but others. He wondered for a second if he should enquire if permission could be granted to visit this section also, but changed his mind as Mr Smitherleigh called back for him, asking *is there a problem?*

'No. No. Just coming.' And Mr Cribbs smiled to himself before joining the others for the only lunch he would eat in his life prepared by the certifiably insane.

Matthew, frustrated by this section, flicks through the pages to discover that the diary entries finish abruptly on March 18th 1871.

He turns to the last few pages of the book, written up by the secretary of the local history society. Good God. The architect Samuel Cribbs was actually found *murdered* – his throat slit; the body discovered in his study at home by the housekeeper – the expression on Mr Cribbs' face, noted in the papers of the day, as 'one of complete surprise'.

The notes mention rumours initially of suicide – that perhaps the architect's obsession with the hospital had got the better of him – but then an escape was reported. One of the patients, who had been incarcerated at Millrose Mount from his teens, had managed to escape in the laundry, hiding in one of the wheeled trolleys that was removed daily along a tunnel which Mr Cribbs had so carefully designed for the purpose.

This patient, suffering some severe personality disorder, apparently developed a fixation with the architect – an obsession which had been fuelled by his kindliness and the interest he showed, especially in the work carried out in the kitchens. Mr Cribbs had made the innocent yet ultimately fatal mistake of praising the patient's bread-making skills. This had apparently been interpreted as some kind of love at first sight, which initially proved a positive thread in the young man's life until Mr Cribbs neglected to tour the kitchens on his subsequent visits. Rejection. Unrequited love turned to hate. Too much for the troubled, damaged mind.

The young man had waited in an alleyway close to the architect's home until after dark and then crept inside.

Matthew feels a shiver – the already cool air chilling further around him – and closes the book.

'Enough for today?' The librarian's smile is genuine as Matthew scrapes his chair back, regretting the noise even though there is no one to disturb. Aylesborough library is too small, too tatty and, above all, too cold to attract much business.

The assistant notices him glancing around. 'There's talk of a new library. But we'll believe it when we see it,' she sighs.

In the corner is a display area for posters – an attempt to attract more children, the mention of a reading club – but the offerings all faded. Matthew has seen only pensioners using the place, many of them after the large-print books kept on three shelves directly alongside the desk area.

Sad really. A dreary and disappointing library, and Matthew is just about to depart when there is a commotion in the doorway – loud voices and the shake of umbrellas – as three men, accompanied by the salesman from Millrose Mount Village, sweep into the room.

The men are all wearing suits in various shades of grey. Council types – a supposition confirmed as the library assistant begins busying herself behind the desk, evidently in the presence of her employers.

'What we were thinking…' The tallest of the men is now sweeping ahead of the others to the window area. 'We were thinking that if there could be an area taking in the views. A lot of glass. Something akin to a conservatory? An exhibition area – over here, say. And then there could be seating – for authors' talks and the like.'

The other men are nodding furiously as the man from Mill-rose Mount makes notes on a clipboard. Matthew slides the copy of the diary across the desk to the assistant, waiting for his card to be returned, and is glad when he is finally outside – the smell of the salt spray and the call of the gulls reviving him.

# CHAPTER 10

Kate waits for the sound of Toby's car departing before slipping on her rubber gloves to get everything ready for Martha. In truth, she knows that her house does not need cleaning and knows too that Toby would have got upset – pacing and worrying about her *overdoing it* – had she removed the gloves from their smart new packet before he left. But this is not about what the *house* needs. This is exciting now.

It is a bit like decorating, Kate has discovered. Once you start cleaning one room truly meticulously, only then do you realise just how dirty the rest of the house has become. OK – not *dirty*. Even Kate can see that it is not dirty, *per se*. But once she starts, she always finds something which can be done better. Surfaces to sparkle more brightly. Things to line up more neatly.

And she has come to love the sensation of finishing; not the cleaning itself. Not that. But the feeling, albeit very temporary, of looking around herself and seeing nothing which needs her attention.

Kate tugs her gloves into place. Where to start? The surfaces in the kitchen first. Yes. She is glad now to have remembered an old toothbrush for around the taps. She flicks the switch on the radio, checking the clock to confirm that the afternoon play is just about to begin, and sets to work.

By coincidence the play begins with the sound of running water just as Kate fills her bucket. A man in his bath – singing to his ducks. It is to be a curious play, the kind requiring a certain amount of concentration, and Kate is not sure she is in the mood. She wipes the surfaces, moving all the jars and equipment carefully aside so as not to miss any stray crumbs from the toaster as the man is interrupted in his bath by his wife to say there is a salesman at the door with encyclopaedias. Kate spins the wheel on the radio until she finds some music. Classical. Yes. Better. She gives the radio a quick wipe with her cloth and checks her watch, reminding herself not to miss the TV chat show later.

She sighs. *Josef Karpati.* Today's guest. Her absolute favourite...

For some reason her doll's house comes next into her mind. That had a smart little kitchen – a real little cooker with a door that opened and tiny saucepans inside. Three different sizes. Kate remembers she liked to move the furniture around – rearranging the rooms each week. Sometimes moving the sofa along the back wall but then realising that people would not be able to see the television painted on one of the walls. Infuriatingly immovable.

She squeezes her cloth into the water and wonders what Martha will make of her home – if the clinical shininess will frighten her away; worry her as it does Toby.

*Please, Kate. You've got to stop this. Please.*

For just a moment she pictures them – her and Toby – in the doll's house together, snuggled up in a single bed – the smell of sex and paraffin and sweat. A glow from the ancient heater across the room; a dirty saucepan and a can of beans on the little Belling cooker in the corner of the room. Their clothes on the floor. How had they lived like that? Student bedsits. How had she and Toby ever lived like that?

Kate refills her bucket now and, while the bubbles rise, reaches quickly into the corner cupboard for the mop. She retrieves her old toothbrush from under the sink and smiles as she scrubs at the taps before polishing them with paper towels to see her distorted reflection, leaning forward and then backwards to make her face swell and shrink, before moving on to the floor.

The room is now smelling of lemons and Kate is pleased. She is hungry, regretting skipping lunch, but does not want to make a mess while it all looks so lovely, so finishes the floor and moves into the sitting room while it dries.

An hour later and she is happy. She prepared the spare room yesterday and checked it all again this morning. A mix of books alongside the bed – Hardy. Agatha Christie. One of Toby's spy novels and Jane Austen, of course. Two towels. A box of tissues. Yes. Everything ready.

In the end, to please her, Toby had agreed to a trial period – a month, tops, on the strict understanding Kate will go back to the doctor, and if there is any sign it is proving too much of a strain, then Martha will have to go. *Agreed?*

Kate stares out of the window onto the garden and digs the nails of her right hand into her palm – pushing the picture away. She watches the birds for a moment, as they enjoy the stale bread retrieved from the toaster tray earlier, and then to distract herself she moves back into the utility alongside the kitchen and sets up the ironing board, selecting three of Toby's shirts from the basket while the iron heats. Two are favourites of his – casual; the kind he likes to wear to work when he is not meeting clients. Architecture, Toby likes to argue, is about creativity, and people who want creative should not expect a collar and tie. *Fuddy-duddies*, he complains, struggling into a tie on the days he has formal meetings – pitching for work.

It is good, Kate reflects, that he is working now with Mark. He has always been the politician, able to talk Toby around. Knows him so well. Better than me now, Kate wonders, switching the dial on the iron to steam.

It was her mother who had taught her to iron a man's shirt – *Collar first, Kate, then the cuffs, then the back panel... see...* Toby

wouldn't care, quite frankly, if she put them straight on the hang-
er – would dress happily in crumpled linen – but Kate does not
mind the task these days. Another thing to keep her occupied.
She pictures him, bent over his designs – his brow tensed into the
Y-shaped wrinkle, examining the work from every angle before
stopping suddenly and relaxing, the letter on his brow dissolving
like writing in sand, before smiling and leaning further forward.
Yes. It is good that he at least has his work.

Kate finishes the shirts and then looks out once again onto
the garden – three birds now pecking at the last few crumbs of
toast on the little table bought from the garden centre the week
they moved in. She looks beyond the bird table to the trees, then
to the earth dug by Toby ready for the vegetables he imagines he
might grow, and the thought returns. And this time she cannot
push the image away.

She closes her eyes and can see them perfectly. Muddy feet
across the floor. A child's perfect little prints.

Kate stands the iron up on its rest and steps out of her sandals. Like a sleepwalker, she moves slowly into the garden, wincing
slightly at the cool wind and the cold of the paving stones, then the
wet of the grass and finally the softer warmth of the damp ground
where Toby has been digging. She looks down at her bare feet as
she walks, around and around, until both her feet are warm and
brown, then back across the lawn, and slowly, ever so slowly, across
the perfectly clean floor. Five, six footprints – until she reaches the
doorway to the hall where she turns to examine the trail.

Too big. She feels her shoulders move. Her footprints are too
big…

Kate feels the familiar prickle of tears and fights hard. How
long she is there – struggling to hold them in – Kate is unsure,
but it is like waking from sleep, from a dream, when the doorbell rings. A glance at the clock. Six already. But – didn't she
say seven? Kate stands to see Martha's blurred image through

the patterned glass of the front door. She bites her lip, slips her muddy feet back into her sandals and smooths her hair. Damn. She so wanted to be calm. Ready.

'You all right? I'm not too early, am I?' Martha looks worried as she stands on the doorstep surrounded by several plastic bags and a small rucksack. For a moment she glances at Kate's feet but says nothing and picks up the collection of bags, swinging the rucksack over her left shoulder.

'No. No. Come on in, please. I was just…'

Martha and her bags seem to fill the entire hallway and there is an awkward pause – her guest unsure of which way to turn as Kate freezes.

'Martha, I'm sorry. I was in the middle…'

Kate stops as Martha clocks the muddy prints across the kitchen floor. She turns, 'I've brought some food, Kate. From Maria. If it's not too forward, I thought I'd cook tonight. As a thank you.'

'There's no need, Martha.' Another pause. 'But thank you. Yes. That would be lovely.'

'So is it all right then?' Martha raises one of the plastic bags as Kate looks on, still dazed. 'To put the food away?'

Kate nods as Martha picks her way around the footprints in the kitchen to lay out her food on the worktop next to the sink. There is a large pack of meat, a small plastic container, tomatoes, some fresh herbs and a bottle of red wine.

Kate watches, fascinated, as Martha produces more and more ingredients and looks around her for the fridge.

'Just lasagne, but I have a fabulous recipe. Maria gets wonderful chicken livers for the sauce. Makes it really rich.'

Kate opens the fridge and moves some items to make room. 'Can I get you a drink? Coffee? Or hot chocolate? I was just about to make myself one. A treat – with the works. Cream and marshmallows. I remember you saying you like it.'

'Oh, goodness. Sounds lovely. Yes, please.' Martha crouches down – sorting her ingredients. 'And you're absolutely sure this is OK with your husband? I mean, it's very good of you. Very unexpected.'

And then, as she stretches out her arm, Kate notices for the first time the scars on Martha's wrist. A series of neat, red lines. Martha catches her eye and quickly pulls down the sleeve of her jumper, using her middle finger to hold the cuff in place. Kate suddenly understanding all the baggy clothes. The overly long sleeves.

'So you're quite sure this is OK with Toby? That he doesn't mind?'

Kate smiles weakly. 'Like I said before, Toby's busy setting up his new business. Working quite long hours. To be honest, he's glad for me to have some company.'

Martha turns again to the ingredients, her finger still gripping her sleeve. 'Maria has a fabulous butcher. Best meat locally.'

'So did she just give you all this, then?' Kate tries not to let her eyes wander back to Martha's wrists.

'Yes. She's short-staffed so I helped her out a bit yesterday. Favour for favour. She's got a new oven, so it's a bit chaotic. There. I think that's everything.'

Kate meanwhile begins busying herself with milk for the hot chocolate. 'I expect you're wondering. About the muddy prints?' She feels uneasy for Martha to see this mess but Martha is frowning at something else. The line of three large packing boxes, still sealed in the hallway.

Toby had wanted to put them upstairs – or in the garage – while she decides what to do. But it makes Kate stressed to even think about it. What to do for the best.

'Really should have got myself better sorted by now.' Kate begins fidgeting with her hair, staring at the boxes. 'The truth is I should have had a better clear-out before we packed up the old house. So much stuff. I still can't decide whether this lot should be unpacked or go to the charity shop.'

'Right.' Martha's tone is curious. She glances between the immaculate order of the house – the neatness in the kitchen, and the sitting room visible through the doorway – and back to the cardboard boxes in the hall. Then she tilts her head and reaches out to lightly touch Kate's arm as if by way of reassurance, before glancing at her own small rucksack on the floor and smiling.

'You will have gathered that I don't have that problem myself. Not a lot of stuff, full stop,' Martha is smiling and Kate is grateful for the gesture.

And then once the drinks are ready, Kate is suddenly noticing the time. 'Oh goodness, I hope you don't mind, Martha, but I want to catch something on the television. Toby is going on about getting one of these video recorder things. Have you seen them? All sounds way too complicated to me…'

She leads the way into the sitting room, the bag of marshmallows tucked under her left arm, Martha a step behind as Kate finds the right channel, relieved that the chat show host is still doing his intro.

'There. Think I've only missed five minutes…'

Martha's eyes widen.

'Josef Karpati's on next. Do you like him? We saw him at the Albert Hall once. Amazing.'

Martha reaches out for her mug, her face colouring now as she takes a sip.

'I saw a documentary on him a while back. Fascinating. Do you know that he defected on a bank holiday? All the embassies shut. Right panic it caused. They had to use some emergency protocol at the airport to sort it all out. Can you imagine? And he was engaged for a time to that opera singer – gosh. What was her name? Anyway. It all fell through. He called it off, apparently.'

Kate pauses suddenly as the host begins the introduction and they start to play a clip of Josef Karpati from a recent movie theme.

'You all right, Martha?'

'Yes. Yes. Sorry. Did you say you saw him at the Albert Hall?'

'Yes. Spectacular concert. And *gorgeous* eyes.' Kate is now ripping open the bag of marshmallows with her teeth.

'I beg your pardon?'

'Josef Karpati. Gorgeous eyes, don't you think? I can't help wondering if he wears those coloured contact lenses. I was reading that they use them in Hollywood a lot.'

Martha does not reply, reaching out instead to take a handful of marshmallows, dropping two into the top of her drink and keeping her own eyes firmly down – watching as the sweet, pink cushions begin slowly to melt through the swirl of cream.

Kate meantime is sighing as the chat show host confirms that Josef has brought his famous Stradivarius cello, rumoured to be worth in excess of a million pounds.

# CHAPTER 11

Josef Karpati – international cellist and now dubbed '*Symphony Sex Symbol*' by the tabloid press – is lying at full stretch on his back along the plastic bench seat of the Channel Six TV green room. His eyes are closed as a young woman wearing headphones, which move up and down, synchronised with her chewing gum, sticks her head suddenly around the door. *One minute, Mr Karpati.*

He does not move.

'One minute. They're playing the intro clip, Mr Karpati. Is everything all right?'

'Yes, yes fine. No problem.'

Truth is, Josef Karpati is luxuriating in the pleasure of not having his stylist in the room (who would be chastising him to *sit up, please – that linen suit will look as if you've slept in it, Josef*) – or his publicist, who would be reminding him not to correct the chat show host too abruptly if they happened to describe him as Russian.

*But I'm Czechoslovakian.*

*Yes, of course, Josef. But we don't want people thinking you're a smart-arse.*

*And I don't want people thinking I'm Russian.*

*Look, you can slip it in later – casually – that you're from Czechoslovakia originally. Just don't pick them up on it straight away. Sound too irritated.*

Thankfully – given the circus of talk shows which has become a part of the Josef Karpati roadshow – he has, these days, earned the trust of his 'people' to behave himself without a chaperone. Just pep talks.

'Just remember to laugh when they crack the joke about the embassy,' his publicist reminded him on the phone earlier.

'Of course.'

'And for God's sake give the new album a plug.'

'Of course.'

Josef Karpati sits up now, takes a deep breath and stretches the fingers reportedly insured for a sum close to the value of the Strad cello already on stage and being watched by a security guard off-camera, if the terms of his contract are being honoured.

*If only they would just let me play.* The talk part always so predictable. The joke about his defection to the west. The anecdote about the film score which made his name internationally. How he coped with the tabloid press label. The *symphony sex symbol.* Oh – and how much the bloody Strad was worth these days.

Always that.

'OK. We're on. Walk with me…'

And now he is following his guide along the narrow corridor to the large double doors and out into the black and white set. The black hole of the audience – unseen faces expectant behind the white haze of the blinding lighting rig. The host standing up through the applause, with an outstretched hand and over-stretched smile.

*Remember to unbutton your jacket before you sit. Button. Sit. Right?*

His stylist made him rehearse it before his very first television interview years back. How ridiculous had that felt? A grown man practising his buttons.

Beaming, Josef skilfully addresses the button with his left hand as he sits – the applause fading.

'So – I finally get to meet the famous Russian who defected on a bank holiday. The day all the embassies were shut!' The host

– Josef has temporarily forgotten his name – is roaring with the audience and obligingly Josef shakes his head with mock shame, grinning as if he had *never heard that one before.*

And now he will tell the story for the millionth time. How – yes, he'd nearly poohed his pants when he handed himself in at New York's JFK airport, to be considered for defection to the west, to learn that it was actually a public holiday. That there were no senior embassy officials who could be reached immediately. How in the end the airport people had listened to his pleadings and finally agreed to arrest him, feigning an investigation into his passport and luggage so that he could be held in a secure cell away from his enraged Russian minders until someone with the correct (and adequately senior) embassy credentials could be summoned via the out-of-hours protocol.

He had lain on his back stretched out in that cell too. His mind in turmoil. Had he done the right thing? Would America even want him? He had calculated, following the shockwaves of Nureyev's defection, that this would be his last chance. No more Big Apple. No more Albert Hall. This would be his final trip outside Russia… unless…

Of course, he wouldn't have done it if his mother were still alive. No. He couldn't have done that to her.

'So – that Stradivarius of yours.' A spotlight moves across the stage now to the cello waiting patiently on its stand.

'Is it true that it's worth more than a million pounds these days?'

Oooohs and aaaahs from the audience.

Josef leans forward, looking for the red light to check which camera is taking the close-up. For a moment he allows himself the fantasy that she could be out there. Sitting out there in the audience at home somewhere, smiling to herself. No. Not smiling. What would she be thinking? Disappointed in all this? The showbiz gloss. This new version of himself that he does not even recognise some days.

His therapist (oh, yes – he has managed to acquire one of that most American of habits too) would be shaking his head in despair now. *We've been over this, Josef. Time and time again. You've got to stop this.* Stalking the past, he called it once. Stepping outside the reality of the present… and stalking the past.

Textbook, apparently. Obsessive first love. *All very understandable, but not necessarily true love, Josef. I mean – it was never tested, was it? With this Martha. You didn't have a real relationship with her. You didn't have time, Josef.*

The therapist quoted research. University professors who had proved that obsessing about first love was absurdly common, and yet, in most cases, entirely delusionary. That first relationships became so idealised in some people's minds that they led to a lifetime of dreaming… and disappointment.

'So the cello, Josef?'

His agent was blunter: *She is probably out there with a huge arse and a horde of kids. It is unlikely she even remembers you. That's the truth. Not this picture you hold in your head. Are you listening to me, Josef? This ridiculous fantasy you run away to every time life disappoints you…*

'The Stradivarius?'

*To be frank you should be relieved she hasn't turned up in one of the Sunday papers. I certainly am…*

'Sorry. Sorry. Yes. More than a million pounds, they tell me. But I don't know how you put a price on something like that. And it's not for sale.'

Laughter.

When he had failed to find her…when he defected and still she made no attempt to get in touch, Josef had tried to move on. He had even thought that getting married would lay the ghost. And Alena was, on paper (and certainly according to *Time* magazine), absolutely perfect for him. A soprano. Beautiful. Russian.

The engagement lasted less than a year, their PR people issuing a bland statement about their careers making it difficult to spend enough time together. Truth was something quite different. Josef's heart was never really in it. Haunted, was how Alena had described him. *You're haunted, Josef. And I've had enough of it...*

That had hurt because he had genuinely tried to move on, but the problem with unfinished business was, well – it was so bloody *unfinished. I mean, why couldn't she have just written? All those years ago. Explained. Yes. A Dear John letter, like everyone else. You know. Sorry but I got swept along. Sorry I said all that stuff, Josef. Made those promises. But we were young. I've met someone else. Have a good life.*

The thing was – one night she had said – *No, listen, please, this is important. I know we were young. Too young* – but she had said that she had never felt able to completely fill her lungs until she met him. As if she had only been breathing half of the air around her. *Waiting for something.*

*I mean, how can you say something like that?* Like you mean it. And then not even write a bloody Dear John letter.

After the engagement fell apart, he had tried a few affairs. The illicit thrill his therapist believed was the source of his 'fantasy'. Completely ridiculous. He had actually been *thumped* by one of the husbands.

Had to cancel three concerts on account of the black eye.

'So, Josef. That film score – the one that really started it all for you?'

Josef searches once more for the little red light as they again play, rather too loudly he feels, the oh-so-familiar movie soundtrack.

# CHAPTER 12

Over the coming days, it is the gardening which begins to win Toby over with Martha.

A completely unexpected diversion for them all.

For herself, Kate has never been keen. And now, so overloaded by the OCD nonsense indoors, she has no spare energy for the outside. Just too big a space to control. Though she likes the finished effect, especially terracotta pots of brightly coloured flowers, it is the mess she cannot cope with. All the scratches and the dirt under fingernails. The endless watering. And the blessed weeds.

Toby, meantime, has big ideas but little time.

'Great space,' Martha had observed on her second morning – wide-eyed, taking in the large but barren plot with its spectacular views over fields to the sea in the distance.

The silence and the sideway glances confirmed the sore point.

'I'm wondering if we should get someone in, actually. To make something of it,' Toby said finally. 'Sadly I'm just too busy with work at the moment. You're right. It's a great space. Could be terrific.'

'I'm afraid it was a source of conflict when we bought the place,' Kate winked at Martha as she poured them all coffee. Three matching bright blue mugs. 'Just don't get it, I'm afraid. The whole digging vibe. I would have preferred a smaller garden. But Toby's father had an allotment. He fancies the whole grow-your-own idyll.'

'Well. I don't want to be pushy, or to kick off a domestic. But if you'd like some help, I'd be delighted to make a start.'

Toby raised an eyebrow.

'It's just it's very much my thing. As you know, I work on farms, abroad mostly, but I also do some more formal gardening – here and there.' Martha had sipped her drink. 'You pick up a lot. In fact, there's a place in France that I help with most years in the spring. Dordogne. Sometimes I spend a month there to get things straight for the season. They have a complex for tourists, with a pool. Wonderful place.'

'Ever the one for surprises, Martha. Is there nothing you can't do?' Kate took in a long breath, pleased to see the expression on Toby's face change completely.

'Of course, it's the wrong time of year for much planting – especially after the scorching summer we've had. But it's an ideal time for sorting and planning. Yes. I could definitely draw up some plans for you. See what you think.'

'No, no. We couldn't expect that – Martha.' Toby searched Kate's face for guidance – still evidently nonplussed.

'Nonsense. I'd absolutely love to help. Be my way of saying thank you for the room. I'd be delighted.'

And so over the next few days there is an entirely unexpected shift in the house. An air of excitement and activity – Martha drawing up surprisingly impressive and extensive plans to divide their new garden into a series of 'rooms', each making best use of the space and the direction of the sun. There is to be a zone for sitting and eating, a 'room' for the workaday vegetable plot and greenhouse, another for a tumble of meadow and cottage plants, and a final section which Martha calls the 'tranquil zone'. A scented garden… *Maybe a water feature, if that's your bag? Somewhere to sit and read, Kate?*

The project also provides the perfect momentum for Kate and Martha while Toby is at work. Between her knitting commissions and visits to other friends on the quay, Martha accompanies Kate to garden centres, buying equipment and materials to get things started. This shared purpose gives a welcome structure to their new time together. And though Kate cares not a jot for the detail – the planks and the potting compost and the sheets of A4 plans – she takes instantly to Martha's easy company – in awe of her knowledge, her energy and enthusiasm.

Raised beds are very quickly installed in the 'vegetable zone' and Kate marvels at Martha's practicality, entirely at ease with Toby's power tools. It is not difficult now to see how she manages on her travels. Fitting in so easily. Ever keen.

And yet there is this one big taboo. The one area which sees Toby whispering in bed at night. Worrying still.

Kate doesn't like to press; asking only gently. As an aside. 'I don't mean to pry. It's just I can't help wondering, Martha. Why this kind of life? All the travelling. All the odd-jobbing. When you could clearly do pretty much anything as far as I can see.'

'But I like all the travelling, Kate.'

'Yes, I get that. And I can see the appeal. The freedom. But don't you think sometimes that it would be nice to stay? Don't you miss having a home, Martha? Your own garden? Don't you have family who— '

'I was wondering about the greenhouse?'

'Sorry?'

'It's just we still haven't agreed on where to site the greenhouse. Toby will need to pick one and arrange to have it assembled. It will need a good, solid cement base built. Foundations are beyond me, I'm afraid. But Wendy knows a couple of builders… I'll have a word.'

# CHAPTER 13

And then it comes.

November 23rd. The day the wind is to change. A clear, bright sky and yet: *look. Listen.* This cooler, stronger breeze suddenly. Ready now to swirl them all – around and around and around. Into this tighter space.

Kate and Martha and Toby and Matthew. The quayside shops.

Even Josef Karpati, travelling to yet another country. For yet another chat show. Today in his first-class seat at thirty five thousand feet…

An unkind wind – this. A warning.

A wind which will wake them all much too early. Matthew and Geoffrey first, tossing and turning in their single beds; in their separate homes. Just conscious, as they stir momentarily, of this sudden cold, pulling the blankets up a little higher.

Wendy and Maria next, each rising for a moment to close their bedroom windows, then settling back to sleep. Maria watched by her husband Carlo.

*What is it, darling?*

*Nothing. Just the wind.*

Kate alone sleeps right through it – Toby rolling on his side to watch her for a time, lifting the covers up over her bare shoulder. Ever so gently.

He knows that she still loves him. Feels it. And he loves her too. Very much. Though he cannot make her believe this – Kate instead believing the statistics. That say they cannot stay together now.

She says she wants to let him go. Will not let him touch her. *Eight months and two days…*

He cannot go back to sleep – Toby aware Kate's respite is chemical induced, sighing as he thinks of the sleeping tablets she tucks behind the cotton wool in the medicine cabinet so they can each pretend he does not know of them.

Quietly he slides from the bed. Manners remembered – self-conscious and in deference to their guest, he slips on a bathrobe to creep downstairs, wondering if tea might help. To his surprise, on the landing he finds Martha's door open and inside the covers pushed back from an empty bed. For a second he turns towards the bathroom but that door too is ajar. No light. Toby frowns. Barely five a.m.

Downstairs he can feel the cool of the outdoors even before he turns towards the kitchen to find the back door ajar. And now he feels terribly awkward, hovering for a moment in the hallway – wondering whether to just creep back to bed?

Nearly a month since Martha moved in, and though Toby is grateful for the effort out-of-doors, he misses privacy. Space to talk. To think. To hope. And he is troubled also by this strange puzzle of Martha's background. All this travelling. The fruit-picking. Half nomad, half hippy. Martha still so quick to change the subject when one of his questions strays into the wrong territory. Kate forever warning – *just leave it. Let it be.*

She is an attractive woman – Martha. Striking cheekbones and a perfect nose in profile. And yet she sets out quite deliberately to negate this. Why? The charity clothes. The rucksack and the trail of bags.

No. Toby cannot put his finger on what is truly going on with Martha.

And so he takes a deep breath now, draws his robe tighter around his waist and turns into the kitchen to see her some way down the garden. She is sitting in pyjamas and a thick grey car-

digan on the top step which leads down to the area with the new
raised beds – the only part of the garden which will enjoy full sun
all day in the warmer months.

Now though, despite the cardigan, Toby imagines that Martha must be absolutely freezing – the stone step an ice slab. And
yet she is completely still, her head tilted up to the sky. No shiv-
ers; no outward sign at all of discomfort until she turns, hearing
the door, and Toby to his surprise and immediate embarrassment
can see that she has been crying.

He has no clue what to do. Clears his throat. Martha, in turn,
wipes her face and stands, pulling the cardigan around her to
apologise that *sorry, I couldn't sleep, and I'm sorry, very sorry to
disturb you.*

They stand for more terrible seconds. Toby runs his hand
through his hair.

'Look. Are you sure you're OK, Martha? Would you like me
to fetch Kate? I'll fetch Kate for you…'

'No. Really. I'll be fine.'

'I was planning to make tea. Couldn't sleep either. This wind.'
She finds a weak smile.

But now Toby is panicking. 'Kate hasn't said anything, has
she?'

'What?'

'Doesn't matter.' He is trying to read her face. To regroup.

'Is there something I should know, Toby?'

'No. Not really.' Wishing he had said nothing now. 'Only that
she isn't strong right now.'

'She mentioned that she was on a break from work. But no
details. I haven't asked. Pressed her. I mean…'

'Right. Yes. Well. She'll be fine. Just needs time.' Toby is relieved. He doesn't want Martha knowing their most private business. When Kate is ready to talk more, he wants her to talk to
*him.*

'Look. I'm very grateful, Toby. For the room and everything. I mean – if it's not working for you, you must say. I don't want to cause any problems. I could find somewhere else.'

'No. No. That's not what Kate wants.' It's true. He can see how much Kate likes having Martha around. But he feels worried. If Martha has real problems of her own, he doesn't want Kate taking that on. It's always been Kate's nature. Both a strength and a weakness – to put other people's needs ahead of her own.

'It won't be for very long. I never stay for very long.'

'It's fine, Martha.'

'Kate's very kind.'

'But not strong.'

'Understood.'

The wind howls, rocking the fence at the end of the garden as their eyes meet.

'Then we're good, Martha.'

Two hundred miles away and Glenda, the woman who will always call herself Matthew's mother, is also rising early. It is his birthday. *Her Matthew.* And she gives up any hope of more sleep to leave Matthew's father snoring and to creep downstairs. She makes tea which she cannot drink, closes the windows to the wind – rattling the shutters – and in the end decides to start the cake.

No matter that he is not here.

From the shelf above the fridge she reaches very carefully for the bright pink book which contains the recipe – a treasured legacy written on lined blue writing paper in fading ink. Her grandmother's handwriting so beautiful – long elegant loops for the g's and j's and y's. Glenda traces her finger across the page. In truth she knows this recipe by heart but loves this moment – taking down the book. Inviting her grandmother to help.

Glenda works quietly, removing the lids of tins and cartons as slowly and carefully as possible, weighing the ingredients into separate white, china bowls.

Across two oceans now, and at thirty two thousand feet for Josef Karpati it is technically time for breakfast. Most of the other first-class passengers have already righted their seats and allowed the cabin assistants to store away their blankets and pillows. But Josef is not ready for the next day. The next country. The next studio.

He shakes his head as the stewardess taps his shoulder, coffee pot in hand. And then a jolt from this turbulence. The coffee nearly spilled. *I'm sorry, sir.* He says that it is fine. She is not to worry. Fastens his belt. And then he rolls back towards the window, grateful that the neighbouring seats are unoccupied. He is heading for another five-star hotel which will look precisely like the five-star hotel he has just left. Sometimes he tries to imagine his mother in these suites – rushing from room to room, stroking the marble in the bathrooms. Bouncing on the huge bed. But mostly he does not. Mostly he just wonders what on earth he is doing in this life.

Back in Aylesborough Matthew now wakes fully – surprised and at first disorientated by the still unfamiliar surroundings. The window of his room at Mrs Hill's bed and breakfast is in the wrong place – compared to his room at home, that is – and it still startles him that the light is coming from the wrong direction. Today, it is the light from the street lamp just outside the window – still dark beyond it.

He has Geoffrey to thank for the introduction – sorted it all out that very first day. Mrs Hill takes in only a few guests over the winter months. She is quite a brusque woman on the outside – no family around now to soften her – but she has taken to Matthew, especially since coaxing him to play for her sometimes in the evenings on the little battered upright piano, neglected in the corner of the dining room. Elton John she likes. And the Beatles. *Let it be, Mrs Hill. Let it be.* Her guest house has seen better days – the wallpaper faded and peeling in places – but it is spotless and Mrs Hill cooks heavenly breakfasts; thick, salty bacon and fried eggs with crisp, brown, frilly petticoats.

Matthew wonders if he should tell Mrs Hill that it is his birthday but decides – no. She may think he is fishing for a treat. A fuss. And then the questions. Why is he not spending it with his family? He should phone his mother again today. Yes. He should do that much. But aside from this, he will pretend it is just another day.

Which no one at this moment can know that it is not…

Geoffrey is the first to get the news.

By the time Matthew arrives at work, he is sitting, ashen-faced on an old piano stool which doubles as the seat for the desk in the corner of the shop.

'Everything OK?' Matthew puts his bag down alongside the door to the office as Wendy appears in the doorway. She is holding a letter and only now does Matthew notice the identical brown envelope in Geoffrey's hand.

'So you too, Geoffrey?' Wendy's voice is trembling.

For a moment the two friends just stare at each other.

'Is everything all right? Shall I make tea? Has something happened?'

There is no reaction – and so Matthew retreats to the office to give them some space, flicking on the kettle. Through the crack in the door he watches Geoffrey hug Wendy tightly as she dabs her eyes with a tissue and then they are comparing their letters – Geoffrey pushing his glasses up his nose and tracing paragraphs first on his paper and then Wendy's.

'But they can't do this? Surely?' Wendy is spit whispering now and Matthew struggles to make out the exchange – guilty at eavesdropping but distressed to see them like this.

He can at least provide a really good cup of tea. Yes. And so, just as his mother taught him, Matthew heats the little teapot with boiling water, swirling it around and around three times, anticlockwise, and tipping it into the sink before making the tea. Then, as it stews, he stares for a time at the telephone – wondering if he should phone his mother. From the office. He has already made a brief, second call from the pay phone at Mrs Hill's. Told his mum which town – on the strict understanding she does not tell his father. He peers again through the crack to see Geoffrey and Wendy still whispering together – Geoffrey tapping the letter with the back of his hand. Matthew dials. Three rings. Four. Five…

'Hello?' His mother never quotes the number. Always sounds startled like this – as if she cannot understand the source of the ringing.

'Hello, Mum. Just a quick call again. I'm at work.'

'Oh Matthew. Are you all right?'

'Yes, Mum. I'm fine. Really.'

'Are you coming home today?'

'No, Mum. I'm sorry. Not yet. I can't.'

A long pause.

'I baked you a cake.'

Matthew bites into his lip and clears his throat against the surge in his chest.

'Oh Mum, you shouldn't have done that.'

'Well. Just in case. Never mind. It was no trouble, love.'

Matthew looks at the teapot and can picture the larger blue teapot his mother uses. Tea leaves and a proper strainer. Never been convinced by teabags.

'Look I'm going to have to go, Mum. But I'm fine. I've been up to the hospital. It's closed. Being converted into houses and apartments. And I've got an appointment to see someone in social services. Next week.'

Another long pause.

'Is there any way you could help? The papers, I mean? I'm going to need the adoption papers.'

'Love – they're locked away. Your father… he…'

Matthew puts his hand over the receiver so that she will not hear his breathing. Heavier now. He doesn't want another row with his mother. Not today. Please not today.

'Look – I'm sorry about the cake, Mum. I'll ring you again very soon. I promise.'

'You're eating all right, Matthew?'

'Yes, Mum.' Matthew can picture the cake – tall and spongy with large air bubbles and a thick, oozing layer of chocolate fudge filling. His favourite. Three candles. Four. Thirteen…

'Happy birthday, son.'

She says it too late – over the dialling tone. Like a kiss to a child already fallen asleep.

Matthew finishes the tea quickly and coughs loudly to announce his return from the little office to the shop floor. Both Geoffrey and Wendy reach gratefully for the drinks and look more composed.

'We've had a bit of bad news, Matthew.' Geoffrey sips immediately at his drink. 'The council want us out. Notices to quit. They're not renewing our lease.'

And then, before he can explain further, the bell tinkles the arrival of Maria's husband, Carlo – sweaty and out of breath.

'I'm sorry to intrude. But do you know where Martha is?'

'Martha?' Three voices at once.

'It's Maria. She's gone to the council offices.' Carlo is looking at the letters, still in Wendy and Geoffrey's hands. He pulls a face of knowing. 'So – all of us then? Our café and you two as well?'

'Well – good for Maria.' Wendy's expression changing now. Defiant. 'To go straight to the council. Yes. Good for Maria. That's what we should have done.'

But Carlo is shaking his head.

'No, no. You don't understand.' He looks hesitant. Then embarrassed. And finally afraid.

'She's taken a frying pan.'

# CHAPTER 14

At the Council House reception a very pleasant young lady is now spectacularly out of her depth. Anna-Louise, according to her name badge (Lou to her friends), has only just completed her refresher training. She has been briefed therefore on the very latest advice on how to handle a suspicious package; how to evacuate (without panic) in the event of a fire and how to effect the Heimlich Manoeuvre in the event of choking.

There has been no guidance on how to handle Italian grandmothers brandishing kitchen equipment.

'Can we try to keep calm, please? If you could just *calm yourself…*'

Maria is by now enjoying the support of a not inconsiderable crowd – a jumble of bored and impatient local residents, queuing to air various grievances with council officials. An overweight couple with five children building a mountain out of the spare chairs. An elderly woman muttering about her bins and *oversexed tom cats.*

*They pull out all the rubbish and then howl, I tell you. All night…*

Maria, in no mood to queue, bangs her frying pan on one of the columns stretching floor to ceiling, evidently and ominously playing an essential role in keeping the first floor in position.

'I want to speak to Mr Fullman.' *Smash.* 'Now!'

Though the column in question is painted, suggesting plasterwork, the sound from the frying pan attack – *smash* – is surprisingly tuneful – confirming metal on metal.

Anna-Louise explains that *sorry but there is no way you will be able to see Mr Fullman without an appointment but if you would like to leave a message?* Maria repeats her assault so that a high note is resounding over and over as Wendy, Geoffrey, Carlo and Matthew arrive.

'Top A,' Matthew whispers to Geoffrey, unable to help himself, for all the chaos.

'Oh Maria. Please. This is *not* the way.' Carlo puts both hands up to his head, covering his ears.

'Tell me where else you can buy polenta in Aylesborough?' Maria waves the letter from Mr Fullman's office.

Anna-Louise again presses the little security buzzer beneath her desk.

'You close me down and where will the fishermen go – eh? Who will pay the loan on my new equipment? My new oven?'

'Close you down?' A tall, moustachioed man among the waiting crowd stands up.

'They're not closing down Maria's café?' He is looking around to see if others share his outrage.

Still waving her letter, Maria now recognises the man as a Thursday regular (full breakfast – double sausage, sunnyside eggs)…

'Ending my lease, they are. No consultation. No nothing. Three months' notice and I'm out.'

There are gasps and mutterings among the crowd. Anna-Louise picks up the phone as Maria resumes her onslaught with the frying pan.

'If you don't stop that right now, madam, I'm going to have to call the police.'

'Santa Maria! The *police*?' Carlo makes the sign of the cross.

'Get Mr Fullman down here to see these people. Right now.' The breakfast customer is still standing – jabbing his finger to underline each word. *Right now, do you hear me? Right now.*

Anna-Louise – *to hell with the bloody course* – is now dialling 999 as Martha, breathless, appears in the doorway, Kate close behind.

'We've only just heard…'

Maria meanwhile is following the customer's lead, using the frying pan as percussion to emphasise each of her own words. *My* – smash – *father* – smash – *gave* – smash – *me* – smash – *that* – smash – *café*.

And then suddenly, as she mentions her father, Maria's face changes. Her shoulders begin to shake – her mouth twitching too so that Martha is the first to take on board that her friend is in real trouble.

Deeper trouble than others realise.

There is no time to think. That is the problem.

Looking back later, Martha will confide in Kate that if there had been time to think, she one hundred per cent would not have done it.

But in the absence of time and options, Martha falls back on an old instinct – a buried reflex from long ago. And so, unthinking, and in a moment of unexpected panic, she does what she had once done regularly in times of extreme stress.

Very quietly, and ever so quickly, Martha takes all her clothes off.

The reaction is as inevitable as it is instantaneous. Loud gasps from the adults – some turning away in shock, laughter from two of the errant children, who allow the chair mountain to collapse – and for Anna-Louise temporary paralysis. Phone in hand, she cannot move her jaw as a voice on the line repeatedly enquires after the nature of the emergency. *Fire, ambulance or police? What is the emergency, please? Hello? Hello?*

Carlo is so stunned, it is a few seconds before he has the presence even to turn away.

But for Martha it is only one reaction she cares about. It is Maria she watches. And just as Martha hopes, the shock and the extremity of the gesture stops her friend instantly in her tracks, diluting her stress and slowing her breathing as they share the stage spectacularly now, so that the frying pan is finally inactive as two security guards appear – one of them rushing forward instantly to remove his jacket in an attempt to cover Martha up.

'That's it – show over. Everyone out. Out, please. All of you.' The second security guard holds his arms wide like a farmer controlling a herd of sheep and ushers the stunned crowd towards the door at the other side of the room as Anna-Louise finally finds her voice to explain to the police officer on the phone that there is a naked woman and a woman with a frying pan in the reception hall of the council offices and could someone come, please. *Quickly.*

The security guard's jacket is in fact too short to restore Martha's dignity completely and so while Martha stands still as a statue, eyes locked on Maria, Kate is the only one who does not, through embarrassment, avert her gaze from Martha.

For Kate it is not just the surprise of the streak, but the shock of Martha's body. This lean, fit frame with its flat stomach – the slimness of her hips. This taught, enviably muscular body – toned from the harsh physical work over the summers across Europe. But the biggest and most intriguing surprise?

The faint, smile-shaped caesarean scar on Martha's stomach which precisely matches her own…

# PART TWO

# CHAPTER 15

The first time Martha woke properly in Millrose Mount – sufficiently, that is, to rise above the sedation – she had been there two days already.

She was just eighteen years old.

As she widened her eyes to the shock of the cracks in the high ceiling, with its glaring striplights and the incongruous addition of a large but immobile fan, there was the jolt of déjà vu. Also a nurse towering right alongside her bed.

'Now then, young lady – are you ready to stop with the thrashing and the drama and let us try to help you?'

A blurred tumble of scenes played out in her head. Thrashing, and yes – a lot of shouting. *I need to get back there. I mean it. The police. I need the police.*

Martha's heart and head began to pound in unison as she realised the echo of the voice in the midst of this cascade of jumbled images – of pushing and shoving and of pain, something sharp in her arm – was her own. Her strongest urge still was to sit bolt upright.

And then, heart booming, her mind suddenly stopped. An elastic band stretched and stretched almost to the point of inevitability; the snap imminent but everything paused at the very moment of full extension. She stilled herself. She held her breath. She fought against the panic to let the tension ease ever so slightly, bit by tiny bit, so that she could feel the sweat on her back and smell the odour of stale body. Hers. She stared some more at the cracks in the ceiling. The cobwebs on the dormant fan.

'What day is it?' It was a different version of her own voice again. Raspy and thin. Her throat incredibly dry. She felt woozy and disorientated. Detached and afraid.

'Thursday.'

And then the enormity of it all hit her. The true meaning of the maelstrom of the sounds and the blurred, confused images. The thrashing and the screaming. If it was really Thursday, she had lost two days.

'So, you feeling calmer? Going to behave so we can we can get you up? Have a nice bath. Yes?'

'Yes.'

During that first bath, supervised in silence by the same nurse who kept looking at her watch and tutting, Martha stared down at the caesarean scar on her stomach, ragged and red and magnified through the water, and tried to stop crying – tears dripping into the water. Tried instead to work out the part she would need to play next.

The part that would get her through this nightmare. Undo this mistake. Get her to a phone. Get her to the police. Get. Her. Out.

She honestly thought if she could just find a way to fight the adrenalin and the panic, she would find some way to work this out. But Martha was very young.

And very wrong.

Over the coming days she tried every part she could think of to try to change her new and shocking circumstance. She played up. She played down. She hurt herself. She stopped hurting herself. She screamed. She was quiet. She took her drugs. She spat them out in the nurses' faces.

Nothing changed anything.

On the rare occasions she was taken to the small consulting room to speak to her doctor, he would place in front of her this huge and unrecognisable version of why she was there.

And she would interrupt him and tell the real story and he would shake his head and look at the nurse. More tutting and mumbling about their duty of care and how much they all wanted to help her. To keep her safe. But it was an important first step for her to face up to what had happened…

And Martha would scream that they were liars. The lot of them. *Filthy, stinking liars!* And it would end badly and she would be warned that there would be no privileges going forward.

And the worst truth of all that dawned bright and dreadful in those early, terrible days that rolled into weeks and finally months was that in Millrose Mount Hospital there was not only nothing, apparently, she could do to get herself out but absolutely nothing to do, full stop.

It was this most of all that Martha would come to remember about her two years, three months and two days in Millrose Mount Hospital. Not the fear. Not the injustice. Not even the trauma of those first terrible days, but the insufferable length of each and every day. The endless walking and sitting, with nothing to distract from the terrible thought of her circumstance, and what she had lost, and always with this same question pounding through her head.

*What on earth am I actually supposed to do?*

At first in the broader sense of sheer panic and terror. Also fury. How to make them listen and to let her go. But then later, in the very practical hour-to-hour sense of absolute despair and yes: sheer boredom.

What to do to fill all these hours? To join the dots between breakfast and lunch and dinner.

The problem was worse always at night, when Martha would never feel safe enough to sleep properly. This another of Millrose Mount's shocks, that sometimes male patients would wander into female wards after lights out. The first time this happened, when she was still on one of the higher security admission wards, Martha was incredulous, screaming immediately for help.

The male patient had not come close to her bed – hers thankfully being at the far end of the ward, nearest the window. He had not touched her. But it was the possibility. The very thought of it. Men being able to just wander around at night.

And yet in those early weeks it was she, Martha, who was punished for making a fuss. Given an extra dose of sedative to *calm yourself down, missy.*

All of the problems, Martha soon realised, were down to a motley crew of indifferent staff, an ineffective and inconsistent regime and a lack of the one thing you would expect in such a place. Care.

The daytime staffing rule seemed to be at least two nurses on duty in the little bay of the corridor which divided wards, but at night a single nurse would have to watch two wards – one for all female patients and one on the opposite of the corridor for men. So the door of each ward would have to be left wide open so the nurse could see into both.

At night it was almost always a male nurse in the corridor, which made Martha doubly uncomfortable. Sometimes they would simply fall asleep and sometimes they would just disappear – the rumour being that they liked to play cards with other staff on shift elsewhere.

Sure enough, someone would come running pretty fast if one of the male patients went walkabouts and the screaming started, but the sense of risk and uncertainty meant Martha found it very difficult to ever relax. To sleep properly.

Instead she would snatch naps whenever she could during the day, and at night would lie in bed with tears running down her face as she tried to work out the next strategy. The next part she might play in the hope of getting herself to a phone.

To somehow get a message to Russia, to the only person in the whole world who could help her now.

*To Josef Karpati.*

# CHAPTER 16

Martha had met Josef two days short of her eighteenth birthday. He was just starting out – an unknown, working with her father under an east–west cultural exchange.

Not only did no one know Josef's name back then, but Martha, as she made sandwiches for her father's rehearsal, was quite possibly the least likely person to be impressed by him.

They were ham – the sandwiches. She wrapped them very carefully, sunlight streaming into the kitchen reflecting dancing orbs onto the greaseproof paper. She had been thinking of her mother, trying not to dwell on how things might have evolved if she were still around.

Martha could not remember a time when she and her father had not been at war – an only child fighting for his attention from the day he closed the door of his music room on her toddler form, screaming for her mother *to do something for God's sake. Is there no way you can keep the child quiet while I'm trying to work?*

Martha throughout her schooling had a succession of music teachers who tutted their way through a series of instruments with her – piano, flute and oboe – her natural flair for each matched only by a spectacular refusal to use it. The rows with her father over this as dramatic as Martha intended them to be, but futile also, for even if the grown-up Martha had written *NOTICE ME* in capital letters on her forehead, Charles Ellis would still have failed to read them.

It was music he had chosen to read. Bass clef and treble clef – the childhood clef completely beyond him.

It was only her mother, Jessica, who could calm the turbulent waters between father and daughter, and her loss, so sudden and so utterly unfair when Martha was just thirteen, had left a chasm of silence between them which even the loudest and most spectacular symphony could not penetrate.

*How can anyone die of a cold?* he would lament over and over in hushed tones – to friends, fellow musicians, to neighbours, the vicar, the housekeeper Margaret – though never to Martha.

So few words left for Martha.

Charles Ellis's great professional sadness was in becoming a better conductor than he ever was a soloist. And so to support and to buoy him, it became her mother's habit, as a concert drew close, geography and weather permitting, to take her husband's lunch fresh to the rehearsal hall. Jessica had liked to listen to the new programme, she confided in Martha, and to watch her husband – so absorbed in his work, baton in hand, when he did not know that she was there.

'It is as if the music takes him to another place. Another world entirely, Martha.'

And then, sweeping her daughter's fringe back from her forehead and planting a kiss in the middle there to soften the frown. 'You must try to forgive him, Martha. He cannot help himself.'

It was for her mother she had chosen ham that day – freshly roasted with a coating of mustard and brown sugar as she had taught her; Martha's only comfort this – to keep the food, the house, the routines exactly as they had always been. As if she could pretend that her mother had just popped out to the shops. Would be back any moment. With something for that cold.

The next concert was just three days away and there was much brouhaha over the unexpected cooperation between Charles's own somewhat provincial orchestra and a more prestigious ensemble visiting from Czechoslovakia. How permission had been achieved for this liaison did not stand up to public examination.

That Charles Ellis was on a panel of judges soon to host an important international competition was a key factor, according to international commentators, though strenuously denied by all concerned. What was more at issue, but less widely known, was the ongoing affair between the British-based press officer for the competition and one of the senior figures in charge of security for the visiting musicians.

None of this Martha knew or cared about at the time. All she saw was that the prospect of playing with the cream of the eastern bloc's touring entourage had thrown her father into even more of a tizz than usual.

The clock from the hall chimed twelve – the cue to hurry – and Martha added some tomatoes, an apple and a large chunk of strong cheddar to the blue plastic lunchbox before placing it into the canvas bag which already contained a flask of tea – Earl Grey, not too strong – with slices of lemon wrapped in foil. There was just a light breeze, and for the twenty-minute stroll to the Salvation Army hall Martha dreamt of the eighteenth birthday party she might have enjoyed if her mother were there to organise it. Friends over. Yes. There would have been a gathering of her closest friends, but not a childish party with buns and sandwiches as her father had proposed. No. Her mother would have realised that something very much more sophisticated would be in order. A little dinner party perhaps. Cocktails even. Two days and she would be old enough for cocktails, surely?

She could hear the muted drift of the rehearsal in full swing long before she turned the corner at the bottom of Clarence Street from where the Salvation Army hall came into view.

Canapés. Of course. Her mother would have organised proper, grown-up *canapés*. Martha found herself smiling at the very thought of this. Smoked salmon. Caviar?

Acoustically, it was apparently not too bad, this hall, though the musicians complained it was draughty, some of them even wearing fingerless gloves one season when the heating had packed up completely.

Martha on the whole liked the musicians and her smile broadened as she remembered how very funny they had looked in their coloured gloves – the eclectic jumble of tall and short, fat and thin, with their preening, their perfectionism and their paranoias. In other people, all of this was entirely fascinating to observe. She remembered the first time she had used the cloakroom at one of the rehearsal venues and had happened upon an oboist retching into the bowl. *Oh dear. Should she get someone? Fetch her mother?* Martha, just ten at the time, had been completely mortified but, to her surprise, the woman had simply wiped her mouth and flushed the chain to explain, quite matter-of-fact, *No, thank you, dear. I am always sick before I play. And I feel very much better. Will be fine now, thank you.*

And Martha had watched her then, throughout the rehearsal, with astonishment as she had proved the point – playing quite beautifully. The pink entirely returned to her cheeks.

Yes. Musicians were an interesting if unpredictable bunch – just not cut out for family life, in her father's case.

The first set of double doors to the hall were exceptionally heavy and Martha held the bag of food to her stomach as she turned and pushed with her bottom to ease them open as quietly as she could, using her hand then to slow the shutting mechanism – working against the overhead spring so that it would not slam. God forbid that she should interrupt her father, baton still in hand.

There was a small inner lobby before less substantial glazed double doors to the main hall, and it was here that it happened.

That moment she first saw him. The moment imprinted forever on her brain.

She recognised the piece – her father had played it years back. Though not like this. Nothing like this. And she was standing now in the lobby staring through the glass, uneasy. Unsteady.

Ill-prepared. She could not recall the name of the movement; all she knew was that she had never been forced to listen quite like this before. Felt tricked. Winded. Stripped suddenly of the defence mechanism which had always served her so well where music was concerned.

He had his back to her – the soloist – so that she could see only his hair at first. Curly hair, which moved like waves on the sea, catching the light from a high window as he played – his upper body at one with the music as if swimming. Or dancing. The muscles of his bare arms – flexing. Tensing and relaxing. To. Fro. Taut. Relaxed. Mesmeric – yes; exactly like waves on the surface of the water. His back completely straight and his head stretched so far to the side that the skin of his neck seemed almost translucent – white and unnaturally smooth so that even from this distance she found herself digging her fingers into her palm in response to the overwhelming and ridiculous urge to imagine how it might feel to the touch.

And then the slight turn of the head so that she sees his face. The perfect shape of his jaw. Those eyes…

It was her father's instrument, the cello, but even he, so applauded in his day, had never played like this. For just a moment then Martha had looked beyond the soloist to watch her father – his baton bobbing over the surface of the water – to see the confirmation in his eyes. Yes. The glint of envy, masked as admiration.

And now she was closing her own eyes and could see her mother sitting alone in the midst of the sea of chairs, smiling at her. *See, Martha? Do you see now?* And she was holding her breath. Yes. She, Martha Ellis, who had blamed music for so much unhappiness in her life – standing, staring and holding her breath for it.

And then, just as suddenly as the magic arrived, so it was gone. The hall silent for just a brief pause before the familiar scraping of chairs as the musicians moved to gather up their things. Rising to the surface.

Lunch break.

And Martha was disorientated. Cross with herself and embarrassed too as she pushed her way through the second set of doors, forgetting the noise of the hinge and not expecting, never imagining, what will come next.

Over and over in her dreams she will replay this moment. The excruciating squeak of the door. His turn. And then the smile. Not just the mouth but the ice blue eyes – so pale, like crystals, that, in theory, they should chill, and yet somehow do exactly the opposite. And she wonders if she has rewritten it. Adorned this moment too much. Reinvented it. Or if it really was as she remembers.

That he did not blink. Not once. That she watched and watched, waiting for him to turn away first but he did not.

Ice-blue eyes. Just staring back at her. Unblinking.

And thank God, her father did not notice her yet – blushing and so awkward, wishing that she had combed her hair, checked her reflection in the double doors. Worn something nicer.

Martha looked beyond the soloist to the far corner of the hall where a group of musicians were huddled together, whispering – alongside them a rather odd-looking man in an ill-fitting suit. The minder her father had mentioned? Yes – he must be the minder, for his eyes were darting around the room all the time. For what, she wondered, smiling to herself, in a Salvation Army hall? Still she watched the musicians, wondering why they did not rush off as usual for their lunch – the brass section so keen normally not to miss a moment of time in the pub. And then her father was signalling the way into the back office, with a grey-haired man following him – his oboe still in his hand – and from this distance Martha unable to make out his face.

Only then did she turn back to the young man to find to her astonishment that he was still staring at her. Dear God. Worse. Approaching. And now in her head she was desperately searching for something grown-up to say. Something interesting. Something…

'Hello – I'm Martha. Charles's daughter. Gosh, you play well.' Blushing then – *Oh shut up, Martha. Shut up* – while still he looked. 'What I mean is that it was a good piece. A good choice.' She had no idea if this was true.

And then at last *his* voice – low and with an accent she could not identify.

'Josef Karpati. I am pleased to meet you, Martha.'

He bowed his head as he said her name, dropping the tone of his voice and holding out his hand to shake hers. Did she imagine that he held onto it just a little longer than was customary? Pressed his palm, still warm from the bow, against hers. Did she imagine that?

And then she was gabbling again, trying to explain that her name wasn't truly Martha. Jessica, actually, after her mother, but it had caused such terrible confusion in the house. *I mean – how ridiculous, don't you think? To name a daughter after the mother.* And so in the end she had taken to using her second name. Martha.

At which he smiled again.

'So – your father?' He turned, to confirm that Charles had left the main hall. 'You like to watch him rehearse?'

'Well – yes. No.' Martha's face felt very hot. 'I just bring lunch, actually.' She held up her bag, feeling ridiculous. Did this man never blink? If he moved any closer, he would hear her pulse, surely? She swallowed. Too much fluid in her mouth suddenly. Wondering where on earth so much saliva had appeared from.

'So – what's going on?' Martha signalled with her head to the gathering of musicians still whispering in the corner, gulping now. Dear God, what if she dribbled?

Josef's eyes blinked at last and he signalled for them to move aside – to some seating at the back of the hall, glancing and nodding momentarily towards the minder.

'It is very sad,' he was whispering. Guarded. 'There is a musician who is having problems today? Michael. Do you know
him?'

'Michael on oboe? Yes – he's been playing with Dad for years.'

Josef dropped his head and shoulders and lowered his voice
yet further so that Martha had to lean right forward to hear him.
'I shouldn't perhaps say. But it seems he has…' He was flexing his
fingers and wrist slowly like a mime. 'Pain in his hands. I don't
remember the word?'

'Pain? You mean like arthritis?'

'Yes. That's it. He has been drinking today to help him play.
Your father is upset. Understandably. It is very sad.'

'But the concert's in three days. He's lead oboe. He's always
been lead oboe.'

And then the muffled sound of raised voices from the kitchen
across the hall. What sounded like a fist banging on the table
– the group of remaining musicians across the hall suddenly dis-
persing – heading for the far exit as Martha stood up, her hand
trembling. The door of the music room slamming shut on her
toddler form. Her father's voice so loud. So angry. 'Look – I'm
sorry but I'm going to have to go.'

And now the ice-blue eyes were confused.

'Look – would you mind if I leave these with you, Josef?' She
was passing him the lunchbox. 'It's probably better that I go. If
things are difficult, I mean.'

'I'm sorry, Martha. I've upset you. I didn't mean to upset you.'

Over the years Martha will come to remember this precise
moment more times than she would choose. In Millrose Mount.
Then later, on her travels, when his name is on the front of a
magazine or newspaper. A billboard. Or he pops up on a television through a shop window, catching her unawares.

From the moment Josef becomes famous, Martha will find it
harder and harder to escape what happened between them. And

when she is forced to think again of that very first day, she will wonder if she has rewoven it.

The way he spoke to her. Did he really take her hand yet again just before she rushed away – so that once more she felt the warmth of his skin, which made her stomach turn right over as she dived into cool water to escape, her hair slicked straight? Delicious and cool down her back.

Did you really do that, Josef? *Did you?* Take my hand not once but twice that very first day? Was it, all of it, between us as I replay it? Or is it as I will come to fear. Remembering all of it all wrong.

Adding.

Inventing.

Dreaming?

# CHAPTER 17

The first year in Millrose Mount passed painfully slowly, Martha watching the seasons from her ward window in disbelief. The first autumn leaves. The snow. The first shoots of spring.

Her father visited every few weeks initially, but Martha refused to speak to him and he eventually appeared to give up. Doctors came and went and seemed, over time, also to lose interest in her case – distracted by specialist wards where various intensive and alarming-sounding treatments were under way. Insulin coma. Continuous baths. All sounded monstrous and, to avoid any stepping up of her 'treatment', Martha, for the most part, tried to keep her head down.

She had vague memories growing up of miscarriage-of-justice cases reported in the newspapers. Discussed at the dinner table. Campaigns on behalf of innocent people wrongly jailed. That was exactly what this felt like. A roaring fury inside at the unfairness of losing your liberty. But who was there to fight *her* corner? And what hope without someone out there to speak up for her? The more fuss she made, the more scenes she created, the more she seemed to match their diagnosis.

Just occasionally the impossibility of this no-win cycle would become too much and Martha would try for a stint on isolation – her favourite place. It was a patient called Emily who tipped her off. When a nurse forgot to count the cutlery at lunch, the trick was to take a knife and make just a small cut to the wrist. Nothing serious but just enough to cause a stir.

Isolation meant your own room. A little bit of peace and quiet for a time. A locked door with a viewing hatch at night away from the wandering male patients. But all too soon she would be back on a general ward with nothing to do. Nowhere to go.

Patients, bar those on acute admission wards, were technically given freedom to visit an array of dayrooms. The reality was a frightening hierarchy of privileges allocated randomly by staff and patient bullying which went totally unchecked. An obese male patient would sometimes follow Martha about all day, pestering her for cigarettes.

*I don't smoke. I don't have any cigarettes.*

*You do. You are a liar.*

Martha sometimes demanded to know exactly what medication she was being given. Why they insisted on so many sedatives, and what precisely she was supposed to be being treated for? But such protests were seen as troublemaking, resulting in withdrawal of 'privileges' which meant eating all her meals on the ward. Same stuffy room, all day and all night.

And then, in the second year of her stay, when Martha had drifted into a state of resigned despair, each day simply rolling into the next, a new nurse called Sarah began working at Millrose Mount. And Martha began to allow herself once more to nurture something dangerous; something which as time passed she had learned to bury.

Hope.

Sarah was in her early thirties and confided in Martha that she had worked in smaller, private units before moving, newly married, to the area. She made no secret of her shock at the way Millrose Mount was being run.

She was absolutely horrified when Martha sprang one of her cutlery tricks in a bid for a stint away from the wards, chastising her gently but firmly as she dressed the wound to her wrist.

'You have to stop this, Martha. I know you like isolation but this is not the way to go. Trust me. In the end it will just make things worse. Go on your record and go against you.'

'Things can't get any worse.'

'Trust me they can, Martha.' Sarah bit into a roll of tape and secured the bandage at Martha's wrist.

'I shouldn't even be here.'

She had kind eyes – Sarah. 'I know that, honey. But you have to understand that they've heard it all before. The doctors. It's what everyone says. That they shouldn't be here. They just read the records. And you have to face up to the fact that you *are* here and so we have to find some way to make things better. To help you get better so we can make them review your case. All this just makes it worse.'

'I'm not even ill. I swear.'

'So why don't you talk to me, Martha? Tell me what happened. What went wrong for you?'

'I don't talk about that any more. Not to anyone.' It was true. Martha had learned to close it all down. All her early complaining about the lies over her admission had only ever made her situation worse.

'Listen, Martha. This is important. If you carry on with the cutlery nonsense – the wrists – they will up your meds. They may even put you back on an acute ward.'

'No they won't. They just give me a few days in isolation, which I like.'

'At the moment. But that might change. It's a risky strategy.'

'But there's nothing to do here. *Absolutely nothing.* At least in isolation, I get peace and quiet.' Martha shouted this and Sarah put her finger up to her lips, shook her head and then after a few minutes took a deep breath.

'So how about the new women's dayroom, Martha? The one with the sea view? No men. You could read in there. Don't you like reading?'

Martha paused. Of course she liked reading. Once. There were a million things she had *once* liked, in a parallel world, and could no longer do. Not here.

'Laura has taken charge of the new dayroom already. If I sit down she comes over and says I have taken her seat. I move. She comes over and says that my new seat is her seat. Then she follows me around like musical bloody chairs.'

'I know Laura. She's tricky but she's all right. She's just bored, the same as you are.'

'Laura is not all right, she's insane, Sarah. Bonkers. Also very, very big. She's taken over the new dayroom and she scares the life out of me. If I take her on, she will hurt me.'

'No she won't. I know Laura, honestly. Laura is all mouth, Martha, but it's just to cover up her own insecurities. She has no history of violence. You just have to stand up to her. If you tell her to go away, she'll let you sit down. I've seen it.'

'So why can't you tell her to let me sit down?'

'It doesn't work like that, Martha. Not with Laura. Come on. I'll show you.'

And then Sarah led her to the new dayroom, with its beautiful sea view, and stood in the doorway, making encouraging faces while Martha sat down. Sure enough, within just a couple of minutes Laura moved from her chair opposite and stood, towering over Martha. Six foot and at least fourteen stone.

'That's my chair.'

Martha glanced back to Sarah in the doorway, who again moved her head, to signal encouragement, mouthing – *Go on. Like I told you.*

Martha could feel her heart pounding. She began to imagine it. A blow. Laura lashing out at her. In the doorway, Sarah's eyes widened as she waited. Eventually Martha took a deep breath. 'No, it's not, Laura. It's not your chair – it's my chair.'

Laura narrowed her eyes and for several more minutes just stood there, towering over her, Martha trying very hard not to wince. Not to show her fear. And then, finally, Laura tilted her head and spoke again. 'OK then.'

And to Martha's astonishment, Laura simply returned to her own chair and let her be.

After that Martha spent a lot of time in the new women's dayroom, with its view onto the gardens and the sea beyond. It was nice to have somewhere a bit more pleasant and safer to sit, gazing out at the birds on the lawn and the waves in the distance. But the reading was not a success. The meds made Martha's mind too fuzzy; she found reading quite hard.

And that's when Sarah came up with a new idea. 'For now it can only be allowed when I am free to supervise, Martha. Because of the needles. The rules. But I can manage an hour or so when I'm on shift to sit with you. It's very therapeutic. You might like it.'

And she produced from a bag a set of large needles and a ball of lemon wool.

'Knitting, Martha. I'm going to teach you to knit.'

# CHAPTER 18

Martha remembers her parting from Josef in the same way she remembers their meeting. With absolute clarity and complete confusion.

It was a Wednesday. It was raining. She had been Josef's lover for precisely six months and two days. And it was the house-keeper, Margaret, who found them out.

*'You're not going to tell my father?'*

The panic was very physical. A gut-wrenching terror at the reaction from her father, who, she feared, would experience as much jealousy as paternal concern. That she should be closer now to his protégé than he was.

Margaret, tears welling in her eyes, explained that her decision to overstep the normal boundaries and confront Martha was born of affection rather than interference or judgement. She had assumed far more than a housekeeper's role since Jessica died and had picked their mutual bread-making session, to raise the matter – pummelling her anxiety into the dough as she spoke.

'I should tell him. Your father. It's my duty. You know I should. But – oh Martha. You're so young. And he's a *musician*. You of all people should know from your father what *that* means.' She was punching the ball of dough with her knuckles.

Martha, in the ballet pumps which passed as slippers, was tapping her foot faster and faster, staring at a crack in the tiled floor.

*Tap. Tap. Tap.*

'I'm just saying that if you were my daughter, I would put a stop to this. For your own sake. How long has this been going on? From the very beginning?'

Martha's vision was now blurring as her eyes welled up uncontrollably. *Tap. Tap.* A sick feeling in her stomach. Growing panic so that the crack divided into two then three lines until she could not be sure which was the real one. She was most upset not at being found out, but at Margaret's tone. Talking of this as if it were some sordid, nasty business. As if Josef were taking advantage.

When it was she who had made it all happen. Was *glad* to have made it all happen.

It still astonished the young Martha how easy it had been. Blissfully unaware of the secret romance growing ever more desperate between the British press officer and the Czechoslovakian security chief, no one rumbled the part this liaison had played in a sudden and unexpected change of plans. Out of the blue an extension was suggested for some members of the foreign orchestra.

A quartet was to stay on for this extended tour. Special recitals to promote the forthcoming competition. Josef was to be the star performer. To help the budget and to keep the embassy sweet, Martha's father Charles had offered his home for two of the musicians plus their minder, and no one could have been more surprised and delighted than Martha when the embassy agreed.

*Thank you, fate, thank you…*

Josef arrived at their home two days later with a surprisingly small brown leather suitcase, a violinist who spoke very little English and a minder called Alexander who could not have minded less. 'Isn't he supposed to keep an eye on you?' Martha teased as Alexander made the excuse of needing a walk before disappearing straight after breakfast every morning.

'He is in love,' Josef explained, whispering as Martha's father remained oblivious behind his newspaper across the table. 'And I am not, apparently, considered important enough to run off.'

Later he confided there was talk of a major international tour being planned for the Bolshoi ballet. These smaller, less important trips for neighbouring artists were being used as recces. To test security and international reaction.

'So you're guinea pigs?'

He frowned at that.

'It's an expression, Josef...'

'You're saying I look like a pig?' He pretended to sound hurt. Both of them very well aware of what was happening. Martha unbearably gauche some days, like a foal tripping over its feet – ever conscious of being watched by those extraordinary ice-blue eyes as she moved about the house, pretending to be busy.

Whilst the minder couldn't have been less attentive, infuriatingly it was Martha's father who seemed unwilling to leave Josef any time to himself. What with rehearsals and schedules and long debates over new scores, Charles was in his absolute element with a new star guest for company. Four torturous days of watching and waiting had to be endured before Martha finally overheard her father confirm on the telephone a meeting in town to liaise with a builder over plans to replace the french doors to the garden.

*I must apologise for deserting you, Josef. I could cancel if you prefer.*

*Please, Charles. Don't worry. I will be fine.*

And then, at last – in the conservatory, watering her mother's beloved plants, his footsteps behind her. Her – so absurdly young. So absurdly shy. So absurd overall. Josef much too formal, admiring the plants and the view of the garden, and then suddenly speechless as she turned.

'Would you play for me, Josef?' She couldn't help herself. Wanted to again see that expression on his face when he was lost in the music and she could just watch him.

He had laughed at first. *No, Martha. Please. Not that. We need to talk. I want to talk to you properly...* But then, when she pressed him – *just for me, Josef, please* – a look in his eyes of feigned exasperation, the acknowledgement that he could not, *would not* refuse her, and it was in that moment – the relief in her own eyes; the realisation that she had not been imagining it all.

Adding.

Inventing.

Dreaming.

He was unusually nervous, fluffing a few notes, complaining that she was too distracting, until in the end he closed his eyes and teased that he would have to pretend she was not there. Debussy. He picked the Debussy Sonata – until he was lost again in the music so that she was able to surprise him, her confidence buoyed by the music and the mood and the fear that this might be her only chance – reaching out to touch the long slope of his neck, as she had so longed to that first time at the rehearsal hall.

So that he stopped playing. Shocked. Then pleased. Then not at all surprised – his eyes smiling as he took her hand to kiss it ever so gently. They were interrupted then by the sound of the front door as Alexander returned, but it did not matter. Was decided now.

And it was she who moved things along. Not Josef, as Margaret assumed.

'No – Martha. We mustn't,' he whispered the first time she crept along the hall. Tiptoed into his room – body trembling not with fear at what she was doing, but the fear she could awake now any day to find he would be gone. That memory, which makes her close her eyes, of the very first time she felt his flesh against hers. The shock of the absolute delight of it. Skin to skin.

'He's not a bad person, Margaret. It's not what you think.'

'I wash the sheets, young lady. So don't try to tell me it's not what I think. And it may not be my place, Martha, but you have no mother here to talk to you. Men. Well. You have to be so careful. And this will turn out badly for you, mark my words.

He's a musician. He'll be off soon. Gone. And you're eighteen years old.'

'We're in love.'

There. She'd said it.

'Love? Oh, it's love, is it, Martha? He's said that, has he? That he *loves* you. Going to give it all up, is he? The music. Russia.'

'Czechoslovakia.'

And now Martha's lip was trembling and for just a moment she had wanted to slap Margaret for her sceptical face. Of course, they hadn't had time to make proper plans yet. But there was no question that Josef felt as she did. *I can't believe this*, he would say over and over at night, begging her to stay with him until morning. *I love you so much, Martha. Let me talk to your father. Please, Martha.* Wrapping his arms around her as she insisted it was too dangerous.

That she had to go. *Let me go, Josef* – fighting the urge to laugh. Teasing him and wriggling from the crook of his arms. Wishing too that she could stay but terrified of being found out.

*We can't tell my father.*

And OK, so it was difficult. Dangerous. Her father would go insane. And yes. A *musician*. Wrong job. Wrong country. But Josef wasn't like her father and it was just as her mother had said. You can't help who you love… *And doesn't love always find a way? Isn't that what they say, Margaret? We are going to be together. We are going to find a way…*

Margaret stopped then and wiped her hands on her apron before turning towards the sink with, to Martha's surprise, tears again in her eyes.

'I just wish your mother was here. She'd know what to do.'

'So you're going to tell my father?' Martha straightened her back but Margaret did not reply, instead throwing the dough into the bowl and dabbing at her eyes with her apron as she walked away towards the pantry.

For the next two days, Martha lived on her nerves, awaiting her father and Josef's return from an extended trip to London. Politics. Keeping the embassies sweet. When confronted she would deny everything, but it would still be dangerous. Her father would either have to believe Margaret or sack her – neither option appealing for, deep down, Martha was very fond of Margaret. But the only thing that really mattered now was finding some way to be with Josef.

Just as Charles Ellis predicted, Josef was the subject of growing admiration in musical circles and the Czechoslovakian officials seemed cautiously pleased. These London visits were more and more regular. And when the two returned finally, the taxi from the railway station sweeping up outside with the sullen and ever more love-struck minder moping in the back, Martha found it difficult to read her father's face – to work out whether Margaret had spoken up by telephone as she had threatened. But no.

The chatter in the hallway sounded amiable enough and her father, when he appeared, looked absolutely fine. Instead, unexpectedly, it was Josef who looked ill at ease. Martha was completely thrown by this. She had been so longing to see him. To find a quiet moment to talk to him about what had happened with Margaret. Two minutes inside the house and still he remained extremely agitated, his eyes widening at her, pleading and panicking, as Charles headed for the drinks cabinet. 'We must celebrate.'

'Celebrate?' The young Martha felt a terrible pull inside. Instinct. An immediate physical warning.

'Josef has the most marvellous news. Now – where is it? That single malt I set aside.'

The icy blue eyes were wide now, trying still to reach out to Martha whose wave of foreboding was getting worse and worse as her father explained the news. The change of events, so completely unexpected and for Martha so devastating.

Supper was unbearable – Martha's distress stretched to the point of nausea as she picked at the chicken salad Margaret had left prepared for them. She tried cutting the chicken into tiny pieces but still found the texture too dense. Chewing and chewing but unable to swallow.

She did not go to him that night, needing time to think what on earth to say, and was still awake, her curtains drawn so that she could see the stars, when he crept into her room.

He sat on the edge of her bed, silent, as in her head she traced the shape of a constellation – just as her mother had taught her.

'So,' she was whispering, still staring at the stars. 'It's Russia for Josef Karpati after all.'

# CHAPTER 19

Ironically, it was Sarah's fault really. The stripping. She meant well – so keen to stop Martha's apparent self-harming in Millrose Mount, trying all sorts of things to break the cycle. *Hold a cube of ice in your hand, Martha. It will give you a release when things overwhelm you here. The same high – something to dilute the stress without hurting yourself. I'll leave a flask of ice for you.*

To pacify Sarah, Martha had squeezed the ice in her hand as directed then tried crunching it in her mouth but neither helped. For what Sarah had not understood was the real motivation. Though Martha did suffer genuine despair in Millrose Mount, she never truly wanted to hurt herself. Stealing cutlery to fake self-harm wasn't a cry for help either. It was a calculated means to an end. A cue to a stint in isolation.

For Sarah did not work the night shifts, to see how bad things really got in Millrose. Martha was still afraid on the wards in the dark. And though she worried about Sarah's warnings that her behaviour would only make her records and her situation worse, she continued to believe the isolation wing was the safest place. It had been run by the same little team of staff for years – not especially caring, but at least indifferent, which was the better of the bad hands. No threat. They peered through the viewing hatches of the single units regularly. They provided meals. They played chess and cards and gossiped. For the most part they simply left the patients alone, which suited Martha just fine.

And so, when Sarah was off-shift , Martha came up with a new scheme to earn herself a few days on 'special watch' in isolation. It came to her suddenly on an especially humid summer's day. Nakedness. Something she could choose when it all became too much.

The shock and anger of the older nurse on ward duty made it all the more delicious and she was soon precisely where she wanted to be. Back in isolation, but without the sore arms.

The only problem was the knock-on effect to the knitting. Some of the crueller staff threatened that if she continued to strip off and make a nuisance of herself, they would never let her knit again.

This, Martha realised, would be unbearable. For sitting with Sarah in the dayroom, click-clicking away, had become a little window of sunlight in the whole dark experience. She went into this strange zone when she was knitting. Maybe it was the rhythm. Maybe it was the sense of creating something. But it became a really special and peaceful place, which helped Martha to cope.

'It quite worries me how much I love this,' she told Sarah one day. 'I'm very frightened they will stop it.'

'I won't let that happen, Martha.'

'I was wandering around yesterday, trying to keep away from Mylo. The guy who thinks I have cigarettes?'

'I've reported that he bothers you, Martha. I don't know what else I can do when I'm off-shift.'

'It's OK. He doesn't like walking much so I always shake him off now. I went to the main reception area with all the portraits. And there was this big picture of Samuel Cribbs, the man who designed this place. Weird picture. His eyes follow you whichever way you turn. Bit like some of the staff.'

Sarah smiled, offering Martha a new ball of wool from her bag.

'Anyway, one of the women on my ward said he was murdered. That he haunts the place.'

'Oh for goodness' sake, Martha. I don't think this is a very good topic of conversation. Murder and ghosts. I thought we had agreed to try to stay positive. Talk about the future. About getting you out of here.'

This had become the key strand of their conversations. Sarah's determination to help Martha. To persuade her to behave. Toe the line while Sarah demanded a review of her case. But the problem was the hierarchy. Nursing staff at Millrose technically had very little role or influence in patient treatment. They were there to deliver drugs, to do the doctors' bidding, to supervise and to break up fights. Sarah's pleas for Martha's case to be reviewed had so far fallen on deaf ears. She wasn't even allowed to see her case notes.

But now Sarah was suddenly looking around her and leaning in closer to whisper. 'OK. So I have something to tell you, Martha, but it's an absolute secret and I need to be sure that you won't tell anyone else. Not even when you're cross. Or stressed.'

Martha stopped knitting and turned to look at Sarah more closely.

'I've been in touch with someone I think can help you, but it has to stay between us. OK?'

'OK.' Martha could now feel her heartbeat increasing, acknowledging the surge of the one thing she still feared as much as she desired. The hope, the dream, the very possibility of… getting out.

'There's a doctor coming here secretly to talk to you and some of the other patients. I think he can help. But you are going to have to talk properly to him, Martha. About what happened when they brought you here.'

Martha turned away to gaze out of the window. For a moment she watched a bird gliding from one tree to another. She watched the clouds drifting. She watched the bird swoop again. Then she closed her eyes.

'I know this makes you stressed, Martha. I know you don't like me to ask. That it's hard. But I need you to talk to him about what really happened. Can you do this for me? *Please, Martha.*'

# CHAPTER 20

Josef and Martha's final night together was unbearably bitter-
sweet.

'I don't want us to argue, Josef.'

'So – let me speak to your father, Martha. If we just explain— '

'No, Josef. You don't know him like I know him. He will go
all out to ruin you, if he finds out about us.'

'I don't understand this. And I am not afraid of him.' Josef
was at first determined to persuade Martha to follow *his* plan.
To say no to the invitation to the Moscow State Orchestra and
instead to stay in England – officially or unofficially.

'Why would he want to ruin me? When I explain how I feel.
That I love you. That I want to look after you. Why would he
want to ruin me?'

'Because I am so young and he will feel betrayed… by both of
us. Also – he will be very, very jealous.'

'Jealous? I am not understanding.'

Martha could not find the words to explain either, but she
knew it to be true. That her father would not accept her being
closer to Josef and his extraordinary talent than he was.

'I can stay here and take care of you.'

'How, Josef? When my father throws you out?'

'I will work. Teach music. Work in a café. Anything.'

'And you are sure that will even be possible? That the authorities will allow it? That Moscow will just shrug this off? I have no
money of my own, Josef. None at all.' Martha had just finished
school with vague plans to be a teacher but nothing had yet been

organised. She had not secured a place at college. Was still undecided.

'So we run away. We get jobs. To be together. Say yes, Martha. Just say yes to this. We can do this.'

'No, Josef. It won't work. You will have to give up the music and you will end up hating me.'

'You are mad. I could never be hating you.'

She had turned then to face him, pulling the sheet around her shoulder, fighting the maelstrom of emotions bubbling up within her. Fear. Love. Longing. Despair.

Martha was already a little late with her period, but there was no way she would tell Josef this now. She wasn't particularly worried, assuming it was all the stress. It had happened before when she was worried about exams. It would come to nothing.

Martha closed her eyes and remembered him playing – that first time in the rehearsal hall and later in the conservatory. That extraordinary look on Josef's face as he reached for the cello, carefully positioning the neck on his left shoulder. His eyes changing. On *that other planet* that her mother had spoken of.

'This is what you have been working towards your whole life, Josef. This invitation to join the Moscow State Orchestra – as their soloist. You simply cannot turn this down. I won't let you.'

Josef said nothing for a moment. Looked away.

Martha stood up, the sheet still wrapped around her, and opened the curtains wider. Her bedroom was not overlooked and had a wonderful view of treetops from the distant park beneath the clear night sky. Ever since she was little, Martha liked to sleep with the curtains open so that she could trace the shapes of the constellations as her mother had taught her.

'You can't say no, Josef. It's not even an invitation really, is it? It's what you've always dreamed of. Say no to this and you will be wondering for the rest of your life what you might have become.

And one day, you will look at me and you will wonder if you did the right thing. Giving it up for me.'

'No. Never.'

'I won't let you do it, Josef. I would rather follow you. Come to Russia to be with you. Once you've made a name for yourself. Once you have some influence and can make that happen for us.' Even as she said it, the idea frightened Martha but she tried not to show this in her voice. To be with Josef, she would do anything. Maybe she could teach English in Russia?

'Your father would never allow it, Martha. And Russia. It's not what you imagine. It's a very different kind of life.'

'But I would be happy just to be with you. I don't mind where.'

Josef was silent for a while, his face tense, and so she linked each of their hands, stroking the back of his with her fingers – ever so gently.

'Admit it. It's a better plan than you working in a café here – with my father trying to get you deported.'

'I'm scared, Martha.' Josef closed his eyes, his brow tense. 'I'm scared it won't happen. You won't come. You will meet someone else. That if I leave, something will…'

'Never, Josef. I don't want anyone else.'

'Then let's not wait. Let's run away. Be together now.'

Martha loosened her right hand to put her finger over his lips then, until he again opened his eyes. 'No more arguing, Josef. Please, let's stop this. You need to say yes to Moscow. Which means you will leave tomorrow. This is our last night for a while. Don't let's argue any more. *Please.*'

'And you will really do this for me? Follow me? Come to Russia when I can organise it? You promise me?' He had cupped her face in his hands, his eyes burning into her. Frightened eyes. 'Say that you promise.'

'Yes. I promise you.' Martha meant it.

And that is when she told him – that since her mother's death she had felt as if the air around her was somehow all wrong. As if she couldn't quite breathe it in properly. The air never quite reaching her lungs.

'I didn't breathe properly until I met you, Josef.' She was staring into his face. 'It was as if I was waiting – but I didn't know what for.'

Josef tilted his head. He kissed her fingers. Then her forehead. And then they made love entirely differently. Very slowly. Not with the urgency which normally overtook them both but with this almost unbearable tenderness because neither of them wanted it to end.

Afterwards they were silent for a time, Martha trying to hide how difficult it was not to cry, and he wrapped his arms around her so that they could both see the window. By way of distraction, she pointed out the constellations – how to find the Big Dipper and the Little Dipper and the North Star, just as her mother had taught her. She was shocked that he did not know how to do this, making him promise something also – that, while apart, they would each look up to the night sky and do this. To trace the constellations to find the North Star.

A connection. Yes. Their small and secret thing – until they could be together again.

# CHAPTER 21

The speed with which Martha's life unravelled after Josef's departure left her in a permanent state of dazed disbelief.

Some nights she would look up at the stars in shock – *just a month ago… Just two months ago… Just three…*

Everything moved too fast. No space to breathe. To think. And no time to find a way to get a message to Josef.

Once the appalling truth hit home, that her period was not running late because of stress, Martha had nowhere to turn. In desperation she confided eventually in Margaret, begging for secrecy and advice, but to no avail. Margaret immediately told her father.

Martha was both horrified and terrified, clinging to the hope he would eventually get over the anger sufficiently to support her. He did not.

The extremity of his rage shook her. In a series of shouting matches, Martha at first point blank refused to say who the father was, guessing that Charles would try to ruin Josef's career. But the visiting ensemble were inevitably first suspects and so to distract her father from this Martha eventually came up with a story – saying she had been secretly meeting a local young man who had promised to marry her but had since disappeared.

She was very quickly sent in disgrace to stay with a great-aunt in the country, where she imagined she would have the child. Find some way to get word to Josef?

But – no.

Just before the baby was due, a car was sent to collect her. Martha imagined she would be going home. That her father had, thank heavens, experienced some change of heart. She had been under virtual house arrest, not allowed to send any letters while away, and began now to hope there might, at last, be some way of fixing this. Correspondence from Josef at home? A chance finally to get word to him?

But the car did not take her home. Instead they drove two hours along the coast to a place she had never heard of. Aylesborough-on-sea. Her destination was a large, three-storey Edwardian terrace on the outskirts of town with a distant sea view.

Inside, staff very quickly explained Martha's new circumstance. It had all been arranged by her father. The property in a smart and quiet residential area had been converted into a home for single mothers run by a charity. Martha was *very lucky to get a place. We are here to help you.*

It didn't feel like it.

If disapproval had a smell, this house reeked of it. The staff were religious. Practical. Curt. Disapproving. It was run with military precision, and from the off Martha was warned that sticking to the house rules and daily schedules was non-negotiable.

Martha was to share a dormitory with three other girls – Peggy, Eunice and Alice – although Alice was clearly a made-up name because often when Martha called to her, she didn't respond. Forgot, apparently, to pretend.

Martha's one hope in all of this was that, being in the same terrible boat, the girls would at least be able to help each other. Buoy each other's spirits. Come up with some grand plan together. But she learned very fast that they were not in the same boat at all.

Giving up Josef's child had simply never occurred to Martha. From the earliest flutterings in her belly to the clear kicks and turns as she watched the bump in amazement in the bath at her great-aunt's home, she had fallen in love with this child.

More than anything, she wished she could rewind. Listen to Josef. Follow his plan to run away. But she still absolutely assumed she would find a way to work this out. And so, as time passed and the bump grew and grew, she would whisper to the baby about the life that lay ahead for them. Once she found some way to get word to Josef. Arrange for them to go to Russia. She knew that this would all be a shock for Josef; far from ideal. But she knew too, with absolute certainty, that he would love this child as much as she did.

What appalled Martha – a dark and oppressive cloud forever overhead – was that all babies born at the home were presumed available for adoption. And Alice, along with some of the other girls, couldn't wait to hand theirs over. They even told Martha that they didn't want to stay the six weeks that was allowed after the birth, but the staff in charge of the place said they had to be patient. The families and paperwork took time. Six weeks was the way they all liked it.

Later Martha heard whisperings that this protocol was really to make sure that the babies were healthy. That there were no disabilities. Problems didn't always show up at first, apparently, and the new parents didn't want a disabled baby.

She also heard the staff muttering about 'removals' and at first wondered what on earth they meant. *Three removals today. Busy.* Beds? Chairs? Tables? What?

But no. All too soon she learnt it was the appalling term for a handover day. The adoption itself. New parents coming to collect.

She watched the girls packing up the babies' things and wondered how on earth they could bear it. How some of them seemed so accepting – even relieved – while others cried and cried and cried as they silently folded things. Vests and nappies. Bonnets and booties.

From the start Martha was clear. She told everyone – the other girls and all of the staff – that this wasn't going to happen in her case. She was going to keep her baby. Her plan all hinged on somehow persuading her father to change his mind. Allow her and the baby home. Then she would find some way to secretly get in touch with Josef. Russia, however different and difficult, was better than the alternative life here. They would get married and they would somehow work it out.

*The father will support me*, she told the other girls, who rolled their eyes.

'So that's why he's here right now, is it, Martha? The father? Because he's so keen to support you?' Peggy, who used to sneak out to the rear garden for a cigarette, was bitter. Warned Martha not to build up her hopes. The father of her own baby was a sailor. She had no idea he was married with a family of his own until she told him about the pregnancy. *Didn't see him for dust after that.*

Peggy said they should count their blessings. Said there were worse places; had heard terrible stories of places in Ireland where the girls were made to work from dawn. Forced to scrub and skivvy right to the end of the pregnancy.

At the Aylesborough home all the chores were shared by the girls but the staff were firm rather than cruel. At prayers, which were held daily, the mantra was one of seeking forgiveness and moving forward. *You've made a mistake but you're here to make a fresh start. To put this behind you. You pray for forgiveness. You move on. You are giving a special gift to couples who cannot have their own children.*

Martha could not bear for her baby to be described as a mistake and would find herself digging her nails into her palms. But the home and all those who worked there had one voice. A set script and a set system.

Some of the staff were midwives – most of the babies born on site.

When Martha had complications and had to go to the local hospital for the caesarean she had imagined her father would surely come and visit. In truth she was so angry at him she had no idea how this would make her feel.

But the birth had been traumatic. Made her feel so vulnerable and so very frightened. There was one point when she thought she was going to lose her child.

The baby was in the wrong position, apparently, and as they wheeled her to the operating theatre she could hear the nurse saying – *baby is in distress. The baby is not getting enough oxygen…*

When she woke up from the anaesthetic she honestly thought the child was dead. Tears streaming down her face during this terrible pause, her head pounding and her mouth so very dry, until the nurse suddenly appeared and placed him in her arms. *Here he is.* All pink and perfect.

The relief then. So wishing that her mother was still alive to see this and so badly needing *family* that, yes – she hoped that her father would come. Be different with her.

She needed his support and so was praying that the scare of this emergency would make him reconsider. Soften him. But it did not.

It was Margaret who came. She had knitted a little cardigan. Lemon wool. She had tears in her eyes the whole time but stayed barely ten minutes and had bad news. Found it difficult even to look Martha in the face.

'I'm sorry, Martha, but I've come to tell you that I'm leaving. Moving to a new job in Scotland.'

'He's sacked you, hasn't he? Is that what's happened, Margaret? He isn't coming?'

'Didn't I try to tell you, Martha? Didn't I try to warn you?'

After her return to the charity home, Martha remembers only the rollercoaster of extreme highs and terrible lows – overwhelmed by her beautiful and perfect baby and yet always so very tired and worried. She insisted on breastfeeding, which, though tricky at first, was soon enormously comforting. But several times when she was forced to leave the child in the nursery to complete her chores, she caught the staff giving him a bottle.

This she found devastating, and she complained loudly but was told it was better to help the baby 'adjust'.

Only at night, just occasionally, would Martha get the tiniest glimpse of how her life might have turned out. Snatched and secret moments that she came to treasure.

Sometimes in the early hours Martha would simply get lucky. Just once in a while the timing would work out that the other girls and their babies would be sleeping and she would get a spell feeding on her own.

In those quiet, stolen moments it was just Martha and her son. She would close her eyes then and blank out everything around her. She would try not to think of the daylight hours. Of the noise and the uncertainty and all the bustling about. The work in the kitchens. The enormous pots of stew, the mountains of vegetables to peel. The rows and rows of shoes that would have to be polished every single day. *Why do we need to do this? Who cares about our shoes?*

Instead she would block all of this out and pretend that she was back home with the baby, in a different version of her life. Back in her bedroom with its buttercup wallpaper, her mother humming downstairs in the kitchen. She would stroke the top of her baby's head as he fed, amazed at the soft down of his hair. She would kiss him goodnight, holding her lips against his forehead – breathing in his wonderful scent.

She would look out of the window, high up in that terrace in Aylesborough-on-sea. She would search the night sky for the North Star and later watch the sun come up over the waves far in the distance.

And she would whisper to her child that she would find a way. *I will not let them take you…*

# CHAPTER 22

Sarah's secret in Millrose Mount turned up in the form of a tall and very serious-looking senior doctor called Wesley Clarke. Martha would later learn that Sarah had taken on the dangerous role – rare and brave for the times – of whistle-blower.

Dr Clarke arrived on a Wednesday, to a flurry of panic among the staff. He demanded to see records and to tour all the wards immediately, presenting stamped paperwork which he showed like a detective.

'You are not to say this has anything to do with me, Martha. Understand?' Sarah had brought a new bag of wool and positioned their chairs in a corner of the new dayroom, away from the other groups of female patients.

'So what's going on?'

'I can't say exactly. But he'll be here for a while. He'll be asking to see you and other patients on a one-to-one. I really need you to talk to him, Martha.'

For two days Martha watched the staff huddled and whispering in corners as Dr Wesley Clarke toured Millrose Mount, his face increasingly grave. Staff were very suddenly on their best behaviour. Cutlery was carefully counted at every meal. The doors were opened after breakfast each morning from the corridors onto the enclosed central courtyard so that patients could enjoy fresh air.

Normally it was only Sarah who could be bothered to supervise this ritual. But now everyone was putting on a show.

And then, on the third day, Martha was escorted to a consulting room to find Dr Wesley Clarke seated at the desk in a high-backed leather chair, Sarah standing by the window.

He had a soft, kind voice so unlike the others who seemed always in such a hurry. He asked her how the knitting was going. Martha narrowed her eyes at Sarah, worrying it was some kind of trick question. Afraid of saying the wrong thing.

'Your nurse tells me she feels a tad guilty. That she introduced you to knitting and you have turned it into something of an obsession.' He was smiling. 'I could do with a new jumper, if you're asking.'

Martha laughed. The mood instantly more relaxed.

And then Dr Clarke moved to sit on the edge of the desk. 'I'm not going to beat around the bush here, Martha, because I simply don't have time on my side. Your admission notes are missing. No one seems to be able to tell me about your case in detail.'

'That doesn't surprise me.'

'Why do you say that?'

'Never mind.'

'Ah, but the thing is I do mind, Martha. That's why I'm here.'

Dr Clarke explained that he was carrying out a full review of Millrose Mount, which seemed to have slipped through a net following abolition of the Board of Control. A new regime of inspections was still a work in progress.

'Can you get me out?'

Dr Clarke glanced at Sarah and back to Martha. 'So you would like to leave Millrose?'

'Of course I would like to leave.'

'Not everyone feels that way. Some patients feel safer when they're looked after.'

'We are not looked after here and I am certainly not safe.'

After that Dr Clarke met Martha a number of times. He discussed her refusal to see her father, the self-harm and the stripping, while she in turn told him of her biggest worries. The slack supervision at night. The rumours of assaults. He eventually confided that the few notes available suggested she had presented as delusional with violent and suicidal tendencies. But this was not what he was seeing. What he was seeing, he shared, was merely depression. Worse – despair. Someone who had chosen to withdraw from the world.

'It is the source I need to understand, Martha. If I am going to help you, I need to understand where this all began for you. The trigger.'

Martha liked Dr Clarke but remained wary. Any and every time she had let herself think about the terrible thing that had happened, let alone seek any kind of support, it had always backfired.

Between these consultations Sarah whispered her own updates over their knitting sessions. She said that Dr Clarke was not only a good man but quite possibly Martha's last hope. He ran an outpatient clinic in Essex and, in addition to his inquiry report, he was hoping to move some of Millrose Mount's patients into his care. His work was part of a new approach, moving away from the big institutions and championing the rehabilitation of patients with short-term conditions. But places were strictly limited.

Dr Clarke meantime insisted that Martha's medication was gradually reduced. Day by day she felt better for this – her mind much clearer, her body stronger.

And then she was called into Dr Clarke's temporary office one final time. On his desk was a slim file with the name of the home for single mothers. Sarah was in the corner of the room, her face pale.

Martha closed her eyes and could feel herself drifting.

False hope, Martha had learned, was a terrible thing. A life raft in a stormy sea. You couldn't help but cling to it, of course you couldn't, but the shock of the cold and choking water was all the worse when the raft was suddenly pulled from your grasp.

It happened twice in the home for single mothers.

First there was Eunice's chambermaid plan. Like Martha, Eunice did not want to give up her child.

Eunice came from a large Catholic family. She was a lovely, sunny girl with a keen sense of humour who somehow managed to crack jokes and dry asides to bolster spirits, however difficult the day. She was taller than most of the other girls, with strawberry blonde hair and pale, perfect skin. She also had a bigger bump than anyone had ever seen.

'What have you been doing? Eating for England?' the other girls joked as Eunice manoeuvred her enormous bump in and out of a chair. Those girls who were keen to get their ordeal over with were paranoid about getting their figures back so they could keep their shame a secret. These girls would tease Eunice that she would be sorry for eating for a small country and would find it difficult to shift the weight afterwards.

But through some of her friends Eunice had heard about a London hotel run by a woman apparently sympathetic to the plight of women like Eunice and Martha. The word was that this woman called Hilda would take in young mums as chambermaids and allow them to devise a rota to complete their work and share the childcare. The wages were apparently pretty poor but it was a way to keep their babies. Accommodation and keep was provided.

It sounded perfect.

Martha and Eunice would huddle together at night, working out a plan. Through Eunice's friend, they would write or telephone this Hilda and secure their places as soon as their babies were born. Eunice said she had enough cash for travel and was happy to sub Martha until she had her first wage packet.

Listening in to this scheming, Peggy and Alice were dismissive. Their line was this Hilda was probably a madam who would put them on the game.

But Martha was ready to grab any lifeline and for a while believed she had an option in place which would buy enough time to somehow get word to Josef if her father still refused to take her home.

The problem was in the detail. Eunice worryingly vague.

'Do you have the address yet? Has your friend got hold of the details?'

'Not yet. We think it's south London, south of the river at least. But she's going to try this weekend.'

The weekend came and went. Still no word. The girls in the home were not allowed to make phone calls or send mail unvetted, so there was very little Martha could do herself.

And then Eunice was taken by surprise – giving birth not only a week early… but to twins! No one could believe that this had gone undetected. No wonder she was so huge. The babies were small but healthy – each quite extraordinarily beautiful, with a full head of dark hair and enormous deep blue eyes.

All was mayhem as Eunice's mother came to visit. As soon as it was shared that there was no certainty that the twins could be adopted together, Eunice's mother was having none of it. Tears. Reconciliation. A complete change of heart. All the things that Martha could only dream of. Suddenly Eunice was all tearful exhaustion and exhilaration, packing up all her things to take her babies home.

'I'm so pleased for you, Eunice. Of course I am. But I was just wondering if you think you could find out? About the hotel? About Hilda?'

'I'm so sorry, Martha. Apparently it was just talk. Rumours. Wishful thinking. To be honest, I'm not sure this Hilda ever existed… Really sorry, Martha.'

The next disappointment was even tougher. Three weeks after giving birth herself and settled back into the charity home, Martha was summoned to the visitor lounge to find her father waiting for her. She had been instructed to leave the child in the nursery. Her assigned welfare officer, Megan, was there too.

At first Martha's heart leapt because her father had a basket on his lap full of beautiful baby clothes. She could see a couple of cardigans and booties and hats too. For a moment she thought that, just like Eunice's mother, there had been a softening of heart at last.

'Your father has brought all this for the baby,' Megan began. And Martha felt a surge of complete and utter relief.

'It is a gift for the new parents, Martha. We encourage it. Something nice for you to do for your baby. A gift from your family ready for your baby to take to his *new* family very soon.'

'But he's not going to a new family…'

'I've had some new information through, Martha. Sorry, are you OK? Do you want some water?' Dr Clarke sounded concerned, glancing again at Sarah.

'I'm fine.' A lie. Martha could feel her heart rate increasing. She looked out of the window at Millrose Mount where a bird on the branch of the nearest tree seemed curious as to the nature of their discussion, his head tilted with imagined interest. As if listening in.

'These papers have just come in, but again it's all a bit sketchy. Unsatisfactory. Pages missing as usual…'

Martha kept her head turned towards the window as he paused. She was thinking about how she might cope this time. Another false hope.

'The papers don't explain what happened. To your child.'

The bird waited. Dr Clarke waited.

'I don't talk about that. Sarah knows that I don't talk about any of that any more.'

'And why is that, Martha?'

Still she watched the bird – joined now by a little friend. A twin. The branch shaking with the increase in weight.

'You wouldn't believe me. No one would believe me. At the beginning it was all I talked about in here. Day and night. But it just made everything worse. They said I was a liar. That if I continued with my lies, I would be in here forever.'

A long pause and then Martha turned back to again look Dr Clarke in the eye. A game of tag now. *Your turn.*

'Look, Martha. I'm going to be really honest with you. I have just one more week to file my report. As part of that, I'm going to be pressing for a review of those patients I don't believe suit the Millrose environment at all. You're one of those. But hunches won't do. I need to make a proper case on paper. Not just your improvement off the meds. A clear clinical case. I would like to propose that you are transferred immediately to one of my clinics as an outpatient with supervised but more relaxed accommodation. A transition, hopefully, to you going back to your life, Martha. But I can't do that unless you talk to me. Help me make the case.'

Martha closed her eyes now and listened to the birds outside a different room. Yellow wallpaper like buttercups. A field with her mother holding a flower under her chin. *Do you like butter?* And then the sensation of extreme tiredness. So little sleep. Punch-drunk with tiredness. Her breasts heavy with milk. Emerging from a dream, opening her eyes and smiling with anticipation. Rolling over to face the cot…

And now Sarah looked at Dr Clarke, alarmed, as Martha's breathing changed. More and more rapid. Her chest rising faster and faster. Eyes shut tight.

'Are you OK, Martha?'

'Yes. So you can really help me? Get me out of here?' The whisper was desperate, each word punctuated by heavy, strained breaths as if the air was not reaching her lungs.

'If you talk to me, Martha – yes. I think I can.'

And so she opened her eyes and made herself go back there. To that awful room where she looks again at the cot.

*Empty.*

And she turned back then to Dr Clarke, who had both tenderness and guilt in his eyes, knowing from the look on her face, from the air which was not reaching her lungs and from all the years in this job, that he had cornered her. Left her no choice.

That it was coming…

Martha's story.

Martha's truth.

# PART THREE

# CHAPTER 23

As Kate sits in the reception area of the local police station, her mind is in overdrive. First and foremost she is thinking what the hell she will say now to Toby. How to explain this bizarre and unexpected twist. Martha streaking in a public building…

The irony of the timing feels cruel. Just last night in bed, she and Toby had lain holding hands and he talked about how he was coming round; surprised at the positive impact of Martha's stay.

*I mean it, Kate. I owe you an apology. I was completely dreading it, as you know. Felt that having a stranger around was the last thing we needed right now, but to be honest, you're right. She's quite a puzzle – Martha – but an interesting woman, and it has been lovely to see the change in you.*

That was the point at which he had reached out for her hand in the darkness. For just a moment she had tensed up, dreading that he would try to take it further, which these days always ended so badly. Her in tears. Him apologising. But last night he had just held her hand and they had lain there in the dark talking for quite a long time, and it had actually been very comforting. Nice. Not happy. Not quite that, of course. But it had felt… *all right* for once, and Kate had been so pleased for Toby, that, at least for a little while, there in the darkness, she could offer him something that felt a tiny bit… *all right.*

*I had an idea, Kate. How about we get away – just you and me. To Paris maybe? A week or so. Just go and look at some of the galler-*

*ies and museums. Eat some good food. Drink some good wine. What do you say?*

*Oh, I don't know Toby. I don't know about that...*

*Well, how about you just think about it? I don't mean a holiday. That wouldn't feel right. I do see that. But just a change of scene. Some time away on our own.*

She knew why he had suggested Paris and was silent for a moment.

*I mean... it doesn't have to be Paris, of course. If that would feel too...*

He paused and she found herself clenching his hand and he had clenched hers back and for the first time in a long time, she didn't want to let go.

*What I meant to say was that if Paris wouldn't feel right, we could think of somewhere else.*

*Maybe. I'll have a think. Perhaps – once Martha has got herself sorted.*

And then they had gone to sleep, still holding hands, and it had felt like some small breakthrough.

And now?

'They've been granted bail.' The duty officer reappears at the front desk to confirm that, after three long hours, things are finally moving. 'But they're in court tomorrow. Breach of the peace. Nine thirty.'

Kate takes a deep breath, not at all sure what she should say to Martha; not even sure what she thinks. How best now to go forward.

There is a commotion behind the counter and Kate watches as the door alongside reception finally opens to reveal Martha and Maria, pale and disorientated but arm-in-arm.

Kate cannot help herself – her gaze drifting to Martha's stomach. Thinking of that shock beneath the jumper. The haunting smile of scar tissue...

'We've been *charged*,' Maria gasps in horror as Carlo, seated alongside Kate for the long wait, now moves forward quickly to console his wife.

'We'll get you a good lawyer.' Kate clears her throat and looks away from Martha as the duty officer hands over two large envelopes containing their personal effects. 'I'm sure the magistrates will be lenient. Once they know the full facts.'

'I really am so very sorry, Kate – about all of this.' Martha is checking inside her envelope and Kate can feel that she is staring at her but does not yet feel quite ready to meet her gaze and so picks at some imagined fluff on her coat.

'It's OK. We'll work this out. But you do realise you'll be in the papers, ladies.' Kate checks her watch next, smooths her hair and tucks it into the neck of her coat, ready for the wind outside.

'The papers?' Maria turns to Martha, her expression initially of shock but then a slow change to something else entirely, as if she has just understood the punchline to a joke.

'Of course. The *newspapers*, Carlo.'

And then suddenly Maria is turning to her husband, smiling and cupping his face in both hands before kissing him loudly on the mouth.

'Placards, Carlo. We need to get home and make some placards.'

'Placards?'

'Yes, Carlo.' Maria is grinning broadly now, completely rejuvenated, as Kate finally meets Martha's worried stare. 'Placards. For our *campaign*.'

# CHAPTER 24

At the age of seven Kate contracted nits. Three other girls shared the shame in her class – singled out and sent home by the nit nurse – but Kate took it especially badly, weeping not at the sting of the foul-smelling shampoo her mother scrubbed deep into her hair but at the very physical thought of the invasion; the vivid picture in her head of the tiny beasts creeping across her skull. *They choose the cleanest hair*, her mother reassured as she massaged, night after night, the cocktail of chemicals into her roots. *They look across the class, honestly they do, and when they spy the shiniest, most beautiful hair, they say to themselves – that's where I want to be.*

Kate smiles at the memory of her mother's silver tongue and wonders if it is the same with spiders as she watches two webs being spun expertly across the top of the curtains (hoovered only yesterday). Have they picked her home, these spiders, because it is so clean? Out of spite?

One of the invaders, as if reading her thoughts, pauses momentarily – caught in the sunlight, its silken thread a tiny laser beam. The second – now in shadow, its line invisible – gives the impression of a flying spider. Suspended in mid-air.

'I really am very sorry about this morning, Kate. And so grateful for your help today.' Martha has made the hot chocolate this time – no cream and no marshmallows – and places Kate's mug on the small, low coffee table next to the sofa. Only now does Kate realise just how tired she feels. Sorting out a lawyer has taken most of the day. The on-call solicitor at the police station earlier was OK but Kate has sourced someone a bit more dynamic. She's confident he'll do a good job, but is still very anxious about Toby's reaction, relieved that he has phoned. Is to be late home.

'I should start something for us to eat.' Kate feels the muscle in her neck strain as she reaches too quickly for the drink.

'I'm going to say it was a publicity stunt. The stripping off. The solicitor you found reckons that if I say it was a one-off, for publicity, the magistrates will accept that. I should get a caution or be bound over. No reports. No *psychiatric* reports, I mean.'

Kate immediately feels the frown. Reports? This is the currency of her world. What does Martha know of courts requesting psychiatric reports?

'The thing is, Kate...'

Kate puts her mug back on the coffee table and sits up now, moving her head from side to side to check that she has not pulled the neck muscle too badly.

'The thing is, I was talking to Toby in the garden. He was saying what I already know. That you're not at your best just now. And so I feel awful. You don't need this, clearly. So I feel I should come clean. The truth is – oh God – there's something I should tell you now, Kate, because I am worried it will come out and be misunderstood.'

Kate finally stills herself.

'I suppose I should have mentioned it before. Right at the beginning when you very kindly invited me to stay. But it was a long time ago. And I – the thing is. Oh lord. I was in a psychiatric hospital for a time, Kate. *Millrose Mount* psychiatric hospital.'

Kate can suddenly feel her own pulse. In her fingers against the warmth of the mug in her hand. One. Two. Three. And also in her ear.

'It was such a long time ago. And I promise you that it was never serious. I was never any danger. To others, I mean. More of a mistake really.' Now Martha is talking very quickly. 'And it's all very much in the past, but the solicitor. Well – I felt it was best to come clean with him too. And he reckons there is a chance – only slim – that it could all come out because of this. If the court asks for reports, I mean. Over the streaking.'

Kate, bolt upright and her pulse still pounding, is now wondering how on earth she is going to explain this new twist to Toby. Not just Martha's streak but *this*. Just when he was coming round...

'But why, Martha? Why on earth were you in there?'

The scars on her wrists. Of course. She should have paid more attention. Listened to Toby's worries early on.

'And *Millrose Mount*? I mean, there was that big scandal up there. The TV documentary. Good God, Martha. *Millrose Mount*?' Kate's brow is tense as she tries to remember the details.

It had been in all the papers. Made the national news. Neglect. Allegations of ill treatment. Worse. Abuse. When they were on the beach, Martha had pretended not even to know of this.

'I just don't like to talk about it, Kate. But I promise you – *promise* you –that there's nothing to worry about. Really there isn't. It's in my past and I wasn't involved in any of the stuff that closed the place. I was there much earlier. A long, long time ago.'

Kate turns back to the spiders – the most ambitious now suspended on a line several feet in length.

Martha takes in a long breath. 'Though I'll completely understand if you want me to leave. Go back to the hostel.' She stands. 'I'll pack.'

'No, Martha. That won't help anything.'

Still Kate is worrying what the hell to tell Toby. He will find out soon enough – the story bound to make the papers. Pictures too, if Maria has her way. She is completely fired up now, planning the protest rally for the court hearing like a military coup. For just a second Kate opens her mouth to broach the subject of

Martha's wrists, but then the air seems to chill as she remembers the other scar.

*On her belly. The unexplained child…*

'I'll start a risotto. I think we have some pancetta. And some good mushrooms too. We need to eat.'

'It was a long time ago, Kate. There's nothing for you to worry about. I promise you.'

Kate tries to smile, pausing before heading into the kitchen to start supper.

# CHAPTER 25

Matthew sees her through the glass of the piano shop door just as he is about to turn the sign to 'Closed'.

'Oh my God.'

'What a day.' Geoffrey is emerging from his office, coat over his arm. 'I still can't take it in. Martha streaking at the council offices. Unbelievable.'

And then Geoffrey stands very still as Glenda and Matthew stare at each other through the glass – each frozen – she apparently reluctant to step inside.

'What is it, Matthew?'

'It's my mother.'

'Well, goodness, lad. What on earth are you gawping for? Invite her in. Invite her in.'

Matthew opens the door and Glenda steps silently inside. Tentatively she hugs him, squeezing tight – Matthew pulling away.

Geoffrey looks from one to the other, pausing before stretching out his hand.

'I'm Geoffrey. I own the place. A wonderful boy you have. We feel so lucky to have him here.'

'Oh. Right. Yes… Thank you.' And then Glenda is turning back to Matthew. 'You OK, Matthew? You look well. You have somewhere to stay?'

'I didn't want you to come here— '

'So. Best I'm off, then. Will you close up for me, Matthew? And don't worry about supper later. I expect you'll be wanting some time with your mum now.'

'No. It's fine. I'll see you later as planned, Geoffrey. Eight o'clock?'

'No, no. We can do that another time. I'm sure your mother— '

'No. Eight o'clock is still fine. Thank you, Geoffrey. I'm looking forward to it.'

They stand in silence. All three of them exchanging a stare. Two seconds. Three. Four. Until Geoffrey finally breaks the moment and, smiling at Glenda, is gone.

'I just needed to know that you're OK.'

'I told you on the phone that I'm OK.'

'Well. I'm here now.'

'And Dad. Is he here too?' Matthew is glancing anxiously back through the glass of the door.

'No, love. He's not.'

'Well, that's something, I suppose.' Turning the sign to 'Closed' and bolting the door. 'Look, Mum. I don't know what you were expecting, but I don't want to do this now. You shouldn't have come. I don't want another row.'

'I'm not here for a row.' She is fumbling in her bag. 'I brought you these. I didn't want to risk the post.'

Matthew glances down at the tattered brown envelope.

'There's not much. Just two papers we were given. But they have the name of the agency. The dates and everything. It's all there was.'

'How did you find me?'

'Well, you said Aylesborough. I always realised you'd come here. And when you mentioned on the phone before you had a job in a music shop, I got the train and I asked around.'

Matthew is skimming through the two faded papers, trying to take in the information. Just a few lines. The name of the adoption agency. A faded stamp with the date. Two signatures. Disappointing. Very little detail.

'I never meant to hurt you, Matthew.'

'Well, you did.' Matthew can feel the anger bubbling back up inside him. This is exactly what he didn't want.

'I know that. And I'm really so very, very sorry.'

'How could you not tell me? Twenty years. You lie to me for twenty years. How the bloody hell did you think I would react?'

'We thought it was for the best.' She says this very quietly, looking at the ground.

'Best for *who*?'

'Oh, Matthew.'

And then she sits on one of the piano stools – the whole of her body crumpled over. Shrunken somehow. And slowly and steadily she talks and talks while Matthew says nothing.

She tells him of a different time. Of meeting his father when they were young and hopeful and when everything in their life seemed straightforward.

She tells him of the years they tried for a child. Doctors. Tests. Hospitals. Of the shock. Of the hole in their lives. Of the decision they made to keep the adoption secret, which at the time seemed perfectly fine – and only now, in a different light, seems so wrong. Has all unravelled so horribly.

'It was the norm back then, Matthew. No contact afterwards. No big discussions. It was just how it was.'

She talks and talks. On and on. And the light fades and Matthew, in the end, softens a little and makes tea and offers to find her a room at the bed and breakfast, but she says no. She is going back on the train to stay with her sister. It's all arranged. She's left her suitcase at the station.

'So you're not going back home?'

'No. Not back home, Matthew.'


Two hours later at Geoffrey's, Matthew is still in shock as he watches him cook.

Geoffrey concentrates on the food. 'Everything OK with your mum?'

'Fine. Everything's fine.'

'It was my wife who taught me this.' Very carefully he is separating eggs into two glass bowls before whisking the whites furiously, twisting his face with the effort. Tongue lolling.

They pointedly do small talk. The parts on order for the Steinway. Which sheet music is moving fastest. Whether they should stock more recorders for the schoolchildren.

Matthew is surprised, glancing around, to find the home has a series of very obvious adaptations. Handrails along the main walls, and a stair lift. He doesn't at first like to ask. Geoffrey is a fit man for his age – early sixties, he guesses. And then, as he glances around some more, the explanation smiles from the shelves. Pictures of a younger Geoffrey with his late wife beaming from her wheelchair. By the seaside. By a coach with a cathedral in the background. Where is that?

Matthew leans in. Geoffrey and his wife, each with Mr Whippy-style ice creams. 'Isn't that the Kent coast?' Yes. Matthew recognises the shingle and the wooden posts of Whitstable.

'You know it? Yes. Jean grew up there. Kent. She loved to go back.'

Geoffrey watches his guest lift the picture carefully.

'She had multiple sclerosis.' Geoffrey has now finished whisking, the egg whites bulky and frothy, and puts a dot of butter with a dash of oil in a small frying pan.

'I'm sorry.'

'Don't be. It was a stroke in the end. The MS never stopped her doing anything. Well – most things.' And then Geoffrey turns to smile directly at Matthew. 'Jean would have liked you. Had a very discerning ear. Would have loved to hear you play that Steinway.'

Matthew is now struggling for a moment to set the picture back on the shelf. There is something amiss with the cardboard flap at the back – the angle wrong at first so that the picture nearly falls over and Geoffrey has to step in to help.

So is that why there were no children? Matthew had not liked to ask. There is a hiss as Geoffrey tips the combined eggs in the pan, moving the mixture with a fork as Matthew wanders around the room to look at other pictures and books.

'I hope you don't mind me being nosey.'

'You say that as if I have a choice.' Geoffrey is laughing as he lights the grill above the hot plate and, with a tea towel to protect his hand, lifts the frying pan up to rest under the heat. 'Now. Watch this.'

And so Matthew turns to watch the first omelette rise, puffing up like a feather pillow plumped from all sides. Quickly then Geoffrey uses a spatula to flip the omelette onto a plate, insisting that Matthew should eat while it is still hot as Geoffrey begins cooking his own.

'I still can't get over it. Martha streaking. Whoever would have believed it? I thought that only happened at big sporting events. And Maria. Getting themselves arrested.' Matthew is eyeing the sauce on the table.

'Well, it was a shock for all of us. The eviction letters. Only a month back I phoned the council about the lease renewal. And there wasn't a whisper of a problem.'

'So what do you think's really going on then? And what are you going to do, Geoffrey?'

'Well, the rumour is they're planning some flash new quayside development. With that company up at the old hospital. Trying to reinvent the whole town – attract a better class of visitor. But the council won't confirm anything.'

Geoffrey again moves the pan under the grill.

'Millrose Mount Village, you mean?' Matthew puts his knife and fork together, still hungry and wondering if it would be terribly rude to ask for a second serving. 'I never liked that bloke.'

'Sorry? Who?'

'Oh, nothing. I just went up there. To Millrose Mount – to have a nose. There was a smarmy bloke on sales.'

Geoffrey looks surprised as he moves his own omelette onto a plate and joins Matthew at the table.

'So are you ready to talk about what happened with your mother, then, Matthew? Is everything really all right?'

# CHAPTER 26

Kate and Martha have finished their meal as a key in the door confirms Toby is finally home. Nine thirty. Martha gathers up her wool as Kate stands.

'Sorry, darling. We had risotto. Doesn't keep. I was thinking I could do you a steak?'

'It's OK. I'm not hungry.' Toby's face is white as he puts down a large black folio, watching Martha disappear upstairs.

'We've had quite a day, actually. I'll pour you a drink, shall I? Explain everything.' Kate is aware of speaking too quickly. She is thinking of opening one of the better bottles of wine, or a Scotch maybe, but Toby is already shaking his head.

'It's OK, Kate. Really. I don't want a drink. And I know about today. That's why I'm so late.' His voice is hesitant, face still pale.

'You know about it? What do you mean you know about it?'

'I heard from the council.'

'The council?'

'I'm so sorry, Kate. I really wanted to tell you this morning. Prepare you all. But I was in the most horrible position and in the end I just couldn't risk it.'

'Tell me what? Toby. You're not making any sense.'

'The shops, Kate. I knew about the shops. The leases.'

For a moment there is complete stillness – deep furrows in Toby's forehead. Only when she says nothing does he continue.

'I wasn't sure if the letters would arrive today. So I couldn't risk saying anything. Conflict of interest. I could have got myself sued, plus it would have put you horribly on the spot with your new friends. I knew you would be upset, so I felt it was better not to put you in that position either.'

'Upset? Toby – I still don't understand what on earth you are saying here. How do you know about this?'

'We're working with the council on some new plans. It's all still speculative. Confidential. It's Mark's baby really, not mine. But of course he's kept me in the loop. If it comes off it will be a massive job for us. And to be frank we need it, Kate. I had no idea your new friends would… '

'You're involved? You're telling me you're involved in this?'

'I'm an architect, Kate. This is what I do.'

'So they're going to demolish the shops? Bulldoze them. The lifeblood of the quay. The wool shop, the piano shop and the café. And you're *involved*.'

'You're making it sound as if it's my idea. Believe me, Kate, I would never have taken it on if we'd known about your friends. Like I say, it's Mark's project. And we're just the architects.'

'But the council has its own architects, surely?'

'It's a partnership project. With the Millrose Mount company – the ones developing the hospital site. We've been called in by them as consultants.'

'No, Toby. You're to have nothing to do with this. *Please.* This is people's lives. Wendy lives above that shop. She's got nowhere else to go. And Maria's family too. That café has been in the family for generations. You're to have nothing to do with it. You hear me?'

'It's not that simple. Mark's committed now. Under contract.' Toby is turning on the lamp over the desk in the corner of the room. 'I heard about Martha. The scene at the council office. I heard about that too.'

'So you knew all this was coming. The notices to quit?' Kate ignores the reference to Martha and sits, her hands trembling. 'I can't believe you didn't tell me.'

And then suddenly Toby's face changes in the lamplight.

'I thought… I don't know. I thought we were getting a bit better, Kate. Last night when we were talking, I thought it felt a bit more… '

'And yet you knew about this. About the impact on my new friends, and you didn't say anything.'

'I didn't want to spoil things, Kate. That hope. That tiny sense that we might one day be OK again… '

His expression kills her. His lip trembling. An expression not of anger or blame or disappointment or any of those things that she feels that she deserves but a look of helplessness. Hopelessness. Worse – a man who has, these days, to be grateful that his wife will even hold his hand…

And it is in this moment, this split second, as he stands looking so crushed and so very, very alone – pushed a million miles away from her – that something breaks finally in Kate.

*Eight months and two days.* Since they made love. Since they felt connected properly. Since they stood any real chance of repairing any row they are ever to have again.

'Kate. You were the one who wanted to move here. To start again.'

*Eight months and two days.*

'So that's what I'm doing here, Kate. I'm trying to start a business. To start all over again. For you. For us. I'm just doing what *you* asked me to do.'

And now the room is moving. As if there is some new lens through which she sees it all. Round and round and round. Toby's voice drifting away as Kate closes her eyes…

She is imagining the water. So very, very cold. Swirling all around her.

# CHAPTER 27

At the Channel MusicMaker studio in London it is a young man this time wearing the headphones – dispatched to tell Josef Karpati that it is only *five minutes to air.*

No answer.

The young floor manager named Jack tries again. Earlier he found Mr Karpati stretched out along three of the seats as if asleep, but now the room is empty.

Jack speaks urgently to the studio runner in the corridor that *Mr Karpati is not in the green room and he will check the toilets. He can't be far but warn the director…*

The men's room is at the end of the corridor and Jack is working out how he will excuse the intrusion if tonight's star guest is simply having a piss, but also what his strategy will be if he's drunk, high, or worse. It would not be the first time a guest disappeared to the bathroom to 'settle the nerves'. Just a few weeks earlier Jack discovered two members of a band in the strange new craze that is punk having sex in one of the cubicles.

Today each cubicle door is ajar. No sign of the so-called symphony sex symbol, and as the runner announces *three minutes to air*, Jack's heart is working overtime. His neck on the block.

'Shit. No sign in the toilets.' Jack joins the runner who uses hand signals to convey the problem to the director who can see them both now across the studio floor. The director and the producer stand in the television gallery, faces red with fury.

'He was here,' Jack is gabbling to the runner now. 'I swear. I showed him to the green room fifteen minutes ago. He was fine. Sober. Friendly. Fine… '

'Bloody hell… ' The runner and Jack are both trying to lip read the director who seems to be saying they should have booked Demis Roussos.

*'Try losing Demis fucking Roussos…'*

In a taxi, already five miles away, Josef is stretched out along the back seat, grimacing at the conversation which inevitably lies ahead with his 'team'.

He did not plan this and feels disorientated. But it is too late for regret now. He just couldn't face it. Same routine. Same questions. Same farce…

What he is wondering now is how long it will be before the press are onto it. A live show, unfortunately, which means he may make tomorrow's papers unless his press office are on the ball. Damn. He should phone them soon. Feign illness of some kind? Yes.

Josef stares at the blurring shapes of passing cars, trees and shops. It is just beginning to rain. He watches the droplets create patterns on the window as the taxi waits for a time at traffic lights.

He is thinking that perhaps he could get away with faking amnesia?

The comic absurdity cheers him for a moment and he smiles. Yes. He will phone his agent once he gets to Brighton. He'll think of some story once he finds a hotel – a small place, out of the way, where hopefully he will not be recognised.

He closes his eyes then, remembering his last trip to Brighton not long after his defection. The days spent pacing the streets, looking for Martha. The evening strolls on the pier. The early mornings on the beach, throwing pebbles into the sea. Wondering. Hoping. If he might just get lucky.

*Bump into her.*

# CHAPTER 28

Martha and Kate are up very early.

'I know you didn't want to talk – in the night, Kate – but I heard Toby's car leave and… Well, I've been really worried. Are you all right? You look absolutely exhausted. Is there anything… ?'

'I just need a bit of time. We've been having a very rough patch.' Kate did not go to bed at all. Just lay down fully clothed and cried pretty much the whole of the night, though she will not tell Martha this.

'This is all my fault, isn't it?'

'No, Martha. I promise you that it absolutely isn't. It's mine. Not Toby's. My decision. My fault. No one else's.'

'You should stay home. Get back to bed, Kate.'

'No. That won't help. Honestly. I need to see you through this. I need to be doing something. Let's just concentrate on to-day, Martha. Then we can talk.'

And so they walk in awkward silence, and on arrival at the court precinct there is the shock of placards everywhere. *SAVE OUR SHOPS. MILLROSE MOUNT: LOCALS VERSUS LEECHES.*

The lawyer is loudly demanding that all litigious banners be moved – *we will be done for contempt* – and looks nervous as he spots Martha and Maria, and takes them aside to repeat his pep talk.

'You understand, both of you, that our strategy is one of ex-treme regret? Yes? You are very, very sorry to have lost control. Mortified. That this behaviour – the frying pan and the streaking – was completely out of character. Born of the trauma. And will not be repeated. Peaceful protest only from this point. Yes?'

He then turns to address the crowd being moved to the other side of the road by the court staff.

'No stopping traffic. No stepping into the road. Understand? Any nonsense and I mean it: they will have you in the cells for contempt of court. It won't help your friends. It will make things very, very much worse.'

And then, as they sit in a silent row in the corridor outside court number one, Geoffrey appears, whispering that he has left Matthew in charge of the shop and admitting that for the first time in his life he wishes he smoked.

Kate sits, still in a state of detached shock born of exhaustion, to learn that luck is on their side – the chairman of the magistrates today is Gerald Smith, a self-made man. Twenty five years an ironmonger and leading light in the confederation of small businesses, he retired early only when his prices could not compete with the larger DIY stores springing up all around the neighbourhood. A man who understands shopkeeping.

'A frying pan?'

'Yes, sir.' The prosecutor adjusts his glasses and checks his notes.

'And this brouhaha followed notices to quit their shops?'

'Yes, sir.'

Kate has managed to get a seat at the front of the public gallery and forces a smile of encouragement at Martha as she stands alongside Maria to listen to all the evidence. Finally, the spotlight is back on the chairman of the bench.

'And has your client any history of this kind of behaviour. *Streaking?*' Mr Smith removes his glasses to look very directly at Martha.

'No, sir. Never done anything like this in public before. She is mortified. Embarrassed and mortified. Says it was a spur of the

moment publicity stunt. Something she now deeply regrets, sir.'
The defence lawyer tilts up his chin.

'You realise, do you, that we can't have people damaging
council property and frightening the children?' Mr Smith is still
holding his glasses in his right hand, swinging them to and fro,
to and fro, as he speaks.

Martha and Maria bow their heads and link hands. And then
suddenly Maria looks up, glancing at Wendy, who is behind Kate
in the public gallery.

'It's all right, sir. No more nonsense. We're going to knit a
tree.'

'To knit a *tree*?' Gerald Smith glances to his two colleagues.

'A peaceful protest, sir. No more damage. No more scenes.
Just knitting. We promise.'

They are both bound over to keep the peace. Maria given a
small fine for the damage caused and Martha warned that she
will be supervised by probation and will be back in the dock if
she takes one single step out of line again.

And then, outside, it is Maria who steps forward to speak
to the reporters – from the *Aylesborough Gazette* and a local TV
crew.

'And what did you mean… about knitting a tree?' Several
journalists are speaking at once.

'We are going to be holding a press conference about that,'
Maria is beaming.

Martha exchanges glances with Wendy and Kate, not a clue
what she is talking about.

'Next Monday. Ten a.m. at Wendy's Wool Shop.'

Half an hour later, at Maria's café, there is the air of a fiesta as
Carlo and relatives wrestle huge trays of pasta to thank all their
supporters, the placards now lined up neatly along the wall and
the room heady with the smell of the best coffee in Aylesborough. There is talk of a petition to the local MP, an all-night vigil

on the quay, of sponsored breakfasts and knitathons and moving one of Geoffrey's pianos out on the quay, maybe even onto a fishing boat, for a sponsored musicathon. Of David and Goliath. Of beating *bloody bureaucrats*. And someone is wondering whether in fact a piano would actually sink a fishing boat, with Maria all the while insisting that, no, she has not lost her marbles; that they really are going *to knit a tree* as the central plank of their campaign. And all will be revealed in good time. *Trust me*, and she is throwing back her head, laughing. Enjoying herself.

It is only Martha who seems to notice the change in Kate in the midst of this. Like a sleepwalker now, her eyes glazed and her smile fixed, taking none of it in. Martha tried so hard to help last night, whispering through the door after Toby left, but Kate wanted to be alone.

*Leave me, please. I'm fine.*

And now, with the court case done, Kate is like a foreign student in a sea of voices – looking around her, as if trying to make sense of a language she cannot follow.

Toby is gone. Her decision. Her insistence…

*It's for the best, Toby.*

*I can't leave you, Kate. There is no way I can leave you like this…*

She had imagined it was what she wanted. The right thing to do now; to give at least one of them the small chance of a future. Toby such a good man. A man who deserved better…

'You all right?' Martha puts another cup of coffee in front of Kate but she shakes her head, pushing it away.

'Martha – do you have your key with you?' Kate stands and heads for the door – not even noticing that Martha has followed her. Outside, the wind is strong and as Kate turns, sensing finally her friend's shadow, her hair blown across her face and into her mouth, she says, 'Look. I just need some air. A walk or something.'

'I'll come.'

Kate shakes her head, twisting her hair into a ponytail and tucking it into the back of her collar. 'No. I'm all right. I'll see you back at the house, Martha. Do you have your key? Sorry – did I ask you that already?'

And then, alone at last, Kate is glad of the wind. On the tourist bus once more it makes her eyes water and her cheeks sting. The cold means she is the only one upstairs. The clouds and the gulls all to herself. So that when the bus finally parks in the little square, she feels bereft that the journey and her imaginary swim – out to the lighthouse – should be over so quickly, wishing she could stay up there in the wind forever.

She has not planned this. So tired. Dazed. Forgotten even that it is Mike's shift. A Wednesday. And then his voice is calling up from the well of the little spiral staircase. How sorry he was. And if it was up to him, she could stay there all day. Really, she could. But the driver needed to take the bus back. *Sorry.* And *are you all right? Would you like a coffee?* And *can I help? In any way at all? Oh, Kate – you're crying…*

He does not take advantage. It is Kate who takes advantage.

*Eight months and three days.*

His bedsit is full of books. And they drink tea – good leaf tea which surprises her – and they eat biscuits in bed and then make love again – the crumbs etching little marks in their skin. Sticking to the sweat as Kate watches herself from the ceiling. Hungry. Desperate.

He is gentle. And kind. And utterly bemused. Kate still the foreigner. No language.

And it is not until he sits up, stunned, still with a sheet wrapped around him, explaining all his plans for the future once he's finished the Open University course. Got his degree. His own business, his own flat – waving his arms in huge and hopeful gestures – that Kate begins to cry, realising just how much he reminds her of Toby, in that doll's house long ago. The memory vivid again of their student bedsit. With its little Belling cooker. And she feels the wind in her eyes again and shuts them tight, tears dripping down her cheeks.

*Eight months and three days.*

A pause then in Mike's dreams.

*We're not going to do this again, are we?* He says it softly and Kate keeps her eyes closed. Too tired and too sad to even feel properly ashamed.

*No, Mike. I'm so very sorry…* Does she remember to say it out loud?

And when she opens her eyes, she realises that she must have, for he too looks more confused than is fair.

And Kate is sorry.

Very, very sorry.

For everything.

She walks then, one – maybe two – hours. Barely noticing when the rain begins to fall, and only as the light begins to fade does she finally take the bus home – a dull single-decker – where she knows Martha will be waiting for her.

She remembers how she tried to explain last night to Toby. About Martha. How somehow she just knew inexplicably but instinctively that she would be safe with her. And needed her.

But he was pleading with her. *We can get through this, Kate.* Until in the end she had thumped his chest over and over. And begged him, shouting now, to *go. Please, just go. Please, Toby. I can't be with you. And you need to go. To be happy again. Please, Toby.*

And they both knew it had nothing to do with the Millrose Mount development.

Or the shops and evictions.

Or Martha.

And Toby had cried. Finally, after eight months, he had sat on their sofa, tears pouring down his face – the same seat where Martha sits now, her knitting in a tangle on the floor. The little lamp beside her the only glow in the room.

'Kate – I've been so worried about you.'

And only now does Kate remember it has been raining. Her wet hair, dripping down her neck.

*Eight months and three days.*

She is wondering what it will sound like. Out loud. If the darkness of her dreams can be as thick and choking and dense. If the water will feel as cold. And if the words, when she shares them now with Martha, will sound so black.

Out loud, here in the same lamplight where Toby finally cried.

# CHAPTER 29

Five minutes either way, Kate reckons, and it wouldn't have happened. If she had just had an extra coffee – or looked for the bloody toy – it wouldn't have happened.

He had Toby's hair, you see. Completely straight, so it fell into his eyes so easily. She had tried to cut the fringe once herself but it was a disaster and so she had found this really lovely woman, recommended by a friend, who was so patient with toddlers. Had a special apron with little penguins all over it… and took so much care and time.

The kind of woman who would have looked for Daniel's toy that morning however late she was.

The thing is, they were always late back then. What with the childminder and the job and everything. And they were about to go on holiday, so she couldn't cancel the car service. And when they said there was no gearstick courtesy car – only an automatic – well, what could she do? She begged them to get a different car. She needed to get to the hairdresser's. And the childminder's. And later to work.

And OK, so she'd never driven an automatic, but they were telling her it wasn't hard. *We'll show you. A doddle.* And if they just hurried for the ferry, rather than the bridge, which was always backed up for a mile or so that time of the morning, she would make the hairdresser's still, and the childminder's.

Daniel was whiney because he didn't have his favourite toy. His duck. But she had found him a rabbit and he quite liked rabbits. When he was a baby. And there really wasn't time to look for the duck, was there? *I mean – you can see that, can't you, Martha?* That if she'd looked for the duck, they would have been late for the garage. And missed the hairdresser's. And the whole day would have…

There was only one space left on the ferry and at first the two men had exchanged a weird glance. Muttering something about the barrier. She had asked them if everything was OK. *I did ask. I promise you, Martha, I asked if everything was all right.* But they shrugged it off. Waved her past. *On you go, love…*

And then, at the other side of the estuary, she checked her watch. *Come on. Come on.* Put her foot down hard, impatient…

Daniel must have thought it was a ride. Like the fairground. Or the waterpark.

For as she turned, in that bright and awful flash of realisation, as the car shot the wrong way – *backwards, backwards, backwards* – he did not even look afraid. His trust in her so complete that even as the broken barrier gave way instantly – even as the first person screamed – even in the shock of that moment, as she waited for the splash of the water – he must have thought it was going to be OK.

And that trust in his eyes – looking at her urgently for reassurance as he held on to the rabbit he did not even like – as the car hit the water. The last thing he was to feel in his little hands, ever…

It was the reason she could not bear to look properly at Toby.
*Same eyes, Martha.*
*Do you understand?*
*Our son. Our beautiful Daniel.*
*He had Toby's eyes.*

# CHAPTER 30

Martha has some tinctures in her bag. It takes her a while to decide which one, closing her eyes for a moment to ask the woman who taught her to make them in a farmhouse in France long ago. She can feel again the dew on her feet and the cool breeze of the early morning; the smell on her hands as they gathered the herbs before crushing and boiling. Mixing with the alcohol – brandy and vodka. Then patience. Four weeks. No less. *Wait, Martha, wait.* Fire Cider made of garlic, onion, ginger and horseradish. Another of elderflower, yarrow and peppermint.

*Take this, Kate.* Just a drop on her tongue.

She does not even try to put her to bed this first night. Brings pillows and a blanket from upstairs and sits in the tall chair opposite the sofa, ready to soak the flannel in the bowl of peppermint water when the fever comes. From the rain.

And somewhere else.

Eventually Kate sleeps, her brow tense and hot, only to wake – eyes staring through the objects all around her, through the walls, through the air beyond the garden to the sea – swimming all night through the darkness… *searching, searching…* until calmer, finally, she closes them as Martha presses the flannel against her head. *Sshh, Kate. Hush. Try to rest…*

Only the next day does she move her upstairs. A bath and then bed, where she stays for two days and two nights, Martha sitting with her knitting or a book in the corner – not even retiring to her own room.

And not until Kate sits up herself to sip soup from a mug do they even speak.

'Has Toby phoned?'

'No.'

And then her breathing faster. Heavier.

'I've done the right thing. Don't you think? Asking him to go?'

'Sorry? I'm not understanding.'

'Toby.' Kate's eyes are still a little wild – staring at a spot on the carpet then making a fist with her left hand and tapping at her chin. 'He says he doesn't blame me. But he must. How can he not?'

'Don't do this, Kate. It wasn't your fault. It was terrible. Beyond terrible. But— '

'It *was* my fault. I shouldn't have taken the car. I should have challenged them over the barrier.'

'Stop it, Kate.'

They are silent for a while now.

'I mean – what I'm thinking, what I'm hoping, is that he can be happy again. One day. Don't you think? Toby. He deserves that chance at least. That he may *eventually* be able to get past it? With someone else, I mean?'

Kate is banging her chin quite hard and Martha watches her very closely.

'He wants another baby, Martha.' Kate's voice a whisper now – her eyes still fixed on some picture on the carpet. 'He thinks that one day we should have another child. And I can't. Won't. I mean – look at me? Look at what I've done. How could I *ever...* '

And now Martha has to step in – to hold Kate's hand firmly to stop her from hitting herself so hard, at which Kate turns, eyes still wide and wild, clutching onto Martha's shirt, pulling her closer, her voice almost inaudible. Whispering in her ear.

'They found the toy, Martha.'

And then the scene, tumbling out – twisted and sharp. The picture of the two women police officers at the door, thinking they were doing a kindness. Bringing comfort. The rabbit recovered from the river two days after the car…

And Kate is mumbling about the boxes in the hall. Couldn't remember which one it was in – Martha suddenly realising. *Of course. Why she wouldn't unpack.*

'Daniel didn't even like the bloody rabbit, Martha. I couldn't bear to look at it. Can't bear to even *think* of it.'

'Right. Look at me, Kate. I am going to go through the boxes and find the rabbit. *Look at me, Kate.* Can you hear me?' Gently she is taking hold of Kate's hands, to loosen their grip on her shirt. 'I am going to find the rabbit and I am going to burn it. Are you understanding what I'm saying? Is this what you want? For me to get rid of the rabbit for you?'

And later in the garden – ripping paper into an old dustbin, the only thing she can find, praying it will not be too damp. And then the flames and the smoke rising into the stillness of the night sky.

And as Martha watches it rise – swirling into the blackness to be lost at last, a faint black halo over the wretched old hospital building up on the hill – she tries not to think of the box now opened in the hall.

With the blankets and the toys – realising now about the muddy footprints across the floor. The picture wrapped in tissue of Toby on the beach, carrying a boy on his shoulders with the same kind eyes.

Knowing and understanding only now that look in Kate's eyes on the day they first met. That strange and momentary flicker of recognition and connection.

Understanding now, at last, the reason she is here.

# CHAPTER 31

Matthew is in a small meeting room on the second floor of the Aylesborough Council offices and has never been more nervous. He was warned on the telephone that this initial session with Aylesborough Social Services will be informal – to get the ball rolling and explain the process. *You realise, don't you, that searching for your birth mother is a sensitive and complex path? That there will be no immediate information?*

The woman assigned to his case is Emily – a skinny, smiley type, with thick almost-white hair cut into a neat bob. She is dressed smartly but somewhat over-formally in a suit with a polka dot blouse, a pendant dangling forward as she places a dark brown briefcase on the desk between them, then produces a large hardback notebook and pearlised fountain pen.

'You've been told, I hope, that this meeting is just to explain everything? It's just we worry that people may not realise how long this might take.'

Matthew has crossed his legs now and is rocking his right foot in mid-air.

Emily glances at her notebook as if needing the prompt.

'So, *Matthew* – the first option is for you to obtain a copy of your birth certificate.'

'Yes – that's why I'm here.'

Emily looks down at her notebook again.

'You're fortunate in starting this now, Matthew. Last year this wouldn't even have been allowed. The legislation has only just kicked in.' She is looking a little nervous suddenly.

'What I mean by that is that this process is still very new to all of us. We're still finding our way. And you understand that counselling for you is a compulsory part of the process? You're OK about that?'

'Yes. I was told about the counselling. I'm fine about that. All of it… I just want to get on with it.'

Matthew has read up on the newspaper coverage in the library. The controversy. The fact that some people do not think it wise to allow this. That searching for a birth mother may end in severe disappointment.

Emily explains it is good – very helpful – that he has provided some papers from his adoptive mother. These allow them to more quickly source and contact the correct adoption agency involved. Sadly, there is no guarantee that records will still be held, but it is at least a start.

'So how long will I have to wait for all this? The counselling? The enquiries?' Matthew realises only now that he has again crossed his legs and is jiggling his right foot up and down at an alarming rate. He uncrosses his legs yet again and tries to still both his feet on the floor, but it is difficult. He had expected to make progress today. A proper start.

'It's hard to say.'

'The thing is – I've only just found out about all of this. And I really want to get on with it.'

'I can understand that, Matthew.' Emily is again looking down at his notes, her face softening as she reads. 'It must have been a terrible shock. Did you really have no idea at all?'

Matthew begins tapping his right foot on the floor. Outside, the town hall clock chimes. One, two, three. The note is middle A. He pauses to play the major chord in his head – his hands at the keys of Geoffrey's beloved Steinway for a moment. He releases the pedal with his foot and looks back up at Emily.

'My father didn't want me to know. My adoptive father, I mean. We don't get along very well. Apparently he had reservations about the adoption from the off. My mother has only just told me all this.'

'I see. I really am very sorry, Matthew. This is something you must go over with the counsellor. They will be in touch. And I will be too. As soon as I have anything.' Emily begins to put her papers away. 'It's important not to raise false hopes or issue any guarantees, but I promise we will do everything that we can to help you. And we can contact you at the… piano shop? That's the correct address?'

'Yes.'

'So we'll be in touch, then.' She closes her notebook, smiling. 'And meantime, it would be good if you have someone you can confide in about this. Someone to talk to. While you're waiting for your official counselling.'

Matthew stares at her, no idea how to answer. Is this really it? He could not be more disappointed. No progress. The hint at long delays and all this prodding to *talk about it* when he still doesn't know how he really feels, let alone what he is supposed to say out loud.

# CHAPTER 32

The following morning Martha gets an early phone call from Carlo begging for her help.

'I hate to ask, but Maria just won't listen to me. She is winding herself into such a state again. Please come. She will listen to you, Martha. Please.'

Martha, reluctant to leave Kate for long, arrives at the café to absolute chaos.

'Maria, this is ridiculous.' Carlo, shaking his head, is chopping a mountain of pistachio nuts while, alongside, Maria expertly fashions leaf-shaped biscuits using a metal cutter.

'Don't chop those too small, Carlo.'

'This is supposed to be a campaign launch, Maria.' Carlo pauses to rescue nuts escaping the knife, rolling from the chopping board onto the stainless steel work surface. 'Not a biscuit competition. Tell her, Martha, will you? Up at six, we were.'

'Are you sure they don't look like holly leaves? Martha – be honest with me. I don't want them to look like holly. Just regular leaves.'

'They look terrific, Maria.' Martha catches Carlo's eye to wink. 'I'm sure everything is going to be fine. Shall I make us all a nice cup of coffee? How about that?'

'I'm thinking we won't put pistachio on all the leaves.'

'The important thing is how many people come. Not the blessed biscuits.' Carlo turns again to Martha. 'Do you think many will come?'

'Some people don't like pistachio, do they? And allergies. People are always talking about allergies these days. Some of the children won't want nuts on their biscuits. Think of little Anna. Turns her nose up at anything with bits on.'

'I think we're all probably just a bit nervous, Carlo.' Martha reaches for an apron, widening her eyes at him again as Maria scoops up a lattice of spare pastry dough and works it into a new ball before sprinkling flour ready for the next batch.

'You know that my father named this café after me.' Maria pats the dough before rolling furiously. 'Everyone thought he would use his own name or my mother's. But no. He named it after me. His first daughter. And now they think they can just come along with their fancy ideas and their fancy new plans. Show her the letter, Carlo. Show her what they've come up with.'

Carlo reaches for an envelope on the shelf and shows Martha a single sheaf of council-headed notepaper.

'They think they can fob us off with some council flat and some soulless square box out on an industrial estate? No passing trade. No trade at all. We would be bankrupt within months.' Maria wipes her floury hands down her apron and then continues in Italian to her husband, who is shaking his head. She pauses then, turning back to Martha. 'And the word is they're getting the schools involved in some competition to support the plan for a new library and to rename the new development up at the old hospital. Dirty tactics, I say. It's getting nasty.'

'I am in the doghouse, Martha. For suggesting that maybe we really should think about retirement. Take the flat and forget about the café. Admit defeat. Put our feet up a bit.'

'Retire? Give up? Tell him he is insane, Martha. And look at these biscuits, will you? Half with pistachio? Half without? What do you think?'

'I still don't get why we are even doing biscuits.' Carlo is shaking his head again.

'The theme, Carlo. It's the *theme*.'

Just then the doorbell to the shop rings and Maria jumps, again brushing her hands on her apron. 'Oh my Lord – the tree. It'll be the *tree*.'

Martha watches her rush, almost tripping, through to the front of the shop where four of her regulars – tall, muscular fishermen – are arguing as they try to manoeuvre a huge pine, long since bereft of all needles, into a large tub positioned outside – between the wool shop and the café.

Maria, on tiptoe to secure a better view, waves and then mimes the tipping of a mug with her wrist, to which the supervisor among her volunteers raises a thumb.

Pouring tea from an enormous stainless steel pot in the corner, she brings Martha up to date.

'For once I am so glad that Carlo ignored me. If he had got round to chopping up the Christmas tree as I've been nagging for the best part of the last year, I never would have had the idea.'

She explains that the huge, bare pine has been propped up in the corner of the backyard. A whopper – the café gifted a tree each year by one of their farmer customers. It made for an impressive festive display, but organising for its safe disposal was a trial.

Until this year.

By nine thirty, the tree securely in place, Kate arrives to tell Martha she is feeling better and would like to help Wendy and a team of volunteers to dress the first branch.

They have been knitting furiously since Maria explained her plan – Wendy and Martha coming up with a simple, basic pattern for a leaf, using wool in various shades of green. Lime green, olive, school uniform green, every shade of green. For the campaign launch they had made up little kits to hand out – photocopies of the standard pattern and remnants of wool. The idea is simple: people who support their campaign – to preserve the quay, saving the wool shop, the piano shop and the café – should help them to knit leaves.

*To knit a tree, get it?* And as the bare fir tree is gradually transformed into a glorious multi-coloured woolly oak, the message to the council will be clear. Like a *Blue Peter* fundraising chart.

'Genius,' Wendy declares as the first branch is finished. 'It's so visual. So clever, Maria. So very beautiful!'

Even the fishermen agree that it looks very 'arty', and it is only Carlo who notices that Maria still looks anxious. Only half an hour to go, and aside from the volunteers there are just six people hanging around – helping themselves to the coffee and tea set up on trestle tables, along with two huge trays of the blessed leaf biscuits.

They said ten o'clock to the photographer from the local paper and were hoping that the television crew who covered the court case might return. Carlo checks his watch and winks encouragement at his wife as Martha leads Kate to one side.

'Now are you sure you're up to this, Kate? No one will mind at all if you want to go home. I can say you're unwell.'

Just last night Toby turned up to collect some more of his things and Martha held her breath upstairs in her room as their raised voices drifted up to her. Him begging her to reconsider. *I don't like to leave you like this…* Kate beside herself but insisting he go. *I have Martha. I am OK.* And then retiring early to bed.

'Thanks, Martha, but I'll be fine. I think it will do me good to help. Doing something useful. I need to be doing something.'

Everyone is checking their watches as Maria begins to look more agitated.

'I thought there would be more people here by now. Carlo? Martha? Did you not think more people would be here by now?'

At five to ten, the photographer from the local paper arrives – frowning at the tiny crowd but impressed by the tree. *Yes – it will make a good photo. If I can just get everyone to group together? To make it look a bit busier?*

Maria implores him to wait a bit – fetching coffee and a plate of her leaf biscuits to distract him – while liaising with Wendy. There is no sign of the TV crew. The newsroom assistant non-committal on the phone. Damn. Five more minutes and they will have to start without them.

And then suddenly there is the most enormous hooting sound from the water. The blast is from the east of the quay – and as the small gathering outside the cafe turns simultaneously seaward, there is a raucous cheer as other boats sound their horns in reply.

For heading into the landing point is one of the pleasure boats which during the summer months ferries tourists along the coast for one-hour cruises. They are rarely at sea at this time of year, except for parties and special bookings, but today one of the larger boats is sporting a huge banner made out of sheets with the words *SAVE OUR QUAYSIDE SHOPS* in large black lettering, billowing in the wind.

'Our surprise.' One of the fishermen is beaming at Maria, who has her hands to her mouth now as at least forty people wave and shout from the boat. It is still too far out for her to recognise individuals, but the fisherman explains they are all regulars who use the café. The TV crew are on board too. It has all been fixed as a surprise. A show of support.

And there are tears in Maria's eyes as Carlo steps forward to hug his wife, with Geoffrey and Wendy lining up alongside them for another photograph – Matthew a step behind, grinning in disbelief.

The skipper of the pleasure cruiser has a megaphone to lead the singing of *We shall not, we shall not be moved* as the passengers embark at the end of the quay, the megaphone eventually handed over to Maria.

After thanks, tears, and urging everyone to help themselves to the biscuits, Maria explains about the campaign tree while a group of Wendy's regulars step forward to hand out copies of the leaf pattern, urging the knitters to rope in all their WI friends.

And then there are the interviews. The photos. *If we can just have all the shopkeepers over here by the tree for the picture? And the biscuits? Is it a secret family recipe? Delicious.*

Finally several men help Geoffrey wheel out one of the old pianos from his shop right onto the quayside, Matthew then playing a medley of Beatles hits for a singalong.

A street party. With Martha so happy for her friends – smiling from the back of the crowd as she hears several of the younger women giggling and whispering about Matthew.

*So who is he? Have you noticed his eyes? Gorgeous eyes.*

# CHAPTER 33

Matthew had not planned to tell anyone about his search.

This was, in part, because he was so confused initially about his own feelings. Afraid to think about them too much, let alone try to put them into words.

Some nights he lies under the green candlewick bedspread of the single divan at Mrs Hill's and realises that it has somehow become as much about hiding as searching. He wants to know the truth about his background, but he doesn't want anyone else knowing it.

What frightens him most of all is the fury that shines from his eyes in the mirror some mornings. He had honestly not realised that he was capable of so much anger.

When his mother – *God, it is difficult to call her anything else* – turned up out of the blue at the shop, it had been the horrible maelstrom of confused emotions that had most shaken him. Anger. Relief. Love. Hate. All of this stuff swirling around and around in his head as he stared at her through the glass of the door. He had wanted to hug her. Also shout at her. In the end he had instead kept mostly silent because he was terrified that if he even *started…*

And now?

Now Matthew has simply become tired of getting up every day and pushing the anger down into a tight knot in his stomach. Exhausted by it as the days passed, one after another, with no progress after his meeting with Emily. No word. No news despite his repeated phone calls. And it is this frustration and exhaustion that finally makes her parting words prey on his mind. *It would be good if you had someone to confide in...*

'Can I talk to you about something, Geoffrey?'

He picks their Omelette Thursday – now a regular fixture. Tonight Matthew is beating the egg whites in a glass bowl. They each have their own roles – working side by side, Geoffrey getting the yolks and the omelette pan and grill ready. The plates warming in the oven.

Matthew normally keeps his eye on the clock, keen not to miss *Top of the Pops*. Each week Geoffrey teases him mercilessly about this, but clearly enjoys watching it with him. It amuses him – *what the young people are listening to these days.* He likes to wind Matthew up about the names. *Showaddywaddwotsit? You are kidding me?*

But tonight Matthew has not even checked the time. Mentioned the show. And Geoffrey narrows his eyes.

'Happy to talk about anything, but you will need to put a bit more elbow grease into that, Matthew.' Geoffrey passes him the salt and pepper. 'And remember to go heavy on the pepper.'

'You've never asked why I came to Aylesborough.' Matthew obediently beats more furiously. 'Never pressed me about when my mum came by. Why things are – well, so difficult between us.' His voice is altered by the effort of the beating – masking his nerves.

Geoffrey has completed his own part of the assembly – the yolks in a separate bowl with cheese grated and ready along with some chopped smoky ham.

'Well, to be honest, I rather felt it was up to you, Matthew. When you want to discuss it, I mean.'

'Right. Well. I'm grateful for that. But – the thing is.' Matthew now hands his bowl to Geoffrey, who combines the yolks and the whites as butter sizzles ready in the pan on the gas hob. 'I'm in quite a quandary, actually. The thing is, I had this big falling-out with my parents.'

'Ow!' Jumping back, Geoffrey wipes a splash of hot oil from the back of his hand and adjusts the gas.

'You all right?'

'Yes, fine. Fine. You were saying? A row?'

Matthew coughs and looks away to the view of the garden from the window by the table where Geoffrey has already set their places, both ketchup and brown sauce standing to attention.

'What am I saying? Of course you realise there was a row. The way I was with my mother and everything. But – Geoffrey. Well. It was a very unpleasant row. Very bad.'

Geoffrey lets out a sigh, moves the pan up under the grill, turning to Matthew who is still looking away.

'I'd rather guessed as much, Matthew. And I am very sorry. But from my experience these things nearly always blow over in the end.'

'No. It's not that kind of row. A normal row. You see – I found out that I was adopted, Geoffrey.'

'My goodness.'

'All my life, they kept it a secret. Didn't *tell me*. It only came out in this really terrible argument with my father. Right out of the blue. I want to go to music college. He wants me to go into the business. The butcher's. It all got nasty. Out of hand. And he started saying awful things… *a true son of mine*. Stuff like that.'

Geoffrey moves the pan away from the heat, to turn out the first omelette onto a plate.

'I honestly don't know quite what to say. This sounds terrible. And you really had no idea at all?'

Matthew shakes his head very fast, eyes wide as Geoffrey turns back to the cooker.

'I tell you what – you start. I'll make mine. You eat, Matthew. You need to eat.'

As he makes his own supper, Geoffrey appears to be thinking hard, glancing every now and again at the photograph of his wife on one of the shelves..

'You and Jean. You didn't have children. I don't mean to pry. But did you never consider it? Adopting?'

'I did, yes, but Jean was very against the idea. I think she thought it would be unfair on the child. Her condition. That she would be turned down. The wheelchair and everything. I disagreed.' Now he was staring at a different photograph, Jean beaming at them both from her beloved Whitstable. 'I really can't think of anyone who would have made a better mother. But I didn't want her to think I had any regrets, Matthew. That I minded about not having children. And so I lied to her, Matthew. I told her that I agreed with her. Sometimes people do that, you know. Lie out of love.'

Matthew smiles weakly at the gesture, chewing very slowly.

'My mother even made up stories, Geoffrey. When I was little and asked about when I was born, she made up stories. About us in the hospital together.' He turns to Geoffrey and looks straight into his eyes. 'How could she do that? Make up stories like that.'

Geoffrey shakes his head.

'To be honest – I have absolutely no idea, Matthew. I'm struggling to know what to say here. But when she came here – your mother. It's obvious how much she cares about you. So I can only assume she was trying to protect you.'

And now Matthew's breathing is changing, and he has to put his hand under the table, clenching his fist to control the familiar knot of anger and confusion twisting in his stomach. The anger which made him hit his father that night – a proper, grown-up, fist-clenched blow to the face which had made his nose bleed. His mother with her back against the sink in the kitchen, weeping and pleading with them both to stop.

*Matthew, I'm so sorry, love…*
*Adopted? You're telling me I'm adopted?*
*Well, you didn't really think you were a bloody son of mine?*
*Stop it, Arthur. Stop it. Not like this – please!*

*A son of mine poncing around on a bloody piano all day, not a decent day's work…*

*Stop it, Arthur! Stop it!*

*A bloody nutter, your real mother. In a mental hospital. A bloody nutter, she was…*

Matthew puts his knife and fork together and pushes his plate to the middle of the table.

'I was born here, apparently. In Aylesborough.' Matthew pauses, narrowing his eyes and deciding he is not ready to mention Millrose Mount. 'That's all I know until I can get hold of more of my records. I've been to the council. For help to trace my birth mother. It's allowed now. Some change in the law.' Again he is searching Geoffrey's face for a clue to his thinking. 'My father – my *adoptive* father, that is – has said that he will disown me if I pursue this. That it's ungrateful. Cruel of me.'

And now Geoffrey takes in another deep breath himself, as if understanding everything better – putting a hand onto Matthew's shoulder.

'And you don't know what to do.'

'No. I mean – when I first ran away, after the row, I was so *sure*, Geoffrey. So angry with them both for lying to me. Not telling me. I didn't care what my dad thought. To be honest, I still don't. But my mother explained things a bit more when she came here. Don't get me wrong, I'm still furious with them both for not telling me. But I do understand a little better what my mother was thinking.'

'Go on.'

And now Matthew slowly shares what Glenda told him as they sat awkwardly on piano stools in the shop that day.

How she and Arthur were so happy when they married. Different people. How not being able to have a child slowly somehow sucked all the happiness out of them. Tests confirmed the problem was with Arthur, which seemed to destroy him.

He was dead set against adoption. Didn't want people knowing their business. But about five years into the marriage, when the chance came to move – to set up his own butcher's shop – Glenda had pushed and pushed and pushed. Hatched this plan to tie in an adoption with the move so that people in the new place wouldn't know.

She had promised on her life that the child need never be told – so it would never be anyone's business but their own. Only very close family would know.

Matthew tells how she was crying as she told him how sorry she was now. But the adoption staff had said that it was fine not to tell the child. For the best, actually. They left that entirely up to the parents.

'She must have wanted very much to be a mother.' Geoffrey says this softly. 'I can understand that.'

'But not telling me, Geoffrey. Not even when I grew up and my father seemed to take more and more against me… '

Matthew goes on – understanding even better himself as he sets the story in front of Geoffrey. His father assuming he would want to follow in his footsteps. The butchering. The business. While all Matthew wanted was his music. He hated the butchering. The blood and the sound of the saws. The carcasses with their empty, staring eyes in the cold room. And his father just got angrier and angrier over the years as people raised their eyebrows.

*So where's he get it from? The music? Is that Glenda's side of the family?*

'We just didn't fit, Geoffrey. Me and my father. He always looked so – I don't know. Disappointed in me.'

And now Matthew shares something he has never shared with anyone. That for a few years he had come to wondering if his mother had had an affair. If that was the root of the conflict. That his father wasn't his father. And the truth? He wasn't even terribly upset by this possibility. Felt it was a plausible explanation. Why he and his mother were so close while his father prowled around them both in this permanent state of disappointment.

'But I never for one moment, Geoffrey— ' And now his voice is breaking slightly, looking once again to the garden where two birds are sitting on the bird table, pecking at the seeds. 'Never once did it enter my head that my mother might not be my real mother.'

It is Geoffrey who makes the move to find a handkerchief. Matthew, embarrassed, struggling in his pockets for a tissue to find only a grey, disgusting rag, which makes them both smile. The cue they both need – Geoffrey's hand again on Matthew's shoulder before disappearing to produce a proper cotton affair. Initialled. And ironed. Making them smile at the contrast as Geoffrey moves across the kitchen to turn off the grill while Matthew blows his nose loudly.

'I'm sorry. I've spoiled our supper, Geoffrey. Spoiled everything.'

'Don't be silly. So – your mother? Have you been in touch again? I mean, I don't want to speak out of place here. To suggest I know best. But it seems to me it's important to stay in touch. To keep talking while you try to work through all this.'

'Yes. I've phoned to say I'm OK.'

'Well, that's good. And you know she'd be very welcome here. If she wanted to visit again, I mean.'

'Thank you, Geoffrey. She's gone to stay with her sister. My parents— ' A clearing of the throat. 'They've separated. It was a long time coming.'

'Well, I'm sorry to hear that. A lot for you all to deal with at once.'

And then it is Matthew who changes the subject – needing a breather – blowing his nose again as he asks what Geoffrey really thinks of the council's wretched public meeting, boasting of all the new plans, and whether their campaign stands a chance now.

Geoffrey takes the cue. So that they talk quite frankly of their fears for Maria, as Geoffrey confides that the council has been far cleverer than any of them had anticipated – roping in all the local schools to support the 'gift' of a new library and arts complex, which the town so badly needs. The idea of a competition for a new name. Yes. All very clever.

'But people will see it for what it is, surely? The library, I mean. It's a bribe.' Matthew, the handkerchief tucked into his sleeve, is now making them both tea, reaching for two mugs on the shelf above the sink.

'Of course. But that doesn't change the fact they *want* the library. You should have seen all the teachers at the public meeting I went to, Matthew. Outnumbered Maria's customers – no problem.'

'But you're not giving up, Geoffrey?'

'Of course not. We'll fight as best we can. But it's all right for me. I've got this place. My own home. It's Maria and Wendy I'm worried about.' Geoffrey takes his mug and signals with his hand for them to move into the sitting room where in the corner stands a large box – which, on closer examination, is from Geoffrey's friend in Bath. Matthew screws up his face, not understanding. It must be the first parts for the Steinway. But why hasn't he told him? Brought them straight to the shop? They'd been waiting for weeks. And then, as Geoffrey blushes, the penny begins to drop.

'You'll keep the Steinway, Geoffrey? Whatever happens?'

'Well – I'd like to, of course I would. But one has to be realistic. It's a question of practicalities. My friend's very kindly offered to take it on if… '

'Oh, Geoffrey – *no*.' Matthew puts his tea down and stands.

'I will support Maria and Wendy as best I can. But if it goes the wrong way, I will probably just do a bit of freelance piano tuning. If I lose the shop, I mean.'

'But you could bring it here. The Steinway. To the house. Do it up *here*.'

'If I had the room, yes. But we have to be realistic.'

And now Matthew does a complete spin on the spot, his mind turning also, desperately trying to work something out.

'No. No, stop – Geoffrey. You are not giving up that piano. You hear me… '

Then he is pacing, mind whirling as he speaks, examining the furniture and trying to take in the scale of the room. The doorways. Trying to picture the piano. Hang on. The sitting room has an arch through to the dining area at the back, with french doors onto the garden. *And with the legs off the piano…*

'It could come in through those doors.' Matthew is estimating the measurements in his head. *Yes. There is a back alley with parking behind the terrace.* 'Have you got a tape measure?'

And soon he is working it all out. Drawing a plan on paper. It would be a tight squeeze, sure. Geoffrey would have to put some furniture in storage. But if they imagined the piano at an angle. Took out the door frame, maybe. *Here look, Geoffrey, this way –* he is pretty sure it would fit.

And then Geoffrey can finish doing up the Steinway whatever happens with the council. *Yes?*

Geoffrey's face is at first difficult to read, glancing around the room. At the door. At Matthew, who is sketching out access and layout plans on a piece of paper. For a moment he has to take a very deep breath.

'You are probably the only one who realises, Matthew. That it is losing the Steinway which has been on my mind more than anything.'

'So we don't even contemplate it, Geoffrey. We fight the council. And if we lose, we find some other way.'

So that, as Matthew carries on taking more precise measurements from the room, demanding *some more paper, please*, Geoffrey has to clear his throat as he watches him.

'What you were saying before. Matthew. About your situation.'

'Yes?'

'I don't feel qualified to advise you. I wish I did. But your mother.' He bites his lip. 'The one who brought you up, I mean.' Slowly passing the clean sheet of paper now. 'Seems to me she did a very fine job, Matthew.'

# CHAPTER 34

Kate sits and watches the seagulls on the rooftop of this unfamiliar café waiting for their chance. The locals, wise to them, lean over their food or opt to eat inside, but soon enough a holiday-maker comes unstuck. In shock and then outrage as a gull tries a cheeky swoop for their plate of fish and salad. Kate can hear the inevitable mutterings about *hygiene* and *why isn't something done about this?* and before long there is a heated discussion with the owner of the café as the customer tries for a refund.

*It's a coastal café. We have seagulls.*

*But I can't eat it now.*

*I'm sorry. We don't do refunds...*

Kate looks away to the ocean. Cups her hand around her mug of tea. She is trying to work out how long since that awful scene when Toby left. Two weeks? Or – *God. Is it three already?* So much has happened.

Last night she had a dream about their trip to Paris, and when she woke and turned to the empty space beside her, Kate for just a moment felt almost as if she was back there. In the hotel, waiting for him to come out of the shower. So happy.

They went to Paris to celebrate the pregnancy. 'Our very best cliché,' Toby said in a café as she began eating for two. Mussels and frites. Beautiful little custard tarts with strawberries and cream.

'Are you sure the mussels are safe? In your condition?' Toby had fussed from the beginning, and she had liked that. Being fussed over.

They had gone to the Louvre to see the *Mona Lisa* but had run out of time and missed it. Kate was at the early stage of pregnancy when she needed the loo every five minutes. By the time she had queued, they had closed admissions for the painting.

They had gone instead to another café for yet another custard tart.

'You realise I intend to get very, very fat,' Kate had joked.

And now, in this very different café, which is not a patch on Maria's, Kate cannot believe that she is the same person who once ate custard tarts in a café in Paris. Smiling. Happy. Fussed over.

And she has no idea what she will say to her husband. The terrible and escalating guilt now over the madness of the episode with Mike. Should she tell Toby today? Does she owe him that? Yes, she does. Of course she does.

And then she thinks how very much it will hurt him and feels a lurch deep in the pit of her stomach.

*Why am I such a terrible person?*

She narrows her eyes. Two weeks since Toby left? No. Kate turns back to watch the customer and café owner still in disagreement over the ruined food when something terrible dawns.

No. It really must be three weeks.

And then there is this completely unexpected shudder right through her body. A wave of cold dread as something new begins to take shape.

She fumbles for the diary in her bag. *Oh my God.* Flicking through the pages.

When she was working, Kate used to be meticulous about counting the weeks. Ringing the date in red felt tip. She suffered bad pre-menstrual syndrome so needed to prepare. Every month. *Headache tablets. Hot bath. Brace yourself, Kate.* She was regular as clockwork, so it was just about getting her head into the right place. A trial – the bad stomach cramps and the awful feeling of something crushing her skull – but it was never more than four days. Doable. Just.

But since Daniel? Since the world caved in? She seemed to have a permanent headache and stomach trouble now, taking painkillers most days, so she had stopped using the diary. Instead she was in trouble with her doctor – nagging her to cut back on the headache tablets, warning they could affect the liver, apparently.

Kate had to flick back two months to work it out properly. Now that she did not keep a record, she had grown used to just waiting for the worst.

*Oh my God.* She checked a second time. *No. That couldn't be right.* She took out a pencil and was more careful. Two weeks. Three weeks… Five?

*No.*

So her period was – *Jesus Christ*. More than a week overdue. Ten days. *And she was never overdue. Never…*

'Hello, Kate. Would you like another drink?'

She looks up and cannot speak. Toby is dressed in her favourite shirt of his, and she takes this in first of all. That he has deliberately put on her favourite shirt – the gesture at once kind and also terrible.

'Sorry. Are you all right? I know this is difficult.' He looks nervous. Eyes afraid. 'I'm very grateful, for you agreeing to meet me. I didn't think it would be a good idea to go to Maria's. Is this place OK?'

'Yes. It's fine. Sorry. Another tea. Thank you.' *Ten days? It can't be. No. It would be the stress of everything. That was all it was…*

Kate watches him move inside, queuing at the counter, her heart pounding. She stares at the shape of his back. The broad shoulders. Can picture him at a different counter, ordering coffee in Paris. So many years watching him queuing for her – always glancing back once in a while to catch her eye. To smile. Though not today.

When he returns, it is awful. Awkward. She has nothing to say; is instead fighting panic. The urge to bolt.

He talks again about how sorry he and Mark were for getting involved in the Millrose Mount project. That they would never have done so if they had any idea that Kate's friends were involved. He is trying to speak up for them at council meetings and will share any news that may be helpful.

Kate glances at the newspaper he has put down on the table. The front page has two stories.

One headline questions whether the new Tory leader Maggie Thatcher will ever be prime minister. A woman. Could it ever really happen?

The second story is on the missing star cellist Josef Karpati.

He has apparently very suddenly just vanished. Did a runner from a live TV show, to the amazement of the host, his agent and everyone involved. No one knows why. Today's story is a summary of the cat-and-mouse game now under way as the tabloids thirst for the first picture.

*Have you seen Josef? Reward for first photo…*

'Do you remember we saw him at the Albert Hall?' Toby is looking into her face. So difficult when he does this. Tries to link them to a happier time. *Before.* The Albert Hall. Paris. It is meant well, and yet it always makes her want to cry because it feels surreal that she was ever that other person. Happy.

'Yes. Of course. He's amazing. So – what's the word?'

'No one has any idea. Not even his agent. Just went AWOL for no apparent reason.'

'I suppose it can't be easy. In the spotlight all the time.'

'I miss you, Kate.'

She looks back into his face now and is having to fight really hard not to cry.

'I miss you. And I still love you. But I have something truly awful to tell you, Kate, which is why I invited you here, and I have no idea how to say it.'

Kate feels her heart thumping even harder.

'I was going to write a letter but that felt cowardly. I have been a complete idiot, Kate. So I'm just going to say it. I would have preferred to come to the house, but I know you didn't want that.'

'Say what?'

'I slept with someone else. A one-night stand. It was nothing. It meant absolutely nothing, I mean. Just sex. I was drunk, and very low, but that's no excuse. It was just this stupid, stupid thing, and I feel such a complete arse. And I have been going over and over it in my head. Whether even to tell you. And the thing is – I know you want us to separate, but I don't. I don't want anyone else, Kate. That's not what it was. And I'm more sorry than I can ever explain. What I want – what I've always wanted – is for us to make it through this. And I realise this is the most stupid thing I've ever done. And it's just going to make everything worse. Make you hate me.'

'Who?'

'It doesn't matter who.'

'Of course it does. Is it someone I know?' She can't believe the hypocrisy of how angry she feels. How jealous. How deeply, deeply shocked. Hurt too. How she is already picturing them. Her. Them.

She looks again right into his face and is thinking of the madness with Mike. Feels the words beginning to form...

But they do not come out of her mouth because she is thinking again of the hypocrisy. Also the diary. *Ten days over*... Of the terrible, terrible possibility.

And so, in panic, with everything swirling around and around in her head, she does a cruel thing for which she will later feel terribly ashamed. She does not tell him her own truth. The matching shame. The irony of her own betrayal. Her own madness.

Instead she stands up and says that she cannot talk to him. That *it is too much, Toby.*

She goes home and she collapses on the small chair in the hallway, alongside the packing boxes. Giddy. Stunned. Tears streaming from her face so that Martha hurries from the kitchen.

'What is it, Kate? What on earth's happened?'

'Oh, Martha. I've been such an idiot.' Her voice barely recognisable. Black spots on the periphery of her vision.

'I think I might be pregnant.'

# CHAPTER 35

Five days later, and with no sign still of her period, Kate is sitting in the little waiting area on the second floor of Alyesborough Council offices, fidgeting with leaflets from a stand. It's a shared building with Social Services and the leaflets offer helpline numbers for all manner of difficulties. The noticeboards are similarly bright and bursting with offers of sympathy and support, and the irony is not lost on Kate. Toby always telling her, right throughout their marriage, that she is very good at helping others but not so good at helping herself.

At last there is a click of the office door and a woman with a neat suit and perfect bob is standing, stretching out her hand. Warm smile.

Kate forces a smile back but inside is wishing she could have cancelled. The problem is it would have looked flaky. And she is looking quite flaky enough, professionally.

'Kate Mayhew? Hello – I'm Emily. So good of you to pop in. I'm sorry I'm always so difficult to pin down, but you of all people will know how it is.'

Emily's office's is very like Kate's old office. A clutter of files and folders signalling the overstretched, hand-to-mouth, crisis-to-crisis lifestyle that she found at times so overwhelming.

And misses so much.

Toby doesn't understand why she would ever want to go back to it. After the cruelty of their own experience, he thinks that she should retrain. Try something completely different, something more cheerful. But this is what Kate knows. Where she feels useful.

Yes. What she misses.

'Sorry for the mess.' Emily is walking over to the window, where there is a coffee machine perched on the deep sill. 'Would you like a coffee? It's fresh.'

Kate can feel herself frown and does not know what to make of the instinctive response. For, to her surprise and confusion, she finds that she would like a coffee. And yet she could not touch coffee throughout her pregnancy with Daniel. So what does this mean? Is this good news? The news she has lain in bed waiting for?

'Yes, please. Milk, no sugar.'

'To be perfectly honest, Kate, I very nearly had to call and cancel. But I know that it's been difficult for you, so I thought we could have a quick chat now and book another slot after Christmas. When things have hopefully calmed down a bit here.'

Kate now accepts a mug, sniffing the coffee, again to test her reaction, not knowing what to think. Also wishing that Emily *had* cancelled. Let her off the hook.

'It's all gone a bit chaotic because we've just taken on responsibility for birth mother searches. Did you know? Were you briefed in your old office?' Emily is now sitting.

'Couple of round-robins on it. I think they were arranging a seminar but I left before… '

'Yes. Well, between us, it's the usual cock-up. A much bigger caseload than anyone predicted. No extra resources. Huge backlog… blah, blah. I'm still putting the full team together but it's definitely caught us out. I'm having to be hands-on myself.'

'Right.' Kate tries her drink and is surprised. It tastes OK.

'Got a couple of heart-wrenching cases.' Emily sips her own coffee. 'To be honest, I was all for it. The right to search, I mean. Our first case was wonderful. Couple who were just sixteen when she gave up the child. They married later and went on to have three other children together. Always regretted giving up their first. She was waiting for the new law... the daughter who was adopted. All very touching. But we have some other much trickier cases.' Emily sighs. 'I have a bad feeling about a few of them. Chances are some of the mothers just aren't going to want to know. Huge ask, emotionally.'

'I can't begin to imagine.' Kate is still thinking about the coffee.

'No. Anyway. Let's not talk about that, let's talk about you. So,' Emily opens a cardboard folder in front of her, 'your letter said you would like to get back to work over time. Maybe a transfer here?'

Emily's smile is now changing as she reads the notes in front of her. Kate feels her stomach flip. Knows exactly what the file will say. Not just the awful thing that happened. But the shopping arcade. The reason she was signed off sick.

Kate is aware that her hand is beginning to tremble and so leans forward to place her mug on the edge of Emily's desk.

No one would ever pretend that social work was anything other than challenging, but Kate had always been very good at her job. Steady. Great instinct. Could trust her gut feeling – which was why the whole terrible business of the arcade was such a shock to everyone.

She had never liked the big arcades, actually, and normally avoided them – all those bright lights and the appalling lift music – but that day she had forgotten her umbrella. Couldn't face the high street. Had nothing to do and so spent a lot of time just wandering about. Window shopping. Trudging from bookshop to bookshop.

She saw the mother for the first time on the ground floor outside one of her favourite bookshops. One little boy of about three, a bit older than Daniel would have been, and a girl – maybe eighteen months – in a pushchair. The older child was playing up – refusing to walk nicely alongside the pram – and his mother was losing her patience. Red in the face. Loud voice.

Kate watched them for a while. The little boy was wearing a denim jacket, she remembered. A proper tiny version of a man's Levi's jacket. Quite expensive, it looked. All the right details, with contrast stitching.

*Any more of that, young man, and you'll get your bottom smacked. I mean it.* The mother was clearly struggling, and Kate had to look away. She was picturing a favourite little jacket Daniel had. Darker blue but with similar contrast stitching. The image was so vivid that she could feel a tightening in her chest and so tried to busy herself.

Half an hour later Kate was queuing in the pharmacy for some shaving foam for Toby – it was a lemon and lime version you couldn't buy anywhere else – and through the doorway she saw them again, the mother and two children, across the walkway outside a toy shop opposite. The little boy was lying on his back on the floor and the mother was shouting, reaching for his hand to lift him back onto his feet. Yanked him much too hard, Kate felt, so that he was lifted right off the ground for a moment.

Several women queuing with Kate watched then as the tin of shaving foam dropped to the floor and she ran across to scoop the child into her own arms, marching in the opposite direction from the stunned and now panic-stricken mother. Very soon there was a lot of screaming. The mother and the little boy too. A security guard from the toy shop came to check out the commotion, and all the time Kate was shouting that she was a social worker, formally cautioning the woman, waving her ID from her bag.

'I should have taken much longer off work.' Kate smooths the fabric of her dress. 'There was no excuse. I let myself down. And I let the profession down.'

'You were under a lot of pressure, Kate. We understand that.' Emily pushes the notes away.

The mother called the police. There were no charges. But there was a formal complaint. A suspension initially, and then the mutually-agreed sick leave.

'The thing is, I don't want to rush you. To put you on the spot. I realise the path to getting back to work won't be entirely straightforward. But I just wanted to introduce myself here and to let you know that my aim, in the long run, *is* to get back to work. Once I'm completely strong.'

The relief on Emily's face is tangible. 'Well – you know how short every council is of good social workers. You don't need me to tell you that, Kate. So – in time. Yes. When you're completely strong. When your doctor is happy. We could talk about a new assessment. Some retraining. Supervision.'

'Supervision?'

'Sorry. I know it sounds a little heavy-handed. But there would be quite a few boxes to tick.'

'Of course.' Kate is surprised at how offended she feels. Whenever she thinks of that incident in the arcade, she is truly mortified. That poor child. So confused and screaming for his mother. She would never, ever let anything like that happen again. But the thought of supervision? Everyone knowing that she is no longer trusted?

'But I'm glad you've made the first step. Introduced yourself here. Look – I'm sorry, I don't want to be rude, but I'm due in a meeting very soon. Maybe, as I said, we could talk again properly, at greater length, say after Christmas?'

'That sounds good.'

'Your line manager— ' Emily glances down at the file to confirm the name. 'Louise. She speaks very highly of you. The service can't afford to lose good people. Yes. After Christmas. Why don't you ring in January and we'll fix a longer chat.'

And then, as Kate stands up, she feels it. The flicker of awareness. A change. A dampness. She glances away to the window, understanding the coffee now. Eager to be gone.

Five days since she met Toby. Five days of regret and shame; of constant worrying and wondering.

She had thought that the stomach pangs this morning were nerves about this meeting. In the toilet cubicle now she sits, heart in overdrive as she pulls quickly at her clothing to confirm the stain – large enough to have seeped through ever so slightly to her dress.

So just a late period after all?

*Just?*

She has been willing this moment since meeting Toby. Lying in bed at night willing it. And waiting for it. And praying for it. And now?

As she fumbles in her bag for tampons, she is surprised to feel wetness on her cheeks. Unexpected tears not just of the relief she had imagined but something else.

*No baby.*

No mess to explain to Toby. No terrible decision to make. A lucky reprieve.

But also.

*No baby.*

And as she sorts herself as best she can, the silent tears now dripping onto the fabric of her dress leaving dark, circular rings, she is thinking something else.

It is a thought that is unexpected.

*That she is never going to be a mother again.*

And the thing is, she thought she was already resigned to this, and sure of it. That it was the right decision for her life. Her punishment. Her reckoning.

But suddenly, clearing up the mess and wiping her tears onto her sleeve, it does not feel like something she is so sure of at all.

It just feels like a huge and horrible deep, deep hole into which she is falling.

An hour later, and she decides against the bus home and instead walks through the centre of town.

As the receptionist phones through to the back office, Kate watches the shoppers through the steamy glass – some weighed down with plastic bags, others struggling with umbrellas and leaning forward into the wind.

After a few minutes her regular stylist appears, brushing the evidence of crisps from her skirt as she walks.

'Right. Sorry to keep you, Kate, quick trim, is it?' She is leading the way to the middle seat of a row of three, adjusting the height of the chair before Kate sits down.

'No, Sandra. I want a change.' Kate takes a deep breath. 'Short. All off.'

'Cut it off? Oh, Kate – I'm not sure about that, love.' She is addressing her via the mirror now, drying her hands on a towel before handling Kate's hair gently, stroking the long ringlets which have tightened in the rain.

'I always recommend stages for something this dramatic. How about a bob first? Shoulder length for a few weeks. Get you used to the wind around your neck.' She folds the hair up and turns Kate's head to the side to show her the suggested length.

'No. I've made my mind up, Sandra.'

'Oh, but Kate. It's such a signature, isn't it? Your hair. We are always saying when you come in— '

'Please, Sandra. If you won't do it, I'll only go somewhere else. And if they make a hash of it, I'll be really upset. I trust you.'

Sandra takes a deep breath, staring unblinking now at Kate through the mirror.

'You'll have to stay with the curls. Once the weight's gone, it will be harder to straighten.' She is pulling the hair back in a ponytail. Tilting her head. 'Well, you've certainly got the cheek-bones, Kate. You can take it.'

'Good. So let's do it. Short. Layered but casual.'

And so Sandra is finally smiling her agreement while Kate in contrast lies back against the sink, eyes closed, fighting hard.

*Do not cry, Kate.*

*Do not cry again. Not here.*

# CHAPTER 36

The last time Martha saw her father he was unaware that she was watching him. It was three months into her stay at Millrose Mount, and he was writing the letter she is now holding in her hand in Kate's box room. Determined finally to destroy it.

It is not the first time she has decided this. Many times she has thrown it away, only to change her mind later, and the single sheet of blue Basildon Bond bears testament to her struggle – stained with coffee, tea and leftover food from the various bins in which it has assumed temporary residence down the years.

It was a long time after Millrose Mount that Charles Ellis died. Martha was abroad, settled in to a nomadic existence, and she had learned too late, via a few column inches on the music pages, so was spared the agony of deciding whether she should attend the funeral in her mother's memory. It was drink, apparently. His liver. Ironic, that – given he had once so disapproved of the weakness in others. Martha often wondered if guilt had in the end played a part in his decline, but guessed deep down that it was more likely to have been his ego. The downward turn in his career.

And now only the letter remains.

*What I did, I did for you, Martha. One day you will see that…*

He had looked uncomfortable to Martha that final day – fidgeting in an armchair in the visitors' reception at Millrose Mount, which she could see clearly from her second-floor ward across the courtyard. When finally a doctor appeared, they talked for five, maybe ten minutes, and then he was left alone to write the letter at a desk before it was collected by a nurse.

She had refused to see him. And for this he chastised her in the letter. *I know you are angry, Martha. It is perhaps understandable. But I believe still that what I did, I did for the best.*

He was moving to Austria, he explained. A job he could not turn down. He wrote that he was torn and had never dreamt she would be detained in Millrose Mount for so long. He had imagined a smaller clinic somewhere. For just a few weeks, until she was *better*. He had even investigated the possibility of a transfer to a private establishment, he said, but had been reassured by the staff at Millrose Mount that it was the best and the safest place for her.

She winced at that.

The job in Austria he justified as an opportunity he simply could not turn down. He had, after all, to earn a living still, and he hoped, above all else, that their estrangement would be temporary. That, in time, she would come to understand that what he had done had not been easy but was his duty. As a father.

Martha lies on her bed in the little box room of Kate's house and stares at the single, sorry sheet which has for so many years haunted her. Made her stand in her dreams, a child again outside his music room, longing for a different look in his eye. A different tone to his voice.

She wonders why she has been unable to destroy it and realises that its hold over her is suffocating.

Enough. Martha marches downstairs with the letter and lights the gas on the stove. If she bins it, there is a risk she will retrieve it, as she has done so many times before.

She looks at it and knows that she keeps it because she struggles to let go of the hope that one day she will read it and see something else there. Love? But that is just not going to happen. And so she holds it now over the flame, watching the corner catch initially with satisfaction but then alarm. Fragments of the letter begin to float into the air. She tries to blow on the paper to dampen down the flames, but this only makes things worse. One of the larger pieces of hot ash drifts upwards then sideways before settling against the blind at the window, and Martha is horrified to see that very quickly a singe mark appears – growing and darkening as a flame in the centre fights for breath. Instinctively she drops what is left of the letter in the sink, fills a mug with water and throws it at the blind.

Then, after pausing to be sure the crisis has passed, she puts her hand up to her mouth, surveying the damage.

*Damn… Damn, damn, damn.*

And then, for the first time in as long as she can remember, Martha begins to cry.

# CHAPTER 37

At the corner table of Maria's café a court jester in full jacquard dress of red and yellow stretch jersey is sipping his coffee, the bells of his headdress jangling as he tips his head in deep contemplation of the crossword in front of him.

'Three across. You need to get three across.' Martha elbows Elizabeth the First, who has her hand cupped around her tea, resplendent in a most authentic costume of richly embroidered velvet – the majority of the café's other customers batting not an eyelid. There is just one woman, unfamiliar with Aylesborough's Wednesday Elizabethan market, who is staring at them, trying to work out why no one considers this state of affairs unusual.

'They say it should clear up later.' Maria has a jug of coffee in her hand, from which Queen Elizabeth and Martha gratefully accept top-ups. Maria smiles. The Elizabethan traders are loyal – always taking refuge at her café when rain scuppers trade at the nearby Market Square.

'So – how's the campaign going, Maria?' Martha leans back in her chair, stretching her arms.

'Don't ask.' Maria pulls a face, setting the coffee pot down on the table mat between them, its steam streaming towards the wall with the draught from the door as Sir Francis Drake appears, adjusting his tights somewhat indelicately before urging his fellow traders to budge up.

'But the knitted tree's looking fab, Maria. Half done.'

'Well, according to the local paper, that's old news. I need a new angle apparently.' Maria sounds bitter, recalling the phone call to the reporter who explained that they'd 'done' the knitted tree story and needed something new.

Maria complains that the council seem to be getting space every week advertising *their* side of the row. Sketches of the new library. Sketches of the swish new bistro and posh new shops. Quotes from all and sundry supporting the reinvention of Aylesborough.

'So what do they mean... a new angle?' Martha is frowning now.

'I don't know. I was thinking of a hunger strike.' Maria's face is poker straight. 'But Carlo says it would be months before I'd be in any danger... ' And now she is guffawing – pleased to have caught them all out, her guests only now relaxing into the joke, with Sir Francis Drake admitting he could *do with a hunger strike myself, to fit my balls back into my bloody tights.*

It is then that the jester – Brian from the white elephant stall – makes a sudden move, rummaging through his bag.

'I almost forgot,' he says, handing over a roll of paper for Maria, muttering about a poster and her window space.

Maria sits and Martha reads over her shoulder. It is a poster for the Elizabethan Christmas market, launched annually by a procession of the best-dressed of the traders, supported by the local Elizabethan Society. Set for December 9th. The usual route from the town hall to Market Square.

'This is it.' Maria's face is suddenly brighter.

'I beg your pardon?' Queen Elizabeth is helping herself to yet more coffee, half distracted again by the crossword which she is now reading sideways.

'Let's move the Christmas fair here. To the quay. Make the whole thing – the procession and everything – part of our campaign. We can finish the knitted tree and I could do some authentic Elizabethan food. What do you think, Martha?' Maria's eyes are wide with excitement.

'Elizabethan food?' The traders look from one to another, immediately heartened at anything which involves free grub. Especially Maria's.

'But the route's all agreed with the police. The town hall to Market Square. Same every year.' Martha is frowning.

'Oh, sod the police.'

'*Maria!*' Martha is now looking seriously worried. 'I hope you're not forgetting we are supposed to be on our best behaviour.'

'Oh, come on. It's only two streets away. Let's move it here. Secretly. To the quay. It's just what we need. Please.' She has turned now to Sir Francis Drake. 'Say you'll speak to the others? *Please.*'

'Well – I could have a word with Andrew,' Elizabeth the First shrugs.

Andrew is the secretary of the market and a regular at Maria's.

'But I really think we'd have to notify the police. They shepherd the route, Maria. Make sure we don't get any hassle from the traffic.'

'Oh, I'm sure we can work round that. If we ask permission, they'll just say no. We need an element of surprise on this one. To get that "new angle" for the press – a bit of controversy.'

'I don't know, Maria.' Elizabeth the First is now looking as worried as Martha.

'So you fancy spending your Wednesdays in some fancy bistro, do you, Marj? With a fancy name and fancy prices to go with it?'

'Don't be daft, Maria. You know we all support you.'

'So it's decided then. I'll have a word with Wendy, and Geoffrey at the piano shop. But not a word to anyone else yet. We need to make sure the council don't get wind of this.'

Reluctantly Martha agrees to help check the viability of this new plan with the others. A quick glance through the door at Wendy's as soon as the Elizabethans have left confirms it is not a good time. A small queue of customers has formed and Maria and Martha are both pleased to see one of them helping herself from the large plastic bin which contains remnants of green wool and the pattern for the leaves. Maria mimes to Wendy that she will call back later and, distracted by the poster which she is reading in more detail now, marches briskly round to the piano shop completely unprepared for the shock inside.

'Oh *no*.' Maria puts her hand straight up to her mouth, Martha a step behind her.

Matthew is over by the counter, stacking music books onto the shelves.

'Poor, poor Geoffrey. When on earth did this happen?'

Matthew turns to Maria, his expression one of puzzlement as Geoffrey emerges from the office at the back.

'I don't know what to say, Geoffrey.' Maria has now sat herself down on the wide piano stool beside a rather attractive upright near the shop window. 'How on earth did they get in?'

Matthew now turns to Geoffrey, who returns his expression of puzzlement as Maria surveys the shopfront for damage.

'Came in through the back, did they? We should consider alarms. I've often said to Carlo that alarms would be a good idea. They're expensive, I know, but... '

And only now does the penny drop with Martha as Matthew explodes with laughter.

'She thinks vandals did this.' His tone is teasing as Geoffrey pulls himself up. Defensive. And from his expression, more than a little hurt. 'It's all right, Maria.' Matthew coughs to compose himself, aware from Geoffrey's discomfort that Maria is not the only one alarmed at the current state of the Steinway. 'I know it looks a little scary but Geoffrey assures me he knows how to put it back together.'

'*You* did this?' Maria turns her gaze towards the assortment of wood panels and unrecognisable pieces of inner mechanism spread around a large area of the floor.

Martha has to put her hand up to her mouth to stifle a laugh, not wishing to offend her friend.

'I'm working on the pedals and sorting out some of the keys,' Geoffrey offers sheepishly. 'Obviously it looks a little alarming. Being a grand, I mean. But it's all very scientific. Pretty straight-forward really.'

Maria is shaking her head in disbelief and takes a deep breath – passing the poster to Geoffrey.

'We're taking over the Elizabethan fair for our campaign.'

Matthew joins Geoffrey to read the poster – both frowning.

'I have to put it on the record that I am not at all sure this a good idea,' Martha interjects.

'Oh, come on, it's brilliant. So long as we keep it under wraps. We can harness the history theme. You know – how important the past is. How much we owe to our heritage. There are some fabulous pictures of the quay from way back, which we can get blown up for a display. And I thought we could get Elizabeth the First to do the honours… put the last leaf on the tree, I mean. And was wondering' – she turns to Matthew – 'if you could rustle up some Elizabethan music? Greensleeves. Stuff like that? There's a brass band for the procession, which doesn't really fit, but you could take turns… ' Gabbling now – her mind apparently in overdrive.

'But they use Market Square for the fair, don't they?' Geoffrey looks puzzled.

'Exactly my point.' Martha is glaring at Maria. 'The police shepherd the route.'

'Normally, yes. But not this year. I'm going to sort it all. You're not to fret, Martha. It's the perfect publicity for the campaign. We'll just need a piano outside. In one piece preferably.' She is sighing again at the Steinway parts strewn around the floor, shaking her head. 'But not a word to anyone? OK?'

'You know they've announced the new name?' Geoffrey looks anxious as he shows Martha and Maria the latest copy of the local paper. The story confirms their worst fears. The council gaining the initiative.

The new name has been selected from the competition entries from hundreds of primary school children. Millrose Mount Village is to be renamed Seaview Manor, with the building company setting up a new subsidiary to manage the conversion and the new quayside project.

The council leader is pictured with a crowd of excited schoolchildren holding a banner for the new name. His quote boasts that simplicity is the strength – the new name summing up the key benefit of life in the new-look Aylesborough-on-sea.

'Life with a "view of the sea".'

'Seaview Manor, my arse.' Maria throws the paper back onto the desk. 'Forgive my language, everyone – but this is war.'

# CHAPTER 38

He is wearing a new shirt. And at first Kate is completely thrown by this.

'Sorry. Am I too early? God – you've cut your hair.'

'Yes. I fancied a change. And no – you're not early. Come in.' She is used to knowing all his clothes and it hits her inexplicably hard as she closes the door behind him. Such a small thing. And yet such a huge thing. Just a blink ago that she was in charge of the laundry; knew every single item. At their last meeting, he wore her favourite shirt. So that, as she leads him through to the sitting room, she is absorbing the large and unfamiliar checks of blue and black and thinking of all the shirts she does know; of a hundred baskets of washing and standing at the ironing board, chatting to him in that previous life. Processing the significance.

She's cut her hair.

He has a new shirt.

He's slept with someone.

She's slept with someone.

'I've made a pot of coffee. I'll bring it through. Martha's out – down at the quay with Maria and Wendy. Drawing up more battle plans.'

'Oh right.' He is still staring at her hair as she heads off to the kitchen. By the time she rejoins him with a tray, he is sitting in his favourite high-backed leather chair. 'Mugs would have been fine.'

She stares at the tray with its cups and saucers. The milk jug. 'I was nervous.'

'Me too. I bought a new shirt.'

'So I see.'

Ten seconds of silence. Thirty.

'It's nice. Suits you – the shirt.'

'Thank you. And the hair… '

'I'm still getting used to it. The wind around my neck. Had to buy a scarf.' She tries to read his eyes. 'People seem to like it. Once they get over the shock, that is.'

'I miss you, Kate.'

'Don't. Please.'

'No. I need to say this. It's just I'm so glad you called. I was scared to death that you wouldn't want to speak to me again. I'm so grateful for you ringing— '

'Stop it, Toby. I mean it. You have nothing to be grateful for. And you are not going to like what I have invited you here to say.'

All last night she lay in bed trying to come up with the right words for this; practising it in her head. But there are no right words. No way to soften this.

'I shouldn't have rushed off the way I did, Toby. When we met before. The truth is, I was being a complete coward. And now it's my turn to come clean and your turn to be angry at me. Because the truth, Toby, is not good. The truth – the real reason I rushed off wasn't just anger, or the shock at what you told me, but shame. Because— ' She lets out a little huff of air. Looks away to the window and then back at him. 'I have no idea how to say this. But the truth, Toby, is I did exactly the same thing and I didn't have the courage to tell you.'

'Excuse me?'

'I slept with someone else too, Toby. When we separated. A one-night stand. Like you. Ridiculous. A complete madness. Just sex, I suppose. *Madness*. After I asked you to leave.'

It sounds even worse out loud. The shock on his face is all-consuming; much, much worse than she imagined. As if he has no way to process this.

'You are kidding me? No. You're just saying this to get even? To hit back at me.'

'No, I'm not, Toby.'

'Jesus Christ.' Standing up. 'No... No, Kate. I don't believe you. I mean, we've only been here five minutes. Who the bloody hell do you even know— '

'It doesn't matter who. It was once. It was a mistake – and I am very sorry. And very ashamed. But let's not forget you didn't seem to have any trouble finding someone... ' She wishes immediately that she had not added this. The hypocrisy of this dig.

He shifts onto the other leg, blushing, and then turning his back on her, pacing over to the double doors, looking out onto the garden, hands on his hips.

'This is... *Jesus*, Kate. I just wasn't expecting anything like this.' Turning back towards her, scraping his fingers through his hair. 'I mean, I know this is irrational and hypocritical. I can see that. But I just feel – I don't know... Jeez.'

'Sit down, Toby. Please. There's something else I need to tell you. Get it all over with.'

For a moment he doesn't move – the hurt in his eyes awful, reminding her of that night. That terrible, terrible night with the police and the hospital. All the flashing lights. And the uniforms.

'Please sit down.'

She hears the air sucked slowly into her lungs but it doesn't help. 'I had a scare after this one-night stand. Which is the other reason I panicked and didn't come clean when we met.'

'Scare? What do you mean "scare"? What kind of scare? Christ – you didn't pick something up, did you?' Finally he sits.

'No. I didn't pick anything up, Toby. I'm not entirely stupid. Oh God – this is so terrible, having to say it out loud.'

'What then?'

'We did use protection, but my period ran late. For a couple of weeks. For a few days – a very short time – I actually thought

I might be pregnant. I'm not. Thank God. But I felt I should tell you everything now. I owe you that.'

His face changes – taking in this new significance.

'And I know what you're thinking right now. The enormity. And don't think I haven't felt exactly the same about it. I decide I can't be with you because I don't want any more children and then *this*.'

'So it was definitely a false alarm?'

'Yes. Stress, probably. That's what Martha thinks.'

'You told Martha?'

'I had to tell someone. I was beside myself.'

'Right. Jesus.'

They both stare at the coffee going cold in front of them.

'I don't know what to say, Kate. I just don't know what to say.' His face says it instead; that he is now more fully processing that other version. Her carrying someone else's child after all those nights. Night after night. Side by side. Her not letting him touch her. Shrinking away. *Night, then.*

Only now does she feel wet on her cheeks, using her sleeve to wipe the damp. Sniffing.

A long time seems to pass in which neither of them can think what to say next. Do next.

'I'm going to my parents for a bit, Kate. Couple of weeks. All arranged. I thought it would be a good thing – to regroup. Also to step away from this council project. It's getting intense on the council side. Not nice. So I've handed it all over to Mark. I'm keeping right out of it.' He is speaking in his business tone.

'Thank you. They're having a rough time. Maria and Geoffrey and Wendy. They're nice people.'

'So I hear.'

'Toby. The thing I really need to tell you— '

'I think we've both probably said enough, don't you?'

Kate wipes at her face again and plunges on. 'This one last thing I need to say. What I haven't told Martha, and am struggling even to understand myself, is that when I found I wasn't pregnant, I thought I would just be relieved. I mean – no one wants to be in that situation. To contemplate having a baby like that. And it would have broken your heart. And mine. And I was just praying and praying that it was a false alarm. But when I finally discovered that I was in the clear, I didn't feel how I thought I would feel at all.'

'I don't understand. What are you saying? You're saying you really care for this other man?'

'No. No. Not that. Of course not.'

'Then – what?'

'Oh – it doesn't matter.' Kate isn't even sure herself what she is trying to say. Wishes she knew. Could think more clearly instead of all this confusion.

And then Toby's expression changes slightly. Thinking. Thinking... Glancing away. Then back.

'So, are you saying you feel *differently* now? About one day having another child?'

'No. Not exactly. Oh, I don't know. God – I don't know what I'm saying. I shouldn't have mentioned it. Said anything. I don't know what I think.'

'No. This is important. It's important we talk about this, Kate.'

'But isn't that the problem? We've talked about it for hours and hours, Toby. Over and over. Round and round in circles. You know that you want to have another child one day. I can't. It's why I need to let you go.'

'But why so sure, Kate? It's not even been a year. Why do you feel so certain you have to punish yourself forever? For something that wasn't your fault?'

'It was my fault.'

'It was not. They're taking the ferry company to court. For the barrier. They knew it was broken. They were supposed to cancel the crossing. They should never have— '

'Oh, stuff the barrier, Toby. Stuff the court case. Nothing is going to bring him back. And I'm not like you. I can't just replace him. I just can't do that.'

And then Toby's face is suddenly black. With an anger she has never seen before.

'You think that's what I want? To *replace* Daniel? You really think that's what I think? Oh, Jesus – Kate… ' His voice rising and rising. 'Are we really that far apart now? That you think I think Daniel can be *replaced*? Fuck me, Kate. I mean – I know I'm not great with words. I know I do the bloke thing – hold it in. But I can't believe you would think that of me.'

She just stares. Taken aback at this new anger.

'Jesus Christ, Kate. Do you not know that I think about him all the time? Every day. Every night. Eyes open. Eyes closed. That I don't want to stop thinking about him. Why would I want to stop thinking about Daniel? You seriously think that's why I want another child? To let go of Daniel? Bloody hell, Kate. No one has another child because they want to stop loving the first one… '

He stands. 'I'm sorry, but I need to go. I can't do this any more. I'll be at my parents if you need me.'

# CHAPTER 39

Matthew has never met a journalist before and has only clichés in his head. Occasionally reporters crop up on *Columbo* and *Ironside* – programmes Matthew once loved to watch with his mother. Nearly always pushy, the fictional journalists. Getting in the way. His research into the exposure of the Millrose Mount scandal paints a similar picture of Ross Tyler, the television reporter who finally broke the story. Pushy. Driven.

It wasn't hard to track him down. Still a freelance – listed in London. Always looking out for new stories. And this is what worries Matthew.

Even in that first phone call, he felt paranoid. 'You're not recording this, are you? It's just I need to speak in confidence. I don't want this on the record. Is that the right phrase?'

Matthew outlined only briefly that he had personal reasons to know more about the Millrose Mount investigation and he wondered if it was possible to meet? Called himself Alan White. Heaven only knows where that came from. He had a teacher in primary school called Alan White. Yes. That was it...

Ross Tyler explained the Millrose Mount story was pretty much closed down now and was instantly fishing for Matthew's true motives. He was sharp, which put Matthew on edge – explaining that the story had pretty much taken over his life for a while. But that was four years ago. It had put him on the map in investigative circles, securing him a few contracts, but they had since dried up. Ross said he hadn't actually liked to think

about the wretched place. Millrose Mount's closure in 1973, a
year after his film, had been a full stop. Mission accomplished.

'Though I'd be happy to talk with you, Alan. Where did you
say you are at the moment?'

The café Matthew suggested was just half an hour from the
railway station in Ross's home town. An hour on the train from
Aylesborough. On his day off from the piano shop.

And now here he is. In this rather tatty café, not a patch on
Maria's place, with this tall and very confidant journalist stirring
sugar into his tea.

'So then, Alan. Millrose Mount. You reckon you had a relative
there, you say?'

Though the café has only three other customers, Ross has lowered his voice and Matthew leans forward to cup both his hands
around his own drink – bitter-smelling – suddenly feeling very
out of his depth.

'I don't know that for sure. It's something I'm looking into
at the moment. But it's possible and so I'm worried about the
stories, the implication in your documentary about— ' He
pauses, weighing up how best to explain himself without giving
too much away. The newspaper review of Ross's TV documentary had shaken him – a batch of cuttings obtained through the
library. Not just the appalling neglect the programme exposed
but most especially the allegations of sexual as well as physical
abuse. 'What I'm interested in, Ross, is the mention that babies
may have been born at Millrose Mount. Following the abuse
allegations.'

Ross takes a sharp intake of breath, tilting his head.

'So you think you might be one of those children?'

Matthew is shocked at the directness.

'No. No. Of course not. What I'm asking here is what hard
evidence you had. From all the cuttings I've read, the documentary didn't seem to spell it out. Hard evidence about the babies.'

And now Ross is shifting physically in his seat. Bristling. He reaches for a second sachet of sugar and rips the corner. 'Look. We wouldn't have put those allegations out there if we didn't have evidence. Trust me – if people saw half of what I saw, they would have kept their criticism to themselves.' Some of the sugar has now spilled and Ross uses a napkin to sweep it into a little mound. 'There was at least one young patient who had a baby at Millrose Mount. All confirmed by her doctors. She said the father was a male nurse. An assault, she claimed. We had no reason to disbelieve her. The child was taken into care then adopted later.'

'So why wasn't that in the documentary?'

'She was very unwell. Unstable. Hardly surprising, poor soul, but in the end our lawyers felt there were consent problems. That it might rebound on us to include her full details. Given her mental state.'

'So just the one case?'

'Only one that we confirmed but there were plenty more stories and rumours, going way back. Some said it was just lack of supervision – that there were unchecked relationships between patients, and also patients and staff – but the allegations of abuse went way back. There was a previous inquiry in the 1950s – guy called Wesley Clarke. Very decent chap. But his recommendations were pretty much ignored. His report buried. Four members of staff conveniently resigned to avoid disciplinary action. All hushed up. The authorities were able to hide behind patient confidentiality. We reported what we could, but we weren't able to get hold of all the files.'

'So the case that you did confirm… ' Matthew finishes the last dregs of his awful coffee, heart pounding. 'What was the name?'

'You know I can't give you that.' Ross stirs the remaining sugar from the sachet into his tea, eyebrows arching. 'I don't even know *your* real name.'

Ross finishes his drink, Matthew sitting in silence before pushing away his own empty cup to suggest a walk. Ross says he knows a nice park nearby and so Matthew nods.

The park has an impressive entrance with enormous wrought-iron gates, flowers and leaves shaped expertly around a central date, 1902, then a winding path through an avenue of oaks. It reminds him of a park he visited often as a child with his mother and he smiles, remembering how they stayed too late one day and had to climb the gates after dark to get home – his mother getting stuck when the belt of her mac caught on the railings.

It is a good day, bright and dry, but the park is for the most part deserted, just a few dog walkers throwing sticks and balls. At the first free bench they sit to watch one of the games of fetch at a distance – between them a misshapen heart etched into the wood declaring that at some point in the past Sandra had loved Edward.

'I always wanted a dog when I was a child.'

Ross's tone sounds genuine enough, but Matthew is now very much on his guard. A tactic? To soften him up? To get his name?

'So what makes you think you're linked to Millrose Mount, then?'

'This is still off the record?'

'Off the record.'

'I'm adopted. My parents were told there was a link with Millrose Mount. I'm trying to find out one way or the other if that is true.' It feels dangerous admitting this but he needs help and suspects he is more likely to get it if he is straight now.

'And do you have the name of your real parents yet?'

'No. Not yet. It's taking much longer than I expected.'

Ross swivels his body towards Matthew, reaching into his pocket and holding out his card.

'Look. I realise this is tough for you. But if you get your mother's name, I'll let you know, off the record, whether it matches the case we had on file. Yes or no. I can't give you any more than that.'

Matthew takes the card and looks at it for a while before putting it in his own pocket and turning away again to watch a black Labrador disappear between a range of bushes – its owner calling fruitlessly for it to return.

'Will you at least consider talking to me again? An interview. If you find that there is a link?'

'Look – I'm sorry. I don't want to waste your time.' Matthew stands. 'But I don't want to be in a story. I mean – I realise that's what you do. But I just need to know the truth about myself.'

Ross shrugs. 'Fair enough.'

'Was it really such a bad place, Millrose Mount?' Matthew is looking at him very directly.

And now Ross stretches out his legs as if examining his shoes.

'Six months of my life I gave that story. Half of it unpaid – until I got one of the networks interested. It was like an addiction, Alan. If I'm still calling you Alan? Anyway. I couldn't get the place out of my head. Awful stories. Understaffing. Patients refused access to the bathrooms at night. Nurses playing cards instead of working. Worse. The overuse of drugs to give the staff a quieter life.'

He sits up, tucking his legs back under the bench and looking Matthew in the eye.

'I didn't sensationalise anything in that documentary. Millrose Mount was a bad place. Believe me. It was a bad place.'

# CHAPTER 40

'You come out first.'

'No, you.'

'I feel ridiculous.'

Kate and Martha's voices from behind their neighbouring bedroom doors have a high and slightly hysterical tone.

At the local theatre four days earlier they adopted this same girlish, self-conscious tone as they bartered over who should go first to select their Elizabethan outfits.

It was Maria who insisted – needing her key campaign troops 'in disguise' to infiltrate the Elizabethan procession and help with the surprise detour to the quay.

Aylesborough's only fancy dress hire agency had been tried and ultimately dismissed, displaying only cheap period costumes in thin, shiny fabric. Unconvincing and decidedly unflattering. It was one of Wendy's contacts from the crafty set who knew of the theatre option – that a private booking could be made to hire costumes not needed for current productions.

'You'll have to be courtiers,' the theatre woman ventured as she led them down a narrow corridor to an L-shaped room without windows or any kind of adequate ventilation, packed with row upon row of clothing rails, some of the outfits covered in plastic, others in proper cotton covers – the whole reminiscent of the backroom of a dry-cleaning shop. Ominously, there seemed to be no labelling system. But the woman, who introduced herself as Karen and had been with the theatre ten years, explained that she never forgot a costume and knew where everything was. 'All the medieval peasants have been adapted for the panto.'

'I beg your pardon?' Kate was fingering her hair self-consciously, realising her longer style would have matched the outfits much better.

Karen stopped then and smiled. 'We needed the autumn colours – browns, yellows and oranges. Lower-class colours by the Elizabethan code.'

'You're saying they had different colours for different classes?' Kate was curious now.

'Oh yes,' Karen perked up. 'It was actually illegal for women to wear the wrong colour. Sumptuary Laws called the Statute of Apparel. Queen Elizabeth's own idea. A sort of colour coding to put everyone very neatly in their place. From 1574, I think it was.'

'You're kidding me.' Martha looked suddenly more interested.

'I think red for you.' Karen tipped her head to the side. 'Yes. Scarlet. Influential. Wife of a knight or a gentlewoman of the privy chamber. Here… ' She was swishing through a number of dresses on a rail crushed against the back wall. 'Try this one. There's a cubicle in the corner.'

And turning then to Kate, who was still fingering her new hair.

'And for you? Gold. Yes – wife of a viscount. Or baroness. Will go lovely with the dark hair.'

And now – at Kate's home. No going back.

'You promise you won't laugh.'

'I've seen it already.' Martha finally opens the door to Kate's room to find her standing in front of the full-length mirror.

'I shouldn't have cut my hair.'

'Nonsense. It looks fantastic.'

'And *you*.'

A pause. And now their eyes meet through the mirror.

'Bloody hell, Martha.'

It struck Kate immediately at the theatre and now even more so. Stripped of her disguise, with the playing field properly levelled – Martha, shoulder to shoulder, in her Elizabethan outfit, has no option today but to be what she is.

'You look really beautiful.'

Martha smiles. 'Dear God. I actually don't look too bad, do I? And you – Kate. It is just so lovely to see you smiling again. Been a while. You OK?'

'I'm fine. Well, not fine, but a bit better. I'll manage. I want to do this for Maria, so come on. If we're late, she'll kill us both… '

At the café they are greeted by the farce of a medieval mob, most standing up in deference to the restriction of their undergarments, tucking into bacon sandwiches and sticky pastries, leaning forward awkwardly to avoid spilling grease and sugar down their finery.

There is a proliferation of velvet and taffeta, much of it fur-trimmed and with stitching of gold and silver, which, according to Karen's explanation of the rules, makes this a very distinguished mob indeed. No one below a baron, knight or wife thereof in sight.

'Martha! That's never you? You look stunning.' Maria, resplendent in deep green velvet with a huge frilly white collar, breaks away immediately from the throng to envelope her friend in a bear hug. 'We must have a picture. Carlo. Carlo? Where's the camera?'

Pictures fretted over, argued over and taken finally in triplicate, Maria claps her hands to gather the troops around a map on one of the tables to explain the manoeuvres ahead.

The quay is more or less parallel to the approved site for the fair in Market Square. As a cover, a few traders whose stalls can be packed up most easily and moved later have agreed to set up in the square as normal, so as not to arouse suspicion. A poor turnout will be the excuse if the council or police ask questions.

Meantime other traders are already setting up instead on the quay outside. This is the riskiest part, Martha explains, as several look up through the window to check progress. There are rarely any officials about to notice, but if they are unlucky – a traffic warden, for instance – then, yes, it could all go pear-shaped.

That aside, this was the plan. The band and the official procession are already outside the town hall on the high street. With no history of trouble – traffic or otherwise – the ensemble is normally shepherded by just three or four police officers. The main concern is the junction with Nelson Road, at which point police normally stop the traffic temporarily to let the procession pass.

'We have our first group of "extras" ready just past the junction so that we can lead the procession right instead of left.' Martha is tracing the proposed detour with her finger now. 'See – along towards Prospect Road. The important thing is to take the lead. This will put the police in the middle of the new procession instead of at the front. By the time they catch up with what's happening, our second group of "extras" step in here.' She has marked an X on the map at the junction with Prospect Road. 'Now we have yet another new lead group to hurry the procession the last little bit to the quay. This will in effect push the police further and further back. It should be too late and hopefully too confusing by then to do anything about it. We'll have Elizabeth the First already in position to do the honours at the tree on the quay, and the council and police will just have to live with it. That way, we get all the pictures and the publicity where we want it. *Right here.*'

There is a round of applause as Martha folds the map before dividing her troops into two groups. It is decided Carlo will manage the first detour along with Kate and Martha, while Maria will wait at the final stage, Prospect Road, with the rest. Various shopkeepers have already offered cover for those who need to lie low until they are needed. Someone mumbles about the need for runners but Maria reminds them of the brass band, signal enough for all but the profoundly deaf, surely?

Forty minutes later the plan is in action. Just as predicted, only four officers have been assigned to the task and the procession begins uneventfully with shopkeepers and customers lining the street applauding politely.

There is just one officer standing in the road, as expected, at the junction with Nelson Road, and he is left both stunned and helpless when the procession does not continue on the agreed route but turns right instead.

'No. No – not that way. Left. It's left.' Innocent of the mutiny and assuming a mix-up, his voice is lost as the band turns right, ignoring him completely. Confused and evidently at a loss, the officer then cups his hand over his radio in a bid to make himself understood above the din.

*It's going the wrong way. The Elizabethan procession. It's going the wrong way.*

It is the proximity of two patrol cars that Maria did not anticipate. Two backup cars sit on standby in the taxi rank just one street away, their occupants enjoying the remnants of chip butties when the panicked message comes through that the procession is off course.

The first car is dispatched immediately to the very point at which Maria and her second gang are waiting.

'Hello? So what are you lot doing here? You're supposed to be in Market Square.' The enquiry, with the window down, is at first polite, the police still assuming a misunderstanding until Maria and her followers spin away from the police car, hitch up their long skirts to leg it across the road, ready to join the head of the procession just turning into the street.

Smelling a rat now, the driver of the patrol car pulls across the street to block the road, intending to head off the procession and send it back around to its original destination.

'Go round the side!' Maria is now yelling. 'Round the side of the police car, everyone.'

Obediently the procession splits into two, streaming around the first patrol car, at which point the second vehicle appears further along the street – this time with four officers.

No longer polite, but still hoping for an end to this fiasco, one of the officers points out Maria as the obvious ringleader and begins shouting at her to *stop this at once. You'll cause an accident, madam…*

Another officer, swifter on his feet than the rest, runs across the road to grab Maria by the arm, demanding she accompany him to the patrol car. Panic on her face now, Maria immediately shakes herself free and without thinking pushes the officer backwards, applying the flats of both palms to his chest.

Knocked almost off his feet, the officer's expression and tone changes. And with it the whole mood.

'Right. That's it!' He moves fast to take hold of Maria again.

Across the road the procession struggles past the patrol car, some of the costumed quite happy to ignore the police, others more hesitant now – slowing down. Maria, desperate the momentum should not be lost, is bright red in the face, shouting her encouragement ever louder while struggling again to free herself.

'Don't stop. Go round them. Go round!'

By this time the bulk of the procession has caught up, and in the distance Carlo, pushing desperately through the throng, can just see his wife, now in the grips of two officers, her face puce and her shoulders heaving with the hyperventilation he has seen all too often.

She is not being held especially tightly. The problem for Maria is that she is struggling too hard. And the more she struggles, the more determinedly the officers hold onto her – with traffic tooting its horn in the street opposite. People shouting. The band playing.

Both Martha and Kate, having pushed their way to the front also, are now running past the musicians to catch up with Carlo.

And then everything seems to stop and Martha and Kate freeze. So that they both hear it.

Above the band. Above the traffic. Above all the other shouting. And tooting.

It is a cry no one who was there can ever forget.

The cry from Carlo to his wife. Out of reach…

'Maria! *No… Maria. No!*'

… as she collapses suddenly and completely to the ground.

# CHAPTER 41

At the hospital later, it is his manners which kill everyone.

Martha watches Carlo especially closely and can hardly bear it – greeting each person as he greets them in the café, as if Maria has just popped out the back, leaving him unexpectedly to mind the shop alone.

*So – can I get anyone anything? Coffee? Tea? Newspaper?*

There are four cubicles in intensive care but the partitions paper-thin so that other families who sit sombre and silent alongside their own loved ones' beds turn occasionally, perplexed as Carlo nips in and out, wittering on and on – unable to bear the quiet. So used to Maria filling it for him.

He takes turns with other family members to sit with her, in between shifts pacing the corridor to join the stream of well-wishers; the air stifling and their throats burning as Carlo fights the silence as if it is the enemy – Maria all the while large and lame in her bed with her drips and drains, her husband's babbling punctuated only by the bleep of her monitors just visible through the glass.

*We'll laugh about this one day. Maria on that stretcher in her costume. The doctors say it was a stroke but she could come round any time. We'll know more then. Sorry – did I ask if you want a drink? Coffee? Tea? Her sister's sitting with her at the moment.*

Only family are allowed to sit alongside at first but eventually the rules are relaxed and Wendy is taken through with a little posy of woollen flowers, an intricate affair knitted expertly by her team – white and pink with leaves to match those on Maria's tree. Kate and Martha next.

*Just five minutes. No more.*

Martha thinks she can steel herself. For Maria. But it is even harder than she expected.

And in the end… too much.

In the corridor she feels giddy, staring into the corner where Maria's youngest daughter is cradling the grandchild for whom she, in another life, knitted the christening shawl.

'Come on, Martha. You look as if you need some air.' Kate tilts her head.

Still Martha cannot move. Mesmerised as the mother rocks to and fro. To and fro. The infant sucking on her little finger. Kate is staring at her. Worried eyes. Frowning.

All Martha can feel is that the air seems to be getting hotter and hotter. More and more stifling.

'I'm not ready to go, Kate.'

'I insist. You look unwell yourself. Come on. Let's just walk a little bit and come back later. I mean it – you don't look well at all. It will be the worry. The air will do you good.'

And so, unspeaking, they finally wind their way through the stale tobacco smell of the hospital waiting rooms, outside to the car park, across a large patch of lawn and then up the steep hill to the Ridge, where Martha feels a little better, taking in the clearer air, taking the lead now, striding more purposefully.

It is one of those perfect winter days – too beautiful for the circumstance; the sky completely clear. Not quite cold enough for snow but with the crisp clarity of light that December can sometimes bring, and as they climb higher and higher, the wind rises with them.

They pass many beautiful properties – large, imposing houses turned mostly into offices for accountants; front gardens turned over to sad little car parks with signs warning trespassers of dogs and fines.

Even as Martha guides Kate to the correct street, she is not sure yet that she will say it. Tell her.

'Do you mind if we stop? Rest a minute?'

And then suddenly it is out of her hands. They are on a bench that is not a random choice at all but within sight of the very house. And Martha knows that it is decided.

She stares at the white, double-fronted properly. Always this same surprise inside her that it has changed so little. Same windows. Same columns at the door.

For a time, just watching the waves, Kate is looking the wrong way. But when finally she turns, she realises.

'What on earth is the matter, Martha? I'm really worried about you. You look— '

'That's where I had my child, Kate. Well – not the birth. I had to go to the hospital for that. A complication. It hasn't changed much, Aylesborough Hospital. Surprising. After all these years.' She looks momentarily away but then back at the building. 'I was there with him – that window up on the right. Second floor. There were four of us in there.'

Momentarily she is smiling, as if in another place entirely, while Kate is stilled. Stunned and speechless.

'I'm sorry, Kate. I didn't plan to tell you today. But the hospital. It was too much. Such a shock. To be there again. It's the first time I've been inside since… '

'Oh my God, Martha.'

'That house. The double-fronted one. It was a home for single mums. Run by a church charity. They gave you six weeks with the child.' She repeats the two words very softly like a chant – *six weeks* – and closes her eyes, sniffing the air then. 'They don't tell you, do they? How lovely babies smell.'

Still Kate says nothing.

'I was very young and my father refused to have me home. With the baby. He was very shocked. *Disgraced*, he said… I had nowhere to go. I asked for more time, but six weeks was the rule. The woman who ran the home was very religious. Disapproving. Said there were other girls waiting for the beds.' Martha's speech is monotone now, the smile gone and one foot still in that other place.

'The adoption people came in every single day, explaining to us all how it would work. And most of the girls were relieved. Just wanted it over. To go back to their lives. I couldn't understand that.' She pulls her coat more tightly around her. 'I pleaded with my father, Kate. Begged him. I thought he was just holding out, you see – to make me suffer a bit. For bringing shame on the family. But he was a very angry man. And then one morning I fell asleep. All the feeds. The broken nights, I suppose. And when I woke up… '

And now Kate puts her hand up to her mouth…

Dr Clarke and the nurse Sarah held their breath also as Martha said it out loud that first time – staring unblinking at the birds outside Millrose Mount's iron-framed windows. Sarah opened her mouth as if to say something but Wesley raised his hand as a signal that, *no. We must let Martha speak. Finish her story…*

'I turned over to look at the cot and he was gone, Kate. They had taken him away while I was sleeping. My father's idea, apparently. To help me adjust to the idea of the adoption. He told them I just needed a little nudge. To come round. To accept it.'

Kate's hands – still up to her mouth.

'I know now, of course, that they had no right, no authority whatsoever to do that.' She is reading Kate's face. The shock. The horror. 'And I should have stayed calm. Demanded that they bring him back. In my dreams sometimes, that's exactly what I do, Kate. I rewrite it. I stay calm. And I make them bring him back to me.'

Martha closes her eyes as if to picture this. To make this version real. And then continues speaking with her eyes still closed. 'But I was eighteen years old. And that isn't what happened.'

In Millrose Mount, Sarah's lips were still parted as if to speak – Dr Clarke's hand frozen in mid-air to stop her, the twin birds listening on the branch outside the window. Martha was standing, her breathing still strained but her body seeming to sink from the shoulders as if the skeleton was slowly losing the ability to support the flesh, so that Sarah moved a chair behind her and helped her very gently to sit down, holding her hand.

'I blew it, Kate. Played right into their hands. I went berserk. Screaming. Throwing things. They locked the door then. Shouting for me to calm down. I suppose they were in a panic too. Hadn't expected me to lose it so badly. There was a nurse with them and she was whispering about a sedative and I was afraid they would knock me out and so I punched the nurse in the face and because they were standing between me and the door, I tried to get out of the window. I smashed it with my hand. Cut myself. It was an accident but all I could think of was getting to my baby somehow and when I saw the blood – *so much blood* – all over my arm, and their faces, horrified, I scraped the flesh some more on the glass. And I told them that if they didn't *bring my baby back, right this minute*, I would jump.'

Sarah's hand was trembling now, still holding onto Martha's – Dr Clarke standing up, his face white. All his training, his rules put aside – whispering a promise in his head that he would *get this poor woman out. If it's the last thing I do, I will get her out of this God-forsaken place…* as Martha whispered, 'I wish I had.'

Jumped, that is.

'So *that's* how you ended up… '

'In Millrose Mount – yes. They lied, Kate. All of them. Told the whole story back to front. Said I had tried to jump from that window up there, which was why they took the baby. For his safety. All back to front, to protect themselves. Said I was ill. A danger to myself and the child.' Martha has again closed her eyes. 'And my father… ' Her right hand is clutching the collar of her coat so tightly that the knuckles are white. Another pause then. A breath. A small, disbelieving movement of the chin. 'He supported their story. Their lies. Said it was for the best. A temporary order…I was taken to Millrose Mount by ambulance, I think. I don't remember that very well. But I do remember my father saying I could come home when I was *better*. And it was all behind me.'

Kate now leans forward, her face in her hands, talking to the ground. 'Oh my God, Martha. But that's the kind of stuff that happened in the thirties. Before the war. Not now. Not us. Our generation. There were benefits. By the fifties. I'm sure there were… ' Frantically she is doing the sums in her head. Working out the dates. Trying to figure what the options should have been. 'They should have told you. *Helped* you. And what about the baby's father? Where the bloody hell was the baby's father?'

Martha shifts in her seat now to look more directly at Kate.

'I don't think Maria's going to make it, do you?'

At this Kate's face darkens.

'The father doesn't even know he has a child. He was a musician. Had a chance to make a name for himself – abroad. He didn't want to go. He wanted to stay with me. But he was this amazing person, Kate. This amazing talent. And I didn't want to hold him back. To have him blame me for missing out on this once-in-a-lifetime opportunity… and so I didn't tell him. I wasn't even absolutely sure I was pregnant when he had to leave. So I thought I would be able to tell him everything later, you see. That we could follow him later, once he was established. Me and the baby.' She brushes a strand of hair from her face, blown across her mouth by the wind. 'It was a miscalculation. A big mistake. My biggest.'

Kate stands, turning away also to look again at the sea.

'I just don't know what to say, Martha. This is so terrible. So completely— '

'Have you spoken to Toby? About the pregnancy scare? About how you are really feeling?'

'So that's why you were pushing me to talk to him?'

'Yes. Because I wish so much that I could go back and do it all differently. Because I really do think the truth, however difficult and however awful, is always better. I learned that much too late.'

'Well, I did tell him. And it's worse than ever. He's gone home to his parents. But this is not about me, Martha. Dear God.'

Now they are both staring at the double-fronted house.

'How can I help you, Martha? You need to tell me how I can help you.'

'That's the problem, Kate. No one can. No one ever could. I got stuck in Millrose Mount – partly my own fault. Now I have absolutely no idea what happened to my son… And no way of finding out.'

# CHAPTER 42

'Ice?'

Josef Karpati stares into the stainless steel bucket in which three shrinking cubes float in a small pool of water along with something which may or may not be a peanut. The bartender-cum-owner of the cheap bed and breakfast two blocks back from Brighton seafront stands impatiently with tongs in his hand.

'Er... Yes, please.'

Just one of the small cubes is navigated into his Scotch, seeming to disappear almost immediately. Josef finds a smile – relieved the tongs at least missed the peanut.

He will not complain. In truth, he has struck lucky here. A quiet and shabby establishment run by a man who appears never to watch the news, read the papers or care about classical music. Or tabloids offering cash rewards for information about runaway stars.

'So where are you from, then? I can't place the accent.'

'Yugoslavia.'

'I always wanted to travel.'

Josef smiles again.

'But the wife was never keen. Always said that's what's ruining the business here in Brighton. So many people going abroad for their holidays.' He wipes his hands on his jumper, Josef understanding now the strange markings down the front. 'So what brings you here, then?'

'Just looking up old friends.'

'Right.' He does not look convinced and for a moment Josef is uneasy. On the phone his agent has warned of a complete scrum when he is found. *A bloody pantomime. You need to get your arse back here, Josef, and quickly. The papers have gone bananas.*

Five days' beard growth, a good hat and glasses are fine out-of-doors but he feels vulnerable inside. Can't wear his hat indoors.

'I was wondering where I might get decent fish and chips?'

'Fish and chips?' The owner looks surprised.

'Yes – I was in Brighton a long time ago. Had really good fish and chips, I remember.'

'Well – there's one opposite the old pier. They're good. Pricey, mind. Or there's a sit-down place in West Street I quite like.'

Josef swigs the last of his Scotch and smiles.

'You got your key?'

'Yes. Thank you.'

'I'll see you at breakfast, then?'

'Yes. Lovely.'

The man wipes the bar top with a dirty beer mat, a crescent-shaped streak of grease gleaming in its wake.

'Look, I don't mean to be pushy but do you know what time you'd like breakfast? It's just – I know we say eight till ten. But with only you staying at the moment, it would help if we knew.'

'Oh. I see. Well. Whatever suits.'

'Nine o'clock?'

Josef pushes his glass toward the back of the bar as he stands.

'Nine o' clock is just fine.'


He has forgotten how attractive Brighton is. So many years now since that ridiculous, pointless and depressing trip soon after his defection. Martha's father had so obviously been lying when Josef found him and enquired after her. Challenged him over the letters. Whether any had ever been forwarded.

*We're estranged. She's married to a doctor, Josef. In Brighton somewhere. I don't hear from her. Sorry. And I have no idea what*

CHAPTER 42                   233

*you're talking about. Letters? Why would you be writing to Martha,*
*anyway?*

Charles's eyes had darted about at the door, a liar's eyes. Josef
should have pressed him – but he was obviously drunk.

Reading between the lines of Charles's obituary in the *Times*
a few years back, it appeared it was drink which finally claimed
him. Very sad. An all-too-familiar story. Turning to the bottle
when the career bombed.

Josef stares out to sea and wonders now just as he had wondered that first pointless visit to Brighton… what the bloody hell
he would say to her if he did find her.

*Hello, Martha. So how is your life, then? I hear you married. A*
*doctor. Or was your father lying about that too?*

He pulls down his hat, raises his scarf and leans into the wind
as he turns onto the seafront road to find the chip shop opposite the old pier. Shame to see it like this. Must have been quite
magnificent in its heyday. He imagines for just a second what a
marvellous venue it would be for music. Open air.

Josef sighs. He loves playing out-of-doors, though these
days rarely gets the chance. Too high-risk financially, his agent
explains. More money in the larger, indoor venues. Keeps the
money men happy.

And so now – for just one self-indulgent, stalking-the-past
moment, he imagines playing right here. On the old pier. And
he imagines her dancing. Out-of-doors, with the wind in his
face and her with her head back, laughing. Swirling round
and round out there on the old pier. That tiny mole under her
chin…

The fish is overcooked but the chips are perfect. Crisp on the
outside but soft and so steaming hot inside that he almost burns
his lips.

Josef finishes them sitting on a bench, and in his head tries
to work out some kind of plan. Two years tops, his agent has

predicted on this top-drawer celebrity. *Two more years of this big money, Josef, then it's all over. Yesterday's man.*

So was this it? Was he saying he was calling time early? Had enough? To be honest, he rather liked having money. The problem for now was no time to spend it. No time to do anything. He didn't even have the time to enjoy his music any more.

All those years ago, when he had the invitation to Russia – truth was he should have defected right there and then. He should have refused to listen to Martha. Stayed with her. And OK, so no one would have cared. Noticed even. Someone like him defecting. And he would have been like every other penniless musician and maybe his therapist was right. They would not have made it if he had taken that path. Him and Martha – in the real world. With grown-up responsibilities. But he wishes, above all else, that he had been able to find out. That he had not believed her when she said that she would follow him. Wishes that he had said no to Russia and its state bloody orchestra. And stayed with her.

And now his agent's voice again.

*Fantasy, Josef. I'm sorry. But it's a fucking fantasy, mate.*

He should go back to the B&B. Tomorrow he will remember this moment and wish that he had. But the chips are so salty that he is thirsty again and decides to find a bar. A bar with proper ice.

He keeps his hat on, which is probably the biggest mistake. Conspicuous. Even then he may have got away with it, most of the customers drunk already, but in the corner is a man in his twenties – a man, unbeknown to Josef, in search of a scoop. A man who has spent the last month working earlies on the local evening paper and lates on a tabloid in London, trying to impress the news editor.

*What you need, Frank, is a scoop. Bring me something good and we might talk about a contract. I'm making no promises, but I want something good.*

So he's sitting in this bar, this ambitious journalist, nursing his first lager when in walks his future. His scoop.

'Windy evening?'

Josef nods, pulling down his hat and turning away. Damn. He should have gone straight back to the B&B.

'So – you live here or just visiting?'

'Visiting.' Josef takes a large swig. If he finishes his drink too quickly, it will look even more suspicious.

'Alan.' The man is stretching out his hand.

'Paulo.'

'Oh – you're foreign?'

'Yugoslavia.'

One more long swig and Josef nods again politely. 'Sorry. Got to go.'

Outside he is in a bad movie – the man following him inexpertly – diving, rather obviously, into doorways and behind lamp posts and post boxes when Josef turns. In his room, finally, he phones his agent.

'I think the press have found me. What should I do?'

'Bloody hell, Josef.' A pause. 'OK. First thing is, you tell me right now where you are.'

Josef looks out of the window. Across the road, the man from the bar is getting into a car alongside another man with a large camera bag. He looks beyond them to the night sky and begins to search. For the Big Dipper and the North Star…

'Brighton.' It sounds ridiculous even as he says it. Still he searches the sky and the stars. Ah yes – there it is. The North Star.

'Brighton Beach?'

'No,' Josef keeps his eyes fixed firmly on the North Star. 'Brighton, England.'

# CHAPTER 43

'I see they found him. Josef Karpati.'

Kate is carrying a tray into the conservatory with the day's newspaper tucked under her arm, to find Martha staring out on the garden. Another clear, crisp day but windy – one of the branches of the laurel by the fence intermittently tapping on the edge of a glass roof panel.

'Can never understand it myself. All that money, all that talent, and still they're not happy. They should meet some of the people I deal with in my job. That would open their eyes.'

Martha turns, eyes distant. 'Sorry?'

'They found Josef Karpati. In Brighton. Still no idea why he did a bunk. Weird.'

Martha says nothing.

'Sorry. I'm just rabbiting. Doesn't matter.'

Kate pulls the biscuit tin to her stomach, conscious that the lid cannot be removed without force, the backlash likely to spew biscuits everywhere if she is not careful. It takes three attempts but Martha shakes her head at the collection of ginger nuts and digestives, returning her attention to the garden.

'It's looking good already. The work that you've put in. To the garden, I mean.'

'Yes. It will be nice when it all comes together.'

Silence for a time between them then – Kate sipping her tea, Martha shovelling sugar into hers.

*The thing is, I can only drink tea with vast quantities of sugar.* Kate is thinking back. All those bags.

'Do you think it was fate, Martha? Me getting off that bus? I keep thinking about it. You know – destiny. Fate— '

'It was the knitting.'

'Sorry?'

'The baby clothes for Maria. If I'd been knitting a Leo Sayer tank top, you would have stayed on the bus. It wasn't destiny. Or fate. It was just chance. I mean, I'm really glad it happened. But it was just one of those things.'

'Right.'

Martha seems distant suddenly.

'Well, I'm not entirely sure I can agree with you actually. I mean – I find it hard to believe – given all we've both experienced – been through – that it was just a coincidence.'

Martha merely shrugs. 'Destiny. Fate. It's all nonsense, Kate. Life is just life.'

'But you've really helped me, Martha. More than you know. And I can't help feeling that I am somehow supposed to do the same. That it's what this is about somehow.'

'You've let me live in your house, Kate. A virtual stranger. Do you not think that's enough?'

'No, I don't actually. And you're not a stranger. You're a friend now, Martha. I mean, I realise it's not been long, but I do really think of you as a true friend. And I am just so bloody *angry*. So churned up by what happened to you that I feel there must be something we can do. Something that I am supposed to *do*.'

Martha takes in a long, slow breath, her eyes softening, which gives Kate more courage.

'Look. I hope you don't mind but I've spoken to a few people. Not given your name, obviously. Not given any details or anything away – not without your agreement. But I've put feelers out about that journalist, the one who exposed the Millrose Mount scandal, and I feel pretty sure that if we approached him officially, he would want to take this up for you. Not just the

Millrose Mount dimension but the charity. The adoption people. I mean, it's a real outrage, Martha. Do-gooders playing God. It should be exposed. And there's the European Court of Human Rights. From what I hear, more of this goes on than you would believe. Stuff brushed under the carpet. And this journalist – well, the word is he will *believe* you, Martha. He'd take it up, I'm sure, if… '

'And then there'd be a circus.'

Kate reaches into her sleeve for a tissue and wipes her nose.

'OK – they'd want a story – yes. I'm not going to pretend they wouldn't. But they have the resources, Martha, these people. The contacts. The clout. Links to politicians and so on. I mean – we don't even know if they broke the law over the adoption.'

The problem whenever they discussed the details – over and over – was Martha genuinely could not remember whether she signed anything. Any forms. Papers. So it was difficult to know for sure if rules had been flouted or if anti-depressants, or whatever medication they put her on, had clouded everything.

'It certainly needs looking into properly, Martha. And there's not much we can do on our own. And I just feel… '

Martha looks across at her, silent now, so that Kate shakes her head, tucking the tissue back into her sleeve.

'You know the law's just changed, Kate? Allowing searches for birth parents?'

'Yes – I read about that. So can we use this new law? To investigate the status of the adoption?'

'Apparently not. I looked into it all. It's for the *children,* not the mothers. Adopted children are allowed access to their records now, but it's a one-way street. It may come one day for the mothers, but not yet.'

'So you're the mother, but you don't count?'

Kate stands up and walks over to the window, hands on her hips.

'The only hope I have, Kate, is that technically now my son could come looking for me. It's been my only hope. All these years. The reason I come to Aylesborough every winter. Kidding myself that he might find out something and come looking.'

'We need to do something more. This is ridiculous. So unfair. Is there nowhere we can at least register your details?'

'I've done that. I write every single year.' Martha turns her gaze to the window again. 'Just before his birthday – to the charity headquarters who keep adoption records. For all I know, they throw the letters straight in the bin. But I write.' She brushes her skirt. 'Then I come here for the winter – just in case. Wendy lets me use her address at the wool shop as a point of contact.'

At last Kate understands. That very first day she was introduced to Wendy. *No letters.*

'So Wendy knows?'

'No, of course not. I just told her it was important to be able to provide an address. For next-of-kin issues. Lawyers. Banks. That sort of thing. She's never pressed for an explanation.'

'Martha, do you mind me asking again? About the father? Why you never considered tracing him – when you got out of Millrose Mount, I mean? He might be able to help you with this.'

Martha shifts in her seat. 'I think about it sometimes. But then I try to imagine what the hell I would say. "By the way, we have a child but I don't know where he is." No, Kate. No point. It would just spread the hurt.'

'And did you never hear from him again?'

'No, never.'

'And on your travels, Martha. I hope you don't mind my asking. But did you not have other relationships? Ever think about settling?'

'I travelled because I needed freedom, Kate. Because Millrose Mount made me terrified of the alternative. And yes – I had a few relationships. But… I don't know. I never wanted to stay in one place and nothing ever came close. I know that may sound ridiculous, because I was very young when I was with my child's father. But it's the truth. Nothing has ever come close… '

And then Martha checks her watch suddenly. 'Oh – Christ. It's never that time.'

Hurrying through to the hall for her coat and scarf, Kate following. Martha is sharing the running of the café with a small team so that Carlo can stay full-time at the hospital, where Maria remains stable. There has been no official word or development from the council since the parade drama, but the family's solicitor has won an extension on the eviction order, given the family's new and terrible circumstances.

'You know I'll help any time you need me.' Kate originally offered to pitch in full-time also, but has so far not been needed – so many other relatives and friends keen to do their bit for Carlo.

'Any time we're short, I'll let you know. Promise.' Martha wraps her scarf twice round her neck. 'Look, Kate. Please don't think I'm not grateful. You wanting to help. But, and I know it sounds strange, the thing is – if I do ever find him – my son… ' A slow exhalation of breath. 'I don't want him to think I *expect* anything of him. That anyone else is involved. A journalist. An agenda. Does that make any sense?'

And then, before Kate can say that she understands absolutely, Martha is waving and is gone, the door slamming with the wind.

Kate sits down on the bottom step of the stairs and closes her eyes to the echo of Martha's presence. It is something which has always both puzzled and pleased her – this very physical sensation when someone leaves the room. Someone you care for.

She read a theory somewhere that human energy is absorbed by its surroundings, leaving behind a sort of physical shadow – a resonance. And though it is more likely to be the contrast of the silence which feels so very odd at times like this, she likes to sit very still until the sensation passes.

And so she waits, thinking of Martha. And thinking also of Toby, who she misses more with every passing day.

# CHAPTER 44

And then suddenly, the next morning, there it is on the doormat.

It is a shock at first for Kate to see his handwriting there on the envelope. On their doormat.

Married life hasn't presented the need for letters. Kate and Toby have hardly been apart since their wedding. And yet, staring at the letter now, Kate is remembering that when they were first together, they wrote often. Kate spent a few months in France as part of her final year at university, and they missed each other horribly; sent postcards and letters all the time. Sometimes every few days. She loved to take photographs and often enclosed a series of random shots. A good meal. A pretty pattern of clouds. A shop window display.

Kate was a good deal less confident back them. Yet she felt so very close and so very comfortable with Toby that she put all of her insecurities in her letters. Goodness. Until this moment she has forgotten about them. They were open and chatty and con-fessional – those letters. How she worried what everyone thought of her French. Of her clothes. Her blessed hair. And in compari-son to this, how much she loved everything about France. The way the women all around her seemed always to look so stylish and self-assured. How she wished with all of her heart that she could be like that. And how she wondered some days if it was an act. If anyone was really that lucky – to feel so sure of themselves? Or whether it was a mask? What did Toby think?

And there is a shudder of connection and surprise and déjà vu as she opens the envelope to find Toby remembers all this also; referencing the very same thing.

*Do you remember how you used to write to me from France, Kate? All those amazing and rambling letters. I so loved them. Still have most of them but sadly not all. Feel very cross with myself now that I did not keep every single one…*

He writes honestly then, on the second page, about how confused and hurt and knocked sideways he is about her confession. How he never saw that coming but regrets parting the way they did, leaving without talking more, because he is beginning slowly to see how hypocritical he's been. And so he wants to keep up some line of communication between them and has decided to write letters.

*It doesn't matter if you don't want to write back. I just need to do this…*

The letter then rambles on – warm and chatty. How his father is now into stamp collecting and seems to think distraction is what Toby needs, dragging him around endless antique fairs and auctions. His mother meantime trying to fatten him up. *You are what you eat, Toby.*

And then, at the end of this first letter, he says how very sorry he is that they have somehow never found a way to be in tune over how to grieve. How to even talk about it.

*Is there a right way or a wrong way? I have no idea, Kate. I only know that for some reason I couldn't cry and I remember how much this upset you. I don't know why. Maybe I thought that if I gave into it, I would never recover. That you needed me to be strong. I don't know. But I cope in my own way, Kate, and that is by picturing him in the present tense. Every day. I close my eyes and I picture him colouring at that little red plastic table we bought. Driving us mad with that bloody drum.*

*I hold his picture in my head, clear and bright as if he is still here, Kate. That's what I do. That's how I cope. That's what works for me.*

*And I need you to know that I have honestly never blamed you for what happened. I have blamed God. The ferry. The barrier. Fate. But never you…*

*You have to believe that.*

Kate reads this first letter over and over that day and goes to bed, shocked and dazed that it has taken a separation for him to say these things.

It was ridiculous and unfair of her but, yes: in the midst of all the madness, it had always really bothered her that in the early days Toby didn't cry. She couldn't understand it.

In the blur of those terrible first days, she remembered very little. Snatched images. Finding Daniel's favourite pyjamas in the washing machine. Being helped to a car after causing an appalling scene at the funeral; trying to stop them from lowering the coffin into the ground.

*You are not to let them do that. You hear me! Toby. You have to stop them. Stop them doing that…*

Mostly just a blur, which probably had a lot to do with medication, which was a blessing at first because it just made her sleep so much. But later – not so great because her body started to reject sleep, as if it was over-rested. Too full up of sleep. And then lying in bed, between sleep, it became too hard to stop all those terrible images from surfacing.

And that's when she got up and started the cleaning. At first just a jolly good clean to fill up a day. And then another day. Followed by the obsessing. Scrubbing and bleaching until her skin burned red and angry.

All this Toby watched – helpless and broken – with visitors and friends and relatives calling in from time to time with cakes and cards and casseroles. *Let her do it her way. Whatever works.*

And Toby didn't cry. That's the one thing she remembers incredibly clearly. Sometimes his eyes would bulge as he struggled. But always he stopped it. Fought it.

'Why don't you cry? What's the matter with you? Why don't you just cry?' She remembers hurling the words at him one night and slapping his arm as if watching him cry was somehow necessary.

The truth was she wanted to be punished. She wanted him to be much angrier at her. She wanted Toby to hate her as much as she hated herself. Justice. But Toby was strong. He held in the tears and he kept on loving her and this was the thing she could neither understand nor cope with. His kindness and forgiveness, despite the terrible, terrible thing she had done. The bomb she had exploded in all of their lives.

Instead Toby turned all his fury on the ferry company, and the garage, and saw a lawyer and Trading Standards, and started this blue box folder which he kept on the top of a pine wardrobe in their room.

*This must never happen to anyone else, Kate. I am going to make sure this never happens again.*

At two a.m. Kate gets up and puts on the bedside lamp to read Toby's letter all over again. She strokes the pages and she realises something dangerous immediately. That deep in her heart, she would like to write back to him…

But she knows this wouldn't be fair. Because he wants another child and it would give him hope and she wants Toby to be happy again and she can't believe this would be possible together now.

And then, just a few days later, another letter arrives and this time Martha notices.

'Another letter from Toby? That's good.'

'Is it?'

'Why don't you write back?'

'I don't want to encourage him.'

'Why ever not, Kate?'

And over the coming days, as more letters arrive, Kate doesn't know what to feel. She tells Martha that it is still hopeless between her and Toby; way, way too complicated. While Martha, with so many problems of her own, just knits – *click, click.*

'But you still love him, Kate? What's complicated about that?'

And then the letters stop  and Kate is completely thrown. She has become used to and comforted by them.

And now Kate doesn't know what on earth to think. Or feel.

Isn't this what she wants?

For Toby to give up on them too?

# CHAPTER 45

Matthew refuses to meet Emily at the council offices. It feels like a small but important gesture for Maria and all of the people who have been so kind to him in Aylesborough.

He has not visited the hospital. Does not know Maria well enough. Too shy and awkward to know quite how to handle this. Just more anger suddenly. More churning inside over how unfair everything seems. Shocked especially at how distressed Geoffrey is. Wendy and all the others too.

They whisper a lot – everyone terrified to admit out loud the terrible fear that Maria may not recover. Have another, even bigger stroke? And the whole business unsettles Matthew so badly that he has phoned his mother a few times, needing to hear her voice. Touch base. Suggesting that she may like to visit again soon? Realising very suddenly that life does not always give you the opportunity to patch things up, however angry you feel.

She is doing OK – his mum. Staying permanently at her sister's. New job, dressmaking for a dry-cleaner's, apparently, which she loves. She used to do a lot of that, years back. Dressmaking. She mentions that there is going to be a divorce but *you're not to worry. I am going to be just fine. It is for the best. Something I should have done a long time ago, Matthew.*

'I'm sorry but I'm not coming to the council offices, Emily. No way.'

She was surprised on the phone, at first, but then regretful when he explained. *A very sad business, Matthew. I didn't realise the woman who collapsed was a friend of yours. Yes, of course. I understand completely.*

But she says they need privacy for this next meeting, rejecting the quayside café, and seems pleased when he suggests the piano shop during lunchtime closing. Geoffrey will be out piano tuning. They can have the back office to themselves. Good.

And now she looks strangely out of proportion perched in her smart suit on the stool among the packing boxes, and Matthew wonders if he should have set two chairs at the desk in the showroom, to make it feel a little more comfortable. Emily says no. *This is fine.* More private. A deep breath then from both of them as she removes his file from her briefcase – her smiling encouragement.

'As I said on the phone, we've had the birth records through and I've been able to make a few more enquiries on your behalf. Now. One step at a time. This is your original birth certificate, Matthew.'

She places a document on the small table and turns it around, pushing it towards Matthew, still smiling her encouragement.

'Take your time. It's a lot to take in.'

Matthew glances over the document and then reads it through more slowly. Once. Twice. Three times. Concentrating. Heart pounding.

He looks up at Emily.

'*Richard?* My name is Richard?' It hadn't occurred to him. That there would be a different name. And now he feels stupid. Realising that, of course…

'That's the name your birth mother gave you, yes. It's very common for adoptive parents to change it. You weren't expecting that? I should probably have said.'

'I didn't think about it.'

*Richard. Richard. Richard?* He turns the name over and over in his head, checking it against his reflection in an imaginary mirror, unable to make it fit.

And then his mother's name. *Jessica.* He says that out loud too. *Jessica Martha Ellis.* Spinster.

The section for the father's name is blank and Emily, who is following Matthew's expression closely, explains that this is not at all unusual – the father's name often omitted. *Your mother would have needed his permission. Very often it just wasn't possible. She was single, remember. We don't know the circumstances regarding your father.*

At this reference Matthew feels suddenly and unexpectedly quite light-headed. He tries breathing more slowly but very soon the sensation becomes stronger. Borderline dizzy. He has not told Emily, not even Geoffrey, about the extent of his research into Millrose Mount. His meeting with the journalist. The new fear which has overtaken any worries about a hereditary mental condition. The dark thought which haunts him now at night – that he may actually be the result of a crime. Part of the Millrose Mount abuse scandal. The real reason his mother did not want him. Gave him up.

And now Emily is frowning. 'Are you all right, Matthew? I'll fetch some water, shall I? As I say – it's a lot to take in. Is there a tap?'

'Through there. In the little kitchen.'

There is the sound of running water. *Richard Ellis.* Matthew shakes his head against the dots forming on the periphery of his vision as Emily passes the glass of water, urging him to sip and breathe slowly. 'Now there is more news, but we need to take this slowly, Matthew. Have a drink first.'

*More news.* Matthew is obedient, sipping at the water with his eyes closed for a moment. In front of him the entrance to Millrose Mount. He is trying not to think of it. The idea of a man and a woman side by side at a window above it.

'OK now?'

'Yes, I'm fine. Really. I'll be fine. Go on.'

'The address given when your birth was registered was here in Aylesborough. You noticed that, I'm sure.'

Matthew stares back down at the paper, struggling to make his eyes focus properly.

'Millrose Mount? Is it linked to Millrose Mount? This address. This place?'

'No. Well – not as far as we know. The house is an accountant's office now, but I've run some checks and in the fifties it was a home for single mothers run by a charity.'

'So my mother wasn't in Millrose Mount when I was born?'

'Well, it doesn't look that way, Matthew. But we can't know for sure. Has your adoptive mother been able to help?'

'She says that's what they were both told. She and my father. That my mother was in Millrose Mount and that's why I was available for adoption.'

'Right. Well, it's a puzzle, that's for sure. I just don't know. All I can say…' Here she pauses, as if weighing something up, trying to assess how he is coping.

'Go on. Please go on.'

'Well – I've been in touch with the adoption agency used by the charity which ran the home. They're no longer operational but they hold records at a headquarters in Hertfordshire.' Emily has put her hand back inside the A4 envelope.

'There was a fire, Matthew, which I'm afraid destroyed a lot of old records, but they ran a check on the names and— ' She is withdrawing two blue envelopes from the file. 'They came up with these.' Emily takes a deep breath. 'They're letters from your mother, Matthew, asking for information about you.'

Matthew can feel his pulse suddenly manifesting itself in his head, chest and fingers. Very slowly he reaches out his right hand, watching it as if it does not belong to his body, Emily again smiling encouragement.

'The most recent is dated two years ago – the other, almost identical, from several years back. Would you like me to read them out?'

'No. No. I'm fine.'

Matthew, his hand trembling, begins to take out the first letter from the envelope, pre-opened very neatly – almost certainly with a knife or proper letter opener. A neat serrated edge.

There is a single sheet inside – the writing remarkably neat also, very upright with long loops below the lines. Fountain pen. Rich blue ink.

'What's most extraordinary, as you will see, Matthew, is the forwarding address.'

He is not listening. Before him just a few short lines, which Matthew, like the birth certificate, scans very quickly and then re-reads more carefully. The temperature in the room suddenly seeming to fall.

*I am writing again with regard to my son Richard Ellis who was adopted through your agency in 1957. I am extremely keen to know if it's possible now to have news of him – to be reassured that he is well and happy. I have written many times before without success and hope you will be able to help me on this occasion. I can be contacted via the address above and would be very happy for my name and this address to be passed on to him and/or his new family, should this be possible.*

'So why was this never sent to me?' Matthew's face is now white.

'It wasn't allowed, Matthew. Adoptions were finalised in the past with a strict rule of no further contact. It was considered best for everyone back then.'

'I don't understand.' He is looking now at the forwarding address.

Emily is shaking her head in shared amazement.

'I know. It's bizarre, isn't it? Very unexpected. So do you know this woman – this Wendy? This wool shop?'

'Yes – yes, I do, as a matter of fact. She's a good friend of Maria. The café owner who's in hospital. So… ' Matthew's eyes are now darting about, as if trying to settle on some imagined explanation somewhere about the room.

'So Wendy from the wool shop knows my real mother?'

'Well – it seems that way. But we can't know what the relationship is exactly.'

Matthew is standing up now, folding the letters back into their envelopes.

'Well, come on – we need to go round there. Ask her. It's just two doors down.'

'No, Matthew. Sit down. *Please.*' Emily's tone is very much more serious now. 'This is a very private, very sensitive matter, Matthew. This Wendy Martin may not know anything about it. She may simply have a forwarding address. We can't go barging in assuming anything. I must also counsel you very strongly to let me handle this next step on your behalf. It's been a long time and I have a responsibility to guard not only your privacy but also Jessica's. I've thought about this, and my advice is that we compose a letter between us and that I take it on your behalf to Wendy Martin to check that she still has a current forwarding address. I can make some careful enquiries without compromising anyone. It's too emotional for you, Matthew. Too much at stake. And we don't want to get this wrong.'

Matthew is using his thumb and forefinger now to pinch his bottom lip over and over. Finally he sits again.

So he *was* born in Aylesborough-on-sea. But what was all this about Wendy? Where the hell did Millrose Mount fit in? And why had the records been mysteriously destroyed? They were just covering up. That was what all this was about. Some bloody cover-up.

'What I suggest is that you have a think tonight about what you might like to say in this first letter to Jessica. To your birth mother. You need to take this slowly. Let it sink in. Talk this through with your friend Geoffrey – yes? Phone the counsellor again if you need to. We can meet again tomorrow – here at the same time, if you like – and then I will take the letter on your behalf. Is that OK? Matthew, are you listening? Are you happy with what I'm suggesting here?'

'Yes. Yes.' His eyes are still glazed, not looking at her.

'And you have your friend Geoffrey you can talk this over with. Or do you want me to phone the counsellor now? Set something up?'

'I'm fine. I'll talk to Geoffrey. He's very supportive.'

Emily stands then to make Matthew a cup of tea with two large spoonfuls of sugar, and stays for a further ten minutes to ensure he seems steadier before explaining that she has to leave for her next appointment.

'Now you're sure you're feeling OK?'

'Yes. Absolutely.'

'It's a lot to take in. More progress than anyone could have expected. So I'll see you tomorrow? Same time?'

Matthew nods as she gathers up her things, then waits six or seven torturous minutes to be sure she will have reached her car – on one of the meters in a neighbouring street, she said – before marching straight around to Wendy's wool shop.

There, he kicks the bottom of the door in frustration – the sign and the locked door confirming half-day closing.

He goes around the back to try the bell to the flat – once, twice, then a long third ring, but there is no reply.

Still holding the two envelopes in his hand, he decides to try the café next. He picked up a bacon sandwich earlier so knows Martha is on duty. She might know where Wendy is.

The lunchtime rush is over – the last two customers leaving from the table closest to the window. Martha, straining under the weight of a large catering-size tray of what looks like macaroni cheese, signals to Matthew that she will be over in just a moment. Still feeling unsteady, he sits at one of the benches in the middle of the café, so that by the time she joins him he is tapping his foot against the table's central support.

He has got better used to Martha now – she seems OK enough. But that business in the council offices. The streak and the court case. He is never quite sure around her. Never completely at ease. He can feel his heart still racing, one hand tightly holding the two letters beneath the table top, the other still rhythmically pinching his lower lip.

'Do you know where Wendy is, Martha? It's just I really need to find her. Urgently.'

'Oh right. No – I'm sorry, Matthew. It's her half day. Is she not at the flat?'

'No – I've tried that.'

Martha looks surprised and then concerned. 'Look – let me get you a drink. Something to eat – yes?'

'No, I'm fine. I ought to get back to the shop.'

'I insist, Matthew. On the house. You can delay opening up the music shop for ten minutes and Wendy might be back then. She's probably at the hospital.'

Martha then puts the macaroni cheese in the oven, to be ready for service later, she explains, and dishes up a large portion of lasagne left over from lunch onto a plate with some salad for Matthew. He is still agitated, not hungry but not wanting to seem rude. Ungrateful.

Martha smiles encouragement as she puts it down, whereupon Matthew instinctively lifts his hand still clutching the letters above the table, ready to take the cutlery she is holding out.

That Martha should recognise her own writing straight away is no surprise. That she should recognise also the address of the charity headquarters is perhaps more so. But what is most surprising is how she reacts.

Much later, given the grave consequence, she will agonise over and over about why she speaks up now so aggressively. Why it does not occur to her, the blood draining from her face, that Matthew could possibly have legitimate business with the letters. *Her letters.*

'Where did you get those?'

She spits the words, lunging forward to snatch the letters from him, his instinct to pull back his hand, a look of intense shock on his face.

Her only explanation, when she relates this scene later to Kate, is that her brain simply cannot, *will not*, compute any option other than that Matthew has intercepted a reply meant for her via Wendy and in doing so has happened upon her most private business.

'I'm sorry, but that's mine, Matthew. And you have absolutely no right… '

Matthew looks at the letters, which he has stretched out of Martha's reach, and then back at her.

'"*Mine*"? You know these letters?'

Again he stares at the writing, narrowing his eyes as if a new shape begins to take form from the neat and careful writing.

Then, and only then, does Martha pull back her hand.

*No.*

She closes her eyes. *No way.* Absolutely not. She would have known. If there was one thing, all these years, she has been absolutely certain about it is that she will *know*. Straight away.

She opens her eyes to see his – wide and unblinking. His skin suddenly pale.

'Jessica *Martha* Ellis.'

Matthew says the name very quietly, eyes still unblinking.

'*You're* Jessica Martha Ellis?'

And then he is pushing the plate away, standing up. It is as if suddenly the room is too small for them both.

Martha steps back – needing more space also, the room shrinking, shrinking between them. He straightens his back now and is staring at her, waiting for a response – words he cannot know she has rehearsed a million times under a million skies across a million miles but are gone now.

Mute.

'Well?' His eyes becoming wilder.

She opens her mouth but nothing will come out. She is thinking of all the times she has seen him round about. At the piano shop. On the quay. At the café. How could she not have known? No…

Matthew is clenching his free fist. 'All this time and you have nothing to say to me?'

Martha is frowning, her head tilted. Yellow wallpaper. Her mother holding the buttercup under her chin. The smell of him still in her nostrils. The feel of his hair still on her fingers. The cot empty.

She is feeling suddenly a little dizzy and closes her eyes.

No. She would know him.

'I'm sorry, Matthew. But there must be a mistake.'

# CHAPTER 46

Kate answers on the fifth ring. It is several minutes before Martha makes any sense at all, fifteen more before Kate can negotiate the afternoon traffic and find a parking space near the quay.

The chairs, kicked over by Matthew as he fled, still lie on their sides alongside the overturned plate, food splattered across the floor – Martha sitting at the bench nearest the serving counter, staring blankly ahead.

'I couldn't speak, Kate. I just couldn't speak to him.'

Kate moves behind the counter to fetch water which she insists Martha drinks before continuing. Martha takes just a couple of sips before standing up.

'There's no time, Kate. We have to find him.'

They try the piano shop first. Locked up. And then in the car as they drive fruitlessly around the town – by the park, the Ridge, the bed and breakfast, all the places they can think of – Kate is trying to reassure Martha that she mustn't blame herself. It was the shock.

*Shock can paralyse, Martha. The body is a strange instrument.*

Forty minutes and Kate insists they drive back to the quay to check if Geoffrey has returned – he their best hope to second-guess where Matthew might go.

'So – tell me again exactly what Matthew said?'

Martha, dazed, is shaking her head, not hearing. Rocking. To. Fro. To. Fro. 'Oh God. I've messed up so badly, Kate. I've really, really messed this up… '

'Martha, listen. You've had a big shock. But I need you to look at me. And to listen. We have to find Matthew to make sure he's OK – yes? So try to breathe more slowly. And to think. Yes? What exactly did he say when he ran off? Why was he so angry?'

Still she is shaking her head.

'I told him it must be a mistake. *Why* did I say that? I should never have said that.'

Unable to find a meter, Kate abandons the car at a precarious angle on a double yellow line and leads Martha by the arm back round to the café – sitting her at a table before checking at the piano shop. She reappears just a few minutes later with Geoffrey, white-faced, behind her.

'It's all right, Martha. I've told Geoffrey everything.' And then, turning to him. 'So do you have any idea where he might have gone?'

'You've tried the B&B?'

'Yes – no sign.'

'We could try my house. He might have gone there.'

They take Kate's car again – Geoffrey having walked to work to enjoy the fine skies. En route Kate very gently tries to coax Martha to go over why it had gone so very badly.

'He wanted to know who his father was. He was very upset. Really worked up.'

'And you told him?'

'*No.*' The tone is incredulous – only later understanding and wishing, wishing with all her heart, that she had.

And now Martha's breathing is becoming strained again.

'His eyes, Kate. He looked so... I don't know— '

'Take deep breaths, Martha. Breathe more slowly.'

'Oh my God. This is my son, Kate. *My son.* We have to find him... ' Tears now – so that Kate reaches out her arm to rest it on Martha's as she drives.

It takes about twenty minutes through the traffic to make it to Geoffrey's home – his face registering confusion then alarm as they pull up outside.

'My car's gone.'

An anxiety deepening but unspoken as Geoffrey fumbles for his keys, all of them then rushing through the house from room to room. Bumping into one another. Each room empty.

On the pavement outside again as Kate helps Martha, unsteady on her feet, back inside the car, a neighbour of Geoffrey's appears after watching the scene from his window.

'So – broke down, did you?'

'Sorry?' Geoffrey is holding the driver's door for Kate.

'Well, I saw your friend. The lad – Matthew, isn't it? – loading petrol cans in the boot. Run out of fuel, did you? In that piano van? Would have offered to help but I'm waiting in for a repair man. Washing machine,' he rolls his eyes. 'Everything all right now?'

'Yes. Yes, thank you. Listen – when did you say that was?'

The neighbour checks his watch, pulling a face. 'About an hour ago now.'

In the car, Martha has her head in her hands.

'We'd better call the police.' Kate directs this as a question to Geoffrey, whose expression suggests he is trying to weigh up the danger Matthew is in … versus the trouble he could be in if they involve the police.

'He must have taken my keys from the shop.'

'And the petrol cans? What the hell is that about?'

'God knows. I should never have left them in the garage. They were for an old generator. Full – both of them.'

'*Oh dear God…* '

And now Kate turns to Martha, lifting up her head gently.

'You said he got really upset when he was talking about his father – yes?'

'Yes.'

'Come on – think, Martha. What *exactly* did he say?'

'He was wound up suddenly about Millrose Mount.' Her face is screwed up. Confused. 'How did he even know I was in Millrose Mount? You didn't tell him, did you?'

'No – of course not.'

And then Martha pauses, looking about the car as if trying to figure something out. 'He said something very odd. He asked if his real father was at Millrose Mount too.' Then looking up at Kate, frowning. 'Why on earth would he ask me that?'

On a good day the drive up to the old hospital takes less than ten minutes, but every set of traffic lights seems against them. None of the three want to believe they will find Matthew there. Geoffrey has seen him poring over his cuttings, bad-mouthing the place, the company, the project, after Maria was taken ill. But none of them can know the darker fear – the mistake about his origin – which has taken deeper and deeper root in Matthew's head since his meeting with the journalist.

And so even as they turn the corner and see Geoffrey's car and the pall of smoke just emerging from the upper windows of the derelict building, they cannot make this fit.

Not with Matthew.

Kate pulls alongside the same telephone box Matthew used to phone his mother on his first visit to Millrose Mount. She leaves Geoffrey there to phone for help – driving Martha right up to the main steps.

Before she can stop her, Martha runs so fast up the first flight – trying to take the steps two by two but miscalculating – that she misses her stride, twisting her full weight over onto her right ankle. She tries immediately to continue but the ankle is twisted. Way too painful – no longer able to take her weight.

'Oh dear God…'

Just then, as Kate bends down to help, there is a loud crack from inside the building and to the far right a pane of glass shatters, spraying glass over the grass frontage, a few fragments landing just feet from the two women.

Martha tries again to stand but the pain is too strong. Kate looks up at the windows to the right, a red glow now from inside – as Geoffrey catches up with them, out of breath.

'Dear God.' Staring in disbelief still at the building. The smoke. 'They're on their way. The fire brigade. But we need to get you both back a bit. Wait for the truck. It's too dangerous this side. I'll see if there's another way in round the back.'

'No. It's all boarded up round there. It'll be too late.' Martha is clutching her ankle, Kate turning then to watch them all reflected in the glass above Millrose Mount's entrance.

She looks down the hill, calculating it will be five, ten minutes maybe before help arrives. Maybe longer. There is no conscious decision. Just instinct. So that as Geoffrey tries to stop her, grabbing her arm – *don't be insane, Kate* – she pushes him away just hard enough to get a head start up the steps.

# CHAPTER 47

Later, when people ask for the details – the police; the firemen; Martha and Geoffrey – she will lie. She will tell no one quite how badly she miscalculated. What it is really like.

Inside.

Geoffrey had been right – *insane* – for it is night-time on the other side of the double doors, the smoke so dense she can hardly make out the shape of the hall. Where it ends. Where the corridors begin. What is most confusing is that very soon, in this smoke, she has no idea which way to turn. Which way even she has come.

One minute there is a narrow stretch, she remembers that, and then she turns right, holding the bottom of her jumper over her mouth, and it is wider suddenly – two circular windows – and there is a huge portrait on the wall between them of a strange, severe man with a dark cape and hat, standing proud in a large gold frame which reflects what little light there is. Weird eyes – this picture – which seem to follow her everywhere.

She turns right at the portrait – a longer corridor now – and then door after door. All locked. She wonders for just a moment, coughing, if she should turn back. *Insane.* But then she hears it.

The tapping.

The sound, metal on metal, is too faint to be sure of the direction, and infuriatingly, just as she thinks she can source it, it stops. She is in a larger room now, much hotter, the smoke denser and for the first time the colour red. She does not register this for what it is, just acknowledges the colour, the glow through the door at the far end of this room. It is some kind of hall – a dining hall, yes, for there are stacks of chairs, old tables too, and in the middle a little staircase to an upper gallery. A mezzanine level. Part of the structure has collapsed; pieces of wood splintered everywhere like a bonfire. She has the sense of someone watching her and remembers for a moment the portrait.

But then the tapping again. And now, crouching down low to follow the source of the sound, she sees him – deep within the pile of shattered wood that was the stairs – tapping the back of his watch against the pipe of a radiator alongside him.

'Matthew. Oh – thank God. It's Kate. It's all right. I'm going to get you out.'

And then the relief is gone instantly, for she sees that his face, behind a lattice of wood, is not the Matthew she knows at all but a child – a little boy who is crying and Kate realises only now how very young he is.

'I'm sorry, Kate. I'm so sorry. I didn't mean— '

'It's OK. Matthew. I'm going to get you out.'

Quickly, furiously, she begins to hurl bits of wood aside, using both hands now, which means her jumper falls from her mouth and she is coughing more. Some of the pieces of wood are quite heavy, interlinked, and there is creaking and crashing as the bonfire readjusts.

'I was trying to get up the stairs to the window to get out. But they collapsed.' Matthew is trying to help but seems unable to move and only now, as she gets nearer, does she see his leg – a large piece of wood stuck deep into the thigh, blood soaking his trousers. And only now is she truly afraid.

'I can't move. I've tried. You'd better go.' He says this in the tone of one who is old enough to know it is the right thing to say but young enough to hope she will not listen.

And so she continues working slowly, more methodically – piece by piece – both of them coughing as the colour red glows brighter across the room.

She will never tell Martha what she does next. That for a few minutes, with some of the wood refusing to budge, so tired, so sleepy and so much smoke in her lungs, she thinks for a moment that she will rest a bit.

For just a moment she puts her arm around his shoulder. To rest. Two bears in a cave, stroking his hair as he cries. Says over and over how sorry he is.

It is the smoke – choking her lungs and confusing her brain. For how long, she will not remember. All she knows is that for a brief time she is waiting for them both to sleep. Warm at first. Floating. Drifting. Floating. And she is telling him that they must sleep, all the while stroking his hair.

But then something changes and it is no longer warm.

The smoke turns to water and she is very, very cold suddenly. She opens her eyes to look up, not through smoke now, but up through the water to the woman on the hill. For a time, she does not realise that it is her. This woman on the hill with long, wet hair down her back, struggling to free herself from a man in uniform who is holding her so tightly that she cannot escape. And the woman is shouting that she needs to get back in the water, cursing the people who have pulled her out. Shouting for the man to *let her go*.

Lower down, by the ferry, there are two more men in the river, surfacing and shaking their heads. A van. More divers. A crowd is watching – silent. One woman in a red coat turning her daughter's head into her stomach so that the child cannot see what is happening.

And now the woman on the bank is screaming for them to try again.

*Daniel. Daniel. Daniel.* On her knees, begging them. *Please.* Telling them that his seatbelt is stuck and they must try one more time. *I am begging you. Please…*

And Kate looks more closely, to see that it is her. The woman on the hill. And that is when – very suddenly – she stirs. Wakes.

And realises…

'Come on, Matthew, I have to get you out.'

… why she is here.

'Come on.'

For a woman knitting on a bench. And the woman on the hill.

'I can't move.'

'You have to, Matthew. Come on. We *have* to get you out.'

It takes her a while to clear enough space, and then she just pulls – dragging him from under the shoulders, both hands knotted around his chest from behind – ignoring his pleas that it hurts too much.

And she is telling him that he must help. Shuffle on his bottom. And push with his good leg. *Come on, Matthew. Come on. You have to.*

Their progress is incredibly slow – Matthew in such pain, Kate dragging him along and all the time bullying him to bend and stretch his good leg to give them some momentum.

*Come on, Matthew. You have to try.*

The colour red has reached the far curtains now, framing the window just as they make it out of the hall back onto the long corridor. Kate shuts the double doors to try to hold the heat and the smoke, but is then confused. Which way? Shuffling and pulling. Which way?

*Please.*

She can't remember. Can't see.

She closes her eyes – smarting in the smoke – and in her head, in the confusion, is counting *twenty eight, twenty nine, thirty… coming, ready or not…* and then, when she opens her eyes, she sees him. The mysterious figure that is Samuel Cribbs in his big black cloak framed in gold, glinting through the grey in the distance, watching them as they shuffle, pull, shuffle, pull. So she heads for the painting. Remembering now…

And then, exhausted, as they finally turn the corner by the painting – two men suddenly, in masks. Uniforms and masks.

*Over here. They're here.*

Flashing lights, arms guiding her and taking Matthew, and then at last outside on the grass – the air so shockingly sweet it makes her cough worse than the smoke. And as someone puts a blanket around her, and others are lifting Matthew onto a stretcher, she whispers it, head down, so they will not hear. That she *got him out...*

To the blades of grass. To the ants marching in line. And then, her head tilted up to the blue of the sky, streaked now with smoke. To the painting of Samuel Cribbs. To the woman knitting on the bench.

And to the woman on the hill, wet hair down her back.

*That this time...she got him out.*

# CHAPTER 48
## December 1977

'Do you think it will snow for Christmas?'

Kate looks at Martha, fidgeting with a strand of cotton from a button, trying so hard to behave as if this is nothing out of the ordinary. Visiting your son in prison.

'I don't know, Martha.'

They have arrived early today, Kate knowing all the shortcuts now. Matthew has been transferred to an open prison in recognition of his work with the choirs. Such a relief. And no surprise that he is using the music more and more – not just accompanying the prison choirs but running workshops also. His way to cope.

'I love snow. Thought about getting a chalet job once. When I was travelling. Switzerland. You know – cooking for the skiers. But like so many things… ' Martha turns to Kate and tries to find a smile. 'I just never got around to it.'

Kate reaches across to squeeze Martha's hand. She tried so hard to prepare everyone – fearing from the very first that Matthew could face a custodial sentence, but Martha and Geoffrey refused to accept it. They convinced themselves that compassion would win the day. That his clean record and the mitigating circumstance would spare him.

*Dear God, but he is practically a child still.* In the end Geoffrey sold a very good upright piano to fund the best lawyer he could find.

But arson – whatever the context – is arson. Matthew was no child in the eyes of the law and there had been a security guard in Millrose Mount that day. He was at the other end of the building and escaped without injury but that, apparently, was not the point. It was what might have been that troubled the court.

Prison rules took a lot of getting used to. A choice at first. One thirty-minute visit each week or one two-hour visit every twenty-eight days? They opted for the shorter, regular visits, so Martha and Glenda can take turns. And now that he has been transferred here, the rules are more relaxed. With parole, this should be his one and only Christmas…

No visiting is permitted on Christmas Day itself, they learn, and so there is an extended slot today. Martha and Glenda have special permission to split this in two. Glenda first, for half an hour. Then Martha.

Kate keeps the motor running, to try to hold in some heat, and passes a newspaper to Martha, who keeps looking at her watch before glancing at the other visitors gathering over by the entrance – six women waiting in a little group. Talking. Smoking. Swearing.

And then – there she is. Like Martha and Kate, looking lost. Entirely out of place – standing apart from the line, awkward in her smart coat, belted at the waist, black patent handbag, immaculately polished shoes and, most incongruous of all, leather gloves.

Kate catches Martha's eye as Glenda turns – both recognising her instantly from Matthew's photographs. This will be the first time they have met.

'Do you think we go in together or do I wait inside for her to come out? What do you think?'

'I don't know, Martha. I really don't know.'

'I suppose I should go over and speak to her. Work out how we do this. I should have phoned her. Or do you think I should wait? Wait for her? What do you think?'

Martha lets the newspaper fall into the well in front of her feet and clenches her fist so tightly, the knuckles turn completely white.

'It was always going to be difficult, Martha. It's natural to be nervous.'

'Yes.' And then she narrows her eyes. 'She looks lovely, don't you think? Not quite what I was expecting, though. God. This feels strange.'

They have taken it slowly – Matthew and Martha – but with everything now talked through so many times, over and over, they are getting on well. All the gaps filled in much more quickly in these extreme circumstances. All their conversations condensed against the clock – everything now settling into a calmer understanding, spoiled only by this terrible place.

Three more months, the lawyers reckon. Then parole.

Kate keeps quiet but is not especially surprised when, after watching Glenda for a time, Martha suddenly takes a deep breath and gets out of the car.


'You must be Glenda?'

The head turns first, followed by the mac then the strap of the handbag which falls from her shoulder.

'I'm Martha.'

Both of them have seen pictures, but not especially good ones. Matthew playing go-between. Ferrying news. To and fro.

Later they will be honest about this moment. That Glenda is warmer and more homely than Martha expected. And she in turn – younger and very much more beautiful than Glenda imagined.

'It's so good that they allow this extra visiting. For Christmas.' Glenda hitches the strap of her bag back into place, her hand trembling.

'Yes. It is.'

Suddenly there is a bellow from the midst of the group of women, followed by a screech of laughter from a tall woman, her hair tied in a ponytail on the very top of her head. Glenda smiles, her hand still holding the strap of her bag.

'She looks like one of those Tressy dolls.'

Martha laughs. Both smiling now.

'It was good of you to write, Martha. I'm sorry I didn't reply. To be honest, I wondered if I should have phoned. But I didn't really know what to say.' She is looking away now, towards the prison side door where a guard has emerged with the familiar sign detailing all the rules for visiting.

Martha puts her hand into her pocket, feeling around for a tissue and, unable to find one, turns away slightly to hold the back of her hand up to her nose in the cold. Embarrassed. Trying to prevent a drip. Glenda, immediately reading her distress, then rummages into her own bag for help.

'Thank you.' Martha takes the tissue gratefully. 'I didn't expect you to reply. I just felt so responsible. The fire and everything. Matthew misunderstanding about Millrose Mount – getting himself into such a... Well. It all felt like my fault and I wanted to say that I can only imagine how angry you must feel. At me.'

'Yes. Well. Very difficult for all of us.'

Martha blows her nose and they stand for a time – awkward again.

'So much colder today.'

'Yes. Kate, my friend who drives me, is worrying about ice on the way home, but I think we should be all right, providing... '

'I should have told him when he was a child.' Glenda is tugging at the wrists of the smart gloves.'

'Sorry?'

'I should have told him. About the adoption.'

Martha looks at Glenda very intently. Warm, kind eyes.

'That's what I would have said, Martha. Should have said – if I'd replied to your letter, I mean.'

For a time then they just watch the group of smokers, some now stamping their feet against the cold – one of them wearing ridiculous gold, strappy sandals without tights. Her feet blue.

'Did you drive here?'

'No. Train and then a taxi. I don't drive. Matthew's father used to do all the driving, but we're not together any more.'

'Yes. I heard. I'm sorry.'

'Don't be.' Again Glenda is hitching her handbag strap higher. 'It's better. Another thing I should have done a long time ago. Much better for Matthew – when he gets out of here, I mean.'

And then Glenda looks very carefully at Martha's face and her expression softens. 'It's good that you've worked things out. With Matthew. I'm pleased for you, Martha.' She has pushed her chin up and lifts her arm to signal the bag she is carrying. 'I made him a chocolate cake. His favourite. Do you think they will let me give it to him?'

Later Martha will wish that she had said today what is in her head at this moment. That if she had to lose him to anyone, she is glad that it was to Glenda. But is not quite ready to say this. Not today. And so instead she simply says she hopes there is some way they can allow the cake. Even a slice. And she insists that Glenda should go in first as planned. *No – I absolutely insist. It's what Matthew wants. And quite right too…*

Much later, after Martha's turn, there is a scribbled message from Glenda via a guard to thank them for the offer of a lift to the station but she has shared a taxi. *Seemed silly to wait but thank you all the same. I'm very glad we met. A good visit today.*

In the car on the way home, Martha is thinking of her own visit, which went well too – Matthew coping better, full of plans for the Christmas concert. His perfect distraction.

She thinks also, lulled by the engine and the classical music on the car radio, of those much more tense and difficult early visits when there was so much to say and always too little time.

Martha decided very quickly, after Matthew's sentencing, to tell him absolutely everything. Every single detail.

*So they took me from you? When I was tiny?*

*Yes, Matthew. When I was asleep. I had no idea they would go that far…*

She told him of Millrose Mount, and how long it took her to get out and start looking for him properly. The whole story. How she very quickly learned she had no rights. No means to trace him. How, in despair, she took to travelling and had spent her whole life since in limbo, just hoping and praying that somehow one day this reunion would happen. Most important of all, she told him over and over that he was born of love. That he was very much *wanted*. That she would never have given him up voluntarily.

Afterwards things slowly improved between them. On subsequent visits Matthew began to open up. To tell her about his own life. His music and his dream of college. And then on one visit, when she was telling him about those rare, precious times in the middle of the night, feeding him in the charity home all those years ago while looking out at the stars, Matthew suddenly stretched out his hand to the centre of the table. Martha stared at it for a moment, so nervous as she took the cue, slowly placing her own hand on top of his. She could feel tears, first in her eyes and then on her cheeks, and stood up, wanting so much to take him in her arms – but a prison officer stepped forward. *Sit down, please. No standing.* And so Matthew instead took her hand properly in his for the very first time. Held it momentarily very tightly.

On the next visit Martha told him everything about Josef – Matthew's face white in shock. *Josef Karpati? THE Josef Karpati?*

*He wasn't famous then. We were very young. But we were in love…*

And so this new dilemma was born between them. If and when to contact Josef?

Staring now out of the car window, watching the green and brown blur of a field – cattle grazing and a copse of oaks in the distance – Martha still does not know what to do for the best.

Matthew has insisted Josef must not be contacted until he is out of jail. Has cleared his head. He is worried Josef will think they are after his money. *He will probably want nothing to do with me. He will insist on tests. It will be awful...*

Martha has agreed to wait. Enough for now that she has her beautiful boy back in her life. She dares not push the dream. Dares not tell anyone, not Matthew and not even Kate, about the new and dangerous hope which all this talk of Josef has stirred.

For Martha is still in love with Josef Karpati. Has always loved him. And in quiet moments, tossing and turning in the middle of the night in Kate's box room, she cannot help herself. Worrying and wondering if she dares to once more open the door on this.

This question. This dream.

Could it, would it be completely ridiculous to hope after all these years that Josef might have room left in his heart not just for Matthew.

But for her too?

# EPILOGUE
## December 1979

And now once more we follow the wind – this time a softer, gentler breeze that rustles through the few leaves left from autumn.

A breeze that strokes faces – just strong enough to catch loose strands of hair. But not annoying – this. The kind of fresh and welcome breeze that makes the people smile, surprised to say out loud... *Goodness. What a lovely day.*

Sweeping and swirling down to the quay where Geoffrey is arriving, checking his watch and waving to Wendy next door.

Their shops are freshly painted – cream and pale blue. Windows sparkling in the winter sunshine. The leases renewed. Five years. No catches.

It is cold – yes – but with this bright, clear sky. And just along the quay Carlo is wiping down the café's new outdoor tables where people will sit in their coats and their scarves to watch the boats a-bobbing. Setting out. And later coming home. The fishermen smiling. Iceboxes full.

Look closer now and you will see two men heading up the hill, laughing together. Tall and slim with matching, striking eyes. They wave to Geoffrey as he stands at the door of the piano shop, smiling back.

A couple waiting for the café sign to switch to 'Open' watch, mouths gaping.

*It can't be. Josef Karpati?*
*I tell you – it was. Definitely.*

*No. No way…*

The breeze for a time plays with a sweet wrapper, dropped by Maria's granddaughter – now grown chubby and gorgeous, all smiles and tantrums and treasured mischief. The picture of her christening in the shawl knitted by Martha still has pride of place on Maria's mantelpiece upstairs.

The stray wrapper darts along the street. Then stops. Then moves again. *Crackle. Still. Crackle. Still.*

And then our breeze loses interest in the ground and rises higher, higher. Up to the rooftops, to stir the feathers of the birds, watching those tables of the café below.

Across to the quayside now, where a tree with woollen leaves is being admired by tourists new to the town.

*Quite lovely… but why woollen leaves? We must ask. The wool shop – there. Let's ask in there. They'll know.*

Higher and higher now, up through the town to the hill where once stood Millrose Mount Hospital. Gone. Demolished.

The ugly fence and the whole place – gone.

Instead we see a park – neat lawns, trees with bare arms outstretched – and in the middle a white and beautiful thing. A bandstand, with a stunning view of the sea, where very soon Josef Karpati will play a concert for the town.

Secretly he owns it now, this Millrose Mount plot – the developers long ago bankrupt – though the breeze will whisper that *you must not tell.* He doesn't want the fuss – Josef. Or credit or thanks. It is for justice, this thing he has done. This gift.

For the ones that he loves…

And now – ah yes. See. Down below; through the window, there she is.

'Do you think it will?'

'Will what?'

'*Snow.*' Martha's voice is raised as she works on the Christmas tree – Kate busy in the kitchen next door.

All morning Martha has been babbling away. Nerves. Matthew spent his first Christmas free with Glenda – this to be his first in Aylesborough. And she so wants everything to be perfect.

Kate decides enough of the raised voices and walks through, flour-covered hands upright, like a surgeon walking into theatre.

'If you put any more on that tree, it will fall over.' She tilts her head in line with the lean of the tree. 'And no. For the record, I don't think it's going to snow.'

'You really think it's too much?' Martha's tone is deflated, standing back from the tree and tilting her own head to reappraise her work.

'Yes, I think it's too much. But, to be honest, I think that's the point, isn't it?'

'Do you know the bookies have a man standing on the roof of the Met Office with a dinner plate? To check for snow?' Martha removes one bauble and begins squashing all the tissue paper back into a large cardboard box. 'It apparently takes just one flake and they have to pay out.'

'I thought it had to settle.'

'No. One flake. At least that's what I read.'

The doorbell then, and Kate watches Martha's eyes change. It will be Matthew and Josef back from the quay. Hands still aloft, Kate returns to the kitchen where she will smile. And listen.

Surreal, still, to watch them all these days – bickering amiably as if everything that went before is a false memory. Something that happened in a parallel world.

'Good God. What have you done to the tree, Martha?' Matthew is the first to tease. So often taking the mick – the tone affectionate, though always he calls her Martha. Perhaps always will. 'You can hardly see the green. And it's leaning. We're going to have to take some of that off or it's going to take out the window.'

'No way. I've spent hours. Tell him, Josef. It's not leaning. It's just the shape of the tree.'

'Your mother is right in all things, Matthew. This you should know by now. That lean. It is entirely in our imagination,' Josef winks, leaning to the side to mimic the tree and then kissing Martha on the forehead by way of apology. Reaching out also for her hand.

Kate is now beaming as Matthew pops his head around the kitchen door to hand over a Tupperware box. 'Mince pies from Maria.'

'You are kidding me? She's supposed to be taking it easy.' Kate shakes her head.

'Not in her vocabulary. The fishermen have just handed over a motorised wheelchair for Christmas. She is racing children on the quay as we speak. Carlo is going bananas. He says, and I quote— ' Matthew here adopts a rather poor Italian accent. '"Anyone else who has been partially paralysed, Maria, would have the decency to behave just a little bit disabled."'

And now, laughing out loud, Kate shoos him from the kitchen, to return to her biscuits.

Three cutters on the worktop. A tree, an angel and a holly leaf – though the angels are proving a mistake – the deformed first batch cooling on a wire rack more like hunchbacks than angels, staring their disapproval.

She taps out six more leaves and glances at the planning list Martha has pinned to the fridge, reminded of the list they made together for that very first dinner.

Josef Karpati. *In our house for dinner.*

It was Kate who wrote the letter. Matthew and Martha – so nervous, putting it all off and going round and round in circles.

*Right. So I am going to write the bloody letter to Josef's agent. And let's see, shall we? If he doesn't want to know, he doesn't want to know. We have, at least, to find out.*

And then – the phone call within twenty-four hours to say that he was on a plane.

Kate cannot think of it still without this little burst of pure joy inside.

Those eyes on their doorstep. Disbelief as he spoke her name, ever so quietly.

*Martha…*

And now it is Kate's turn – the key in the door and she wipes her hands quickly on a tea towel. Must be Toby, back from the paper shop.

From upstairs there is the familiar shriek of delight. She did not sleep well last night, and is supposed to be napping, but can see out of the window from her cot and Kate is glad she left the sidebar in place. For Molly can get out of bed if she really tries – and she gets herself in such a *state*. So easily overexcited.

And so Kate runs up, two steps at a time, and scoops their daughter onto her hip to carry her down, weaving her way around a book. A doll. A discarded puzzle.

'Daddeeeeee.'

All curls and cuddles – this wriggling and over-excited mass, transferred from her hip to his.

Toby has no newspapers but instead a new kite. Molly can hardly believe it. Already – so many kites.

Kate smiles at her husband. 'You'd better hang on a minute, Toby. I'll get her a thicker jumper and coat. A hat too – it's really cold.'

'Cold enough for snow?' Martha shouts from the conservatory.

'*No.*' Kate is shaking her head, laughing again.

'You'll join us? With the kite on the beach? Gorgeous sky and just enough wind.' Toby is staring at Kate.

'Yes, of course. But you go ahead. I've just got a couple of things to do and I'll be along in just a moment. When the final batch of biscuits is done.'

'OK.' He smiles, still staring at Kate. He kisses her nose and she touches his cheek with her palm before kissing him back on the mouth.

And then, as Kate closes the door, Josef and Matthew start to rehearse. It is a new piece for the concert. They have been practising for days now. Haunting. Beautiful.

The Steinway is allegedly on loan – though Geoffrey shows no sign of wanting it back. *You use it, Matthew. Please. Get yourself ready for music college…*


And now Kate pauses, standing terribly still; she knows this feeling well and knows too exactly what she needs.

It is Martha who notices her grab her coat and her hat, tucking her hair, grown long and wild again, into her collar to head out into the garden… to the bench at the far end, set in the winter sunshine where all the planning and the planting has finally come good. Evergreens and silver-leaved plants which glint in all lights, even this gentle, December glow.

Kate wraps her coat tighter, tighter, and closes her eyes.

'Mind if I join you?' Martha, in coat and hat also, has her knitting as she stands by the bench.

Kate nods.

'I sometimes wonder, Martha, what on earth my life would be if you hadn't made me write back to Toby. Can you imagine?'

Martha sits and sets to work, smoothing the new ball of wool and tucking it inside her bag. *Click, click…*

'It might have taken a bit longer. But he wouldn't have given up on you, Kate. As I've found out myself – the good ones apparently don't.'

Kate smiles and wraps her coat tighter still, closing her eyes once again.

It was the present tense that did it. How, in all those letters, Toby was the only person who still talked about their son in the present tense…

*No one has another child, Kate, because they want to stop loving the first…*

And it was like this sudden flash of understanding.

'I used to look for him in all the wrong places.'

'Sorry?'

'Daniel. I used to look in the wrong places.' Kate is thinking of the imaginary swimming. The bus trips and the dark, dark shadows. A different bench. A different Kate.

'I know, darling.' Martha squeezes her arm. 'But not any more?'

'No. Not any more.'

They sit then, very quietly, and Kate keeps her eyes closed very, very tight.

'I am so very thankful I got off that bus, Martha.' Kate links their arms loosely, eyes still shut.

And as she listens to the music, and the click-clicking of the needles, she feels calmer; soothed and safe, and for a moment almost weightless. Just like the snowflake which may or may not fall on the dinner plate tomorrow.

So that as she thinks now of Daniel, she knows that she will find him easily.

Today by a lake. *Look.* He is smiling and waving, watching the ducks – ripples spreading like soundwaves from the Steinway, stretching out across the water as they splash and they play.

And Kate does not give it a name – this place. Enough that she has found it now. This place to visit. This place to believe in. This place *in her heart* and *in the present tense*, where her son's eyes say always now that he is safe. That he is happy.

And best of all.

Just like her sweet Molly at the beach.

That he is waiting…

## THE END

# A LETTER FROM TERESA

Thank you so much for reading my second novel. A lot of people ask where the idea for a book comes from, and in this case the seeds go back a long way.

When I was a television reporter in London, I was sent once to cover a campaign launch at the House of Commons. A group of women were releasing balloons… each one, I was told, representing a child they could not find. The estrangements were for all sorts of different and heartbreaking reasons, and I have always been slightly haunted by the image. All those balloons…

As for Martha's awful experience? I so wish I could say it could never happen. But my husband is also a journalist and he once interviewed a woman who finally found her birth mother in a psychiatric hospital, sadly too institutionalised to ever be released. She was never mentally ill.

I make no apology for giving my fictional Martha a much happier ending.

I was very touched by the lovely reviews for my debut novel. So – if you've enjoyed this one too, I'd be very grateful if you would share your thoughts on Amazon. It really does help other people to discover my books.

I love to hear from readers, so do feel free to get in touch any time – on Twitter or via my author Facebook page.

With warm wishes,

Teresa Driscoll

www.teresadriscoll.com

@teresadriscoll | teresadriscollauthor

Also, if you'd like to hear about all my latest releases, just sign up here:

www.bookouture.com/teresa-driscoll

# ACKNOWLEDGEMENTS

There are so many people I must thank for supporting me through the writing and editing of this – my second novel.

I always knew this particular book was to be a 'big story' and that working out exactly how to tell it would be a challenge. So special thanks go to my editor Claire Bord, whose expert guidance helped me so much in shaping a complex story into the novel here.

Thanks as always to my gorgeous husband Peter and sons James and Edward for patience, especially when things got a bit feral on the domestic front during editing! A hug too to fellow authors at Bookouture for their terrific camaraderie and to the many writer friends at regular lunches and get-togethers in Devon, who provide invaluable insight and encouragement always.

I must also mention the fabulous blogging community, my lovely book club, and especially the very dear school friends who supported my debut so brilliantly and even cooked some of the recipes from it for a recent reunion. That was very special.

And, as ever, my final thanks go to my agent Madeleine Milburn…who made the dream come true.

Lightning Source UK Ltd.
Milton Keynes UK
UKHW022110060619
343980UK00015B/1835/P